Descent

Tom Dawn was born in Stamford, Lincolnshire in the no man's land between the Baby Boomers and Generation X. He has worked as a journalist, farming contractor and in Information Technology. He moved to Devon in 1987 and has lived there since.

Descent

Tom Dawn

Pomegranate

There is no evidence that we've been placed on this planet to be especially happy or especially normal. And in fact our unhappiness and our strangeness, our anxieties and compulsions, those least fashionable aspects of our personalities, are quite often what lead us to do rather interesting things.
—Jon Ronson, *The Psychopath Test: A Journey Through the Madness Industry*

Under Pressure

He was late again. I saw Pete's dark red Jeep appear through a gap in the trees where the river had eaten into the bank. He sped over the ruddy brown scar which undermined the road's thinly metalled surface. A moment later he had disappeared behind the dense green curtain of vegetation that covered the whole slope down to the water's edge. I checked my watch – it was gone 8 o'clock already.

The others had seen him too, and there was the start of movement as they breathed out, stood up and stretched, the period of waiting coming to an end. A fly which had been buzzing me persistently settled for an instant on my hand to drink from the sheen of perspiration before I waved it away.

A few minutes later Pete turned into the compound, circling smoothly over the rough stones which crunched and ground under his tyres as he pulled neatly into a space. He stepped out and walked over efficiently but unhurried, clean-shaven and in freshly pressed jeans and a brilliant white t-shirt.

"Hi guys – are we all ready to go?" he said, as if he had no idea we'd all been here since half past.

Without answering, Enrique turned his back and set off on foot towards the dam wall, phoning the control room as he went. I stood up and Pete and I walked down to the sandy red bank where we hopped aboard the launch. Leo started the motor which blew out a sooty cloud of diesel exhaust, and we set off towards the diving barge.

The river was wide above the dam wall, but we were working on the nearside today, at a draw-off tower, so there was only a short stretch of water to cross. As we made our way and the shoreline receded, the gently sloping wooded banks came further into view, stretching into the distance. The dull flat empty countryside behind them remained hidden out of sight.

The thin green line of the woods along the water's edge led the eye naturally upstream until, at some distance it faded into the same warm haze which welded the steely sheen of the river to the dusty blue sky. It was an elemental, watery landscape until you looked downstream, where the view was interrupted by the dirty grey of the massive concrete dam wall, looming above us, behind the tower. To an observer on the other side of the dam, the energetic discharge would indicate the huge weight of water which it held back, ready to burst forth. On our side, the boat chugged softly over still tranquil waters which gave no clue about their hidden potential.

We sat on benches opposite each other without talking. I was still feeling moody about having been kept waiting, but not enough to say something about it. Over the top of my book, I noticed Pete stretch out his arm to look at his watch, raise his eyebrows and pull a face. He saw me looking and gave a shrug and a cheeky grin which stood for an apology. I'd seen that expression plenty of times. Lateness was his great weakness.

As we came up to the barge I slid a bookmark into my paperback. Leo cut the engine and cruised the last few metres. The only sound was of water washing past the sides of the boat and lapping against the diving barge. Then the gentle bump between the two vessels as they met. Pete, who was in his wetsuit by now, called out to Victor, already on the barge, to help us offload our kit and climb up.

It was a talent of Pete's, to be so damn likeable and easy-going that it was hard to tick him off. Despite all his experience and skills, he had held onto a naivety which made him seem younger than his years. He didn't wear responsibility too well, but he made up for it with charm instead, notwithstanding slip-ups like today's. Maybe that's why even Enrique was soft on him.

In any case, I owed him, for he had somehow wangled this contract for us both, six thousand miles from home. A bit of warm water work in subtropical South America would see us both right through the winter, he said, a world away from the freezing northern latitudes which were our usual habitat. He was older and had a lot of skills to bargain with, not that we needed them much today, but the work so far had been varied and interesting. Tagging along with him as my mentor over the last few years had been a great learning experience for me, and we got on well together, so we'd become regular buddies.

Enrique caught up within a few minutes, having taken the land route and walked along the wall to our mooring. He climbed nimbly down the ladder and jumped aboard. His hair was still dark and he kept himself in good shape, although he was short and naturally thick-set. He wore a shirt with a collar as a token towards being in charge, but it remained open-necked. He was much older than the rest of us and took a fatherly interest in us all. That included discipline when it was called for. I glanced up at him to see if he had cooled off yet and caught his eye. "What do you call a man who's always late for work?" he asked me in his

3

accented English, obviously aiming the remark at Pete, and not too subtly.

The word tardy sprang to mind and seemed to have an obvious translation, if it kept its meaning, but while I was still wondering whether dilatory might have more of an edge to it, Pete took over: "Mister Bus," he chipped in.

I clapped my hand to my eyes and groaned. "I can tell you're a dad. Please save those for Charlie and Amy," I begged.

English being his second language, Enrique took a little longer to process the joke. His scowl softened as the cogs in his mind went round and then he broke into a smile and laughed a little, in his gruff way. He shook his head and waved a finger in admonishment. "Every time I warn you, it makes no difference, you never listen. One day..." he left the threat hanging. But Pete was forgiven already and Enrique busied himself with the equipment checks.

"Actually Pete," I turned to him, "can we do a swap this morning and I'll do the next turn? I feel like finishing this." I held up my book by way of an explanation. Pete agreed, and Enrique just shrugged to show his assent.

The morning was warming up quickly, so I set up my sun umbrella and plastic deck chair and sat back to admire the scenery, such as it was. The dive barge was crowded with our equipment, including a large compressor, several equipment lockers and Enrique's control cubicle, which provided a little extra shelter from the hot sun. The water flow around the tower was shut off in our designated work area, and as it settled a brownish foam stuck to the edges of the rafts of floating trash which drifted lazily in the calm water around us.

"Did you know that crocodiles actually construct piles of twigs to hide under so they can ambush their prey?" I asked.

4

Pete looked up. "But there's no crocs here, right?"

"There are caimans."

"What's a caiman?"

"A crocodile."

He did a double-take and we both laughed.

♈

We were working with surface-supplied air, pumped to us through a so-called umbilical, which was a bundle of tubes including a lifeline, a gas tube and various bits of wire to allow for two-way communications. Leo and Victor were our line tenders, who helped us both on and off with our equipment and stayed topside at all times. Although I was now the back-up diver, I still had to be ready to jump in at a moment's notice and so I was kitted up fully, and feeling the warmth. The only piece of equipment I skipped at this point was my mask.

Leo and Victor were gossiping with each other in Spanish and although I couldn't keep up with them, I was reasonably certain the conversation was about last night's football. Leo rarely wore anything except his local team's shirt. Their high spirits suggested they were happy with the result.

Meanwhile, Enrique pulled out the job plan, cleared his throat and, when he had our attention, began to read out loud: "Pete, main diver: Descend shot line. Locate mid-level draw-off inlet at 20 metres. Check for flows. Clean trash bar. Ascend and locate top level draw-off at 8 metres. Check for flows. Clean trash bar. Ascend to surface with decompression stops at 6 metres and 3 metres. OK?"

"Yes boss," Pete answered.

"Marc, back-up diver. You seen the emergency plan?"

"Yes boss," I answered.

5

Enrique carried on with the checklist: "Control room and site maintenance confirmed draw-off valves are closed and locked out ... Let's go – *¡Largarse!*" He clapped his hands.

Victor fitted Pete's helmet over his suit, checked the communications channel and Pete was off, climbing down into the water, pausing at the waterline only to check water seals and set the dial on his orange-faced diver's watch. His attitude to time-keeping below the water bore no resemblance to when he was on dry land. Enrique flicked the comms channel over to the speakers on deck and as Pete disappeared from view we listened to the steady hypnotic draw and release of his regulated breathing.

I settled down to a lazy morning and opened my book again. I'd picked up a copy of *Robinson Crusoe* for being set in roughly this part of the world, give or take three thousand miles. I found him surprisingly empathetic: a liberal-minded man for his era. His family wanted him to choose a profession instead of a life of adventure, as some would see it, and it irked me slightly to recall the arguments with my parents when I had made a similarly unwise choice, from their point of view.

The sun climbed higher and the warmth built up. Pete finished clearing the lower section and moved up to start work at the higher level. A lot of vegetation had come down the river in the last few weeks and had collected on the screens which were there to stop it from clogging valves and pipes deeper inside the dam. We were engaged for more skilled work, but it was a simple enough task to clean up the guards while we had our operations set up. I could hear over the deck speakers that Pete was struggling to clear the top-level inlet, which had a large quantity of wedged material, where trash had mixed with sediment. My line tender Leo had taken the launch out a few metres and was using it to help pull the mass of debris clear using a rope and irons which Pete was hooking on from below, as best he could.

After a while, Enrique came up to me. "Marc – this is taking too long. Can you go down? Help move this stuff. I will get Leo back," he said. He turned and waved towards the boat which at that moment was tugging on the ropes.

♈

As he did, a yelp of surprise from Pete burst out of the deck speakers, followed by a cry of alarm and pain. Pete's harness wire twitched and began to straighten like a line when the fisherman's quarry strikes. Victor, Pete's line tender, leapt forward ready to start pulling him in.

In an instant, the atmosphere became charged. Enrique shouted to Leo to hurry back, then he ran for the intercom. In a controlled but urgent voice, he asked Pete to tell him what had happened. All that came back were cries of pain, and then abruptly the sound died completely. Surprised and nonplussed, Enrique toggled the communications between the deck speakers and the small intercom unit, and then back again, but there was still no sound.

Victor called out and we all turned towards him. He was pulling on the line, bringing the umbilical up without resistance. Then the realisation came with a thud: Pete's line was broken.

Whatever was happening down below, we knew we were working against the clock now. Pete had had a reserve cylinder of air with him that might be good for up to an hour, if he was conserving air. Or half that, if his heart was thumping like mine.

Leo had come back to the barge by now and had run over to me. I pulled my face mask over my head and he hooked up my breathing equipment. Enrique placed himself between me and the water. The creases on his face seemed deeper and his eyes bored into me. He pushed a rescue tether into my hand.

"OK Marc. I think maybe something fell on him or the inlet is opened or some other leak pulled him in. You got to get the tether to him now. Be calm. Talk to me, all the time. Start from the wall and work out to the end. You know to test for water flows. Don't hurry. Don't get yourself in trouble. I am calling for another diver now." He pushed a length of frayed rope into my other hand – an impromptu method to check ahead for deadly water flows that could grab you and suddenly suck you in.

"Yes boss," I answered, mechanically.

Enrique had begun calling the control room before I entered the river. I descended headfirst through the green water, between shafts of sunlight which penetrated the upper levels, following the shot line into the darkness. The long-learned discipline of controlling my breathing helped to calm me and the pulse thudding in my ears began to abate. There was near silence down there, except for the hiss of my regulator and the metallic gurgle of air bubbles rising from my mask.

I very quickly reached the point from where the inlet pipe protruded and I began to work my way out more slowly, testing ahead of me. The piece of frayed rope flopped limply and I progressed further along. It was pretty dark and the visibility was poor due to the stirred up sediment. As I reached the end of the pipe, I held my rope-detector ahead of me and felt the tug of a strong current drawing on it. The rope bent and twisted down towards where the trash grille should have been attached to the end of the pipe. Except that the grille wasn't there, the inlet was open and water was being sucked in through it. It was a worst-case scenario: it seemed like the inlet valve must have been opened, even though we'd checked it and seen it locked out. I immediately recalled that the valve mechanism had stuck not fully screwed down. We'd checked it but the operators were sure this valve screw never went all the way down. And so we'd double-checked for water flows already and they were OK too. But I could see now that Pete must have been pulled into the pipe. Quite likely he was trapped inside by the rush of water, sucked into the darkness of the inlet, or possibly even gone right through it. I wasn't sure if that would be possible.

I reported the situation up to Enrique and then began to think how to pass the rescue tether down to where Pete might be, without being pulled in myself. Like when you put a hand over a plug hole in the bath, you would scarcely feel the suction of the water until it suddenly snatched you in with a bang.

How would Pete even be able to see the tether in the dark, if he were capable of looking? An idea came to me. I switched on my spare torch and clipped it onto the end of the tether, then pushed it out in front of the inlet, where the current immediately dragged it in.

That was something, at least. The body of the torch added enough drag for the current to pull the line along down inside the inlet. I could feel a little tension in the line, enough to help it travel into the pipe. I counted hand over hand as I paid it out, until after about twenty feet it became loose and I was no longer sure if it was still travelling. I wound it halfway back in, then tried again. Again it stopped after twenty feet, which wasn't far enough. It wasn't working, but I could think of nothing else to do, other than keep on trying.

And so I persisted. As time ticked by, a feeling of helplessness overtook the initial sense of desperation. Alone in the green depths, an arm's length away from the deadly current, I could neither save Pete nor quit trying. He was my sole responsibility and I couldn't look to anyone else to help. I felt hollow, ashamed of my powerlessness and inability.

My training should have prevented me, but for a while I lost track of time. The nightmare seemed endless. Then eventually I realised that the inlet current was reducing.

"Enrique, what's happening? The water flow is slowing down," I asked through the intercom.

"The guys from the control room are shutting the valve. They think it was jammed maybe," he replied. "Marc, another diver will be with you in a few minutes. If the flow has stopped then I will ask you to go in and look for Pete."

But for being underwater I would have sweated. As it was, I merely shrank inside my suit. I knew someone had to do it, of course. Me. Pete could still be alive inside this steel sarcophagus, just. I checked my watch. I'd been down for nearly an hour. How could so much time have gone by already? But the thought of entering the inlet pipe made me feel sick with dread. The dark waters had played a trick on Pete, hidden the danger until he was in harm's way. The disturbance he made when clearing the trash must have shaken the inlet, dislodged the trash guard. Maybe. The valve was never shut properly, or wedged half open until something had dislodged the blockage. Another maybe, but feeling more likely now. But what if it was still partly blocked, waiting for another disturbance before something else – maybe me – dislodged the last obstacle?

"Enrique, are you sure they've closed it off properly?" I asked.

"Victor has gone to do a visual check," he replied.

Within a few minutes the new diver appeared. They told me his name was Gabriel. He was carrying a spare umbilical and some extra lighting. He would take my place as backup, positioned at the entrance to the inlet, tendering both my line and the spare one while I made my way inside. Confirmation from Enrique followed soon after. It was all clear. Time for me to go in.

With a huge sense of foreboding, I discarded my reserve cylinder before entering the inlet. Without its bulk I would have more manoeuvring space inside the pipe – and face it, if the current flow began again then I was screwed in any case. Gabriel made as if to stop me, but I signed to him to let me get on with it, and to keep quiet about it.

Inside the duct was pitch dark, and my light penetrated only a short distance through the clouds of sediment. It was cramped, without enough room to turn around in. The first twenty feet were clear, and then I found a branch lodged inside the pipe, making a partial blockage against which many smaller pieces of trash had collected. I supposed that was where my torch and tether arrangement had become stuck previously. There was just enough room to squeeze past it without pulling it out, which I was loath to do. This kind of work was no good for anyone with claustrophobia. Then it was a further twenty feet down the pipe to the junction with the main valve, which is where I felt and then saw Pete's motionless body, floating gently in the murky sediment-clouded water. I peered down to the valve and saw it was now fully shut.

Pete had switched his air supply to his reserve cylinder, so he could have lasted for some time while he was pinned there. I went alongside him and connected his helmet to the new air supply, but he was either unconscious or dead, so the main job was to get him out of there quickly. I clipped the safety harness to him so that Gabriel could pull him gently back up the length of the inlet pipe. For myself I had to work my way back up the pipe in reverse, the space inside being too tight for anything else. And so I led, walking with my hands against the inside of the duct, pulling Pete behind me and trying to keep us both from tangling with the umbilicals. Then after I was clear of the lodged branch, his reserve air cylinder caught against it. I don't know why I'd left it attached to him, but I had. I talked to Gabriel who let the tether go slack while I worked Pete loose and then back around the branch. The job was tricky in the near-dark and it was a tight squeeze. It demanded patience and burned time which we couldn't spare. Then, once he was through, I let Gabriel pull us quickly for the rest of the way until, finally, we cleared the entrance and together we took Pete straight up.

When we broke the surface there were suddenly a lot of new faces on the dive platform, and plenty of hands to haul Pete's limp body up and onto it.

Victor had Pete's helmet and harness off in seconds. His skin was quite blue. Then a guy who looked like a medic took over while we all stood and watched. The medic checked his vital signs and rolled him over to get any water out, though there was none. We carried our own defibrillator as part of the medical kit, which he used almost straightaway, although to no effect. Dead is dead, but to give him credit he went on trying for long after I thought there was any point. I began to wish he would leave Pete's body alone, to let him rest in peace.

Enrique meanwhile had checked Pete's reserve air cylinder. "Looks like he ran out of air," he said, his words flatly spoken, but his face showing the weight of worry and concentration. He checked the time and wrote a few words in his logbook.

After a while we loaded Pete's body onto a stretcher on the

launch to take him back to the compound. No-one talked. The drone of the launch motor and the slap of the bow against the water were the only sounds on the river.

An ambulance was waiting for us where we beached and we manhandled the stretcher off the craft and carried Pete up the bank. The medic appeared to be with the ambulance, as far as I could see, and they loaded Pete's body into the back. Enrique agreed to follow them in his pickup to the hospital.

Enrique turned to me. "You have done plenty today. I will go with him," he said. "You go home. Stay there. I will call you tomorrow."

I didn't want to hurry off, or to join the others talking through what they'd just witnessed, and so I waited in my car until they dispersed. Time passed as I watched the river, indifferent to the human tragedy, carry on flowing towards the implacable dam wall. The compound gradually emptied of vehicles, until only Pete's dark red Jeep was left behind.

Aftershock

I was too stunned to function properly and shut myself inside my apartment, where I sat in a daze. I didn't sleep that night, but filled my head with alternative accounts of how things should have been. It should have been me down there, except for my skiving off, for a book for Chrissake. And I was the better swimmer – I might have been able to get myself out of that situation. But I was lying to myself, I knew I had to hold back until it was safe didn't I? I should have tried anyway. All the time I tried to re-imagine everything as if it should or could have happened differently. And at the end of every train of thought I was defeated by the pointlessness of it. What was done was done, and no act of will on my part could deny or change the fact.

When day broke, I was still awake. My scantily furnished bedroom was on the east side, so the dim grey twilight filled quickly with the light of day and I opened the window wider to let more air in. I tried to divert my thoughts by going back to my book.

Providence has provided, in its government of mankind, such narrow bounds to his sight and knowledge of things; though he walks in the midst of so many thousand dangers, the sight of which, if discovered to him, would distract his mind and sink his spirits, he is kept serene

and calm by having the events of things hid from his eyes,
and knowing nothing of the dangers which surround him!

I stuck on this passage, sharing the feeling of despair on discovering that, even as he had gone carelessly about his business, disaster had been stalking him, crept up behind him, and then the evil hour had descended on him, Crusoe, as it had on me. The world seemed so different, looking back, than it had when looking forwards. I felt every bit as marooned and hopeless as if I had been shipwrecked.

But concentration had deserted my tired brain as much as providence had deserted the rest of me. I found myself reading and re-reading the same pages and taking in very little. I dozed briefly, but my dreams were filled with disturbing visions. When I woke again, I stopped reading and gazed out of the window through the fly screen, waiting for something – anything – to happen.

When it did, it was Milena letting herself into the flat. She was the cleaner, the landlord's niece as it happened. We'd had a brief casual liaison before, but like all my previous relationships, it had faded as quickly as it began. Being self-contained, I was always content with my own company, which didn't leave much room for long-term relationships, whether it was with girlfriends or friends from my past. The irregular shifting lifestyle of work as a contractor only added to that.

Milena was humming sweetly to herself when she came in, in her dainty manner. She wore a simple lightweight linen dress which looked cool and showed off her slim arms and shoulders. Her lustrous hair fell about her face until she reached up to tie it back, holding a hairpin in her mouth. At the same moment she saw me watching her through the door of my bedroom.

"Oh! Marc. I didn't know you were in the flat. I'll come

15

back later if you prefer." Her English was good, tinged with an east coast American accent from the time when she'd lived there.

"I was sent home from work. There was an accident yesterday. Fatal."

She walked into my room, looking concerned. "You look tired," she said. I nodded. "Was it someone you knew? Are you OK?" I was too choked to say, just nodded again. Although Pete rented the flat above mine, I didn't think Milena knew him. She perched herself on the edge of the bed and stroked my head. "It must be a big shock. Your work can be quite dangerous, can't it?" I put my hand on her lap and she took it. Her soft and gentle manner belied the fact that her arms were strong and her hands rough from hard work. She kept her nails short but well-shaped.

"When are you going back to work, do you know?" she asked.

"I've no idea, I'm waiting for Enrique to call me," I answered, feeling downcast and slightly sick at the prospect of going back to the dam and into the water again. "I suppose he has the legal stuff to do first. Maybe some safety inspections."

"*Pobrecito*, it would be better for you to be doing something instead of just sitting here," she said. I looked up at her, her soft eyes looked straight into mine and a faint smile teased the corner of her mouth. A feeling swept through me as much of relief for the diversion as it was of desire, as I reached out and drew her towards me.

Familiar as we had been to each other, and however briefly, it only served to increase the excitement and anticipation of re-discovery as we removed our few items of clothing. The day was warm and humid and the sun streamed in through my open window. As our movements together

16

increased, a sheen of sweat began to form on our skin, shining in the bright light. Our bodies slipped against each other's and blended together in a rising tide of passion.

We lay in each other's arms for a long time after. I'd forgotten the fascination of the soft dark hair of her armpits. Feeling her tender loving presence beside me was like an opiate. An overpowering feeling of guilt was growing inside me, and I wanted to stave off the pain. She took me outside of myself, which is what I wanted now. She was warm, relaxed and drowsy and I drew comfort from sharing the feeling with her.

"Marc, how much longer are you working here?" she asked, after a while.

"Contract runs out in six weeks."

"And then you do what?"

"I go home and start looking for work again."

"That's what I thought." She sat up, swung her legs out of the bed and started pulling her clothes on again. I didn't want her to go.

"Shall we meet up later? I'd like to take you out somewhere," I offered, apologetically.

"OK, call me." She spoke airily and left without looking back, although I could tell she liked that. Yet within minutes of her leaving I had fallen into a mood as dark and despondent as ever.

♈

The sun had moved around to the other side of the building by the time Enrique appeared. He accepted the offer of a coffee and took a seat at my kitchenette table while I assembled the expresso machine and lit a gas ring under it. It was one of the few pieces of kitchenware which I'd bought

17

since moving into the flat, as I usually ate in the café along the street.

He told me a little about how deaths were registered here, and what it meant for our team. It transpired there would be two investigations, with Enrique in the middle of both of them, to cover the interests of the owners of the dam as well as our employer's insurers.

"It's a lot of paperwork, not just for me," he said. "I got some things for you to sign, here." He slid several sheets of printed paper onto the table.

"And we are cleared to start work again tomorrow. Better to do something, no?" he asked. I nodded, but I shuddered at the thought of it. A pervasive image had settled in my mind of a deadly current hidden in the gloom, beginning to tug on my limbs and suck me down into the darkness, and the thought began to tug on my imagination even as we talked about the return to work. Enrique slurped his coffee noisily and I pushed the thought aside, picking up the paper from the table.

Enrique, or someone, had drafted a surprisingly short witness statement on my behalf, with a space left for me to sign. There was also a legal agreement, forbidding me to discuss the accident with Pete's family or their representatives, on pain of losing my contract and more besides. Lots of small print ensued and I realised I was not the only person who had been up all night. There was also a growing realisation of what the intention behind these papers added up to, and my blood began to boil.

"You're kidding me, right?" I demanded. "This is a company whitewash, a stitch-up. But for why? We didn't do anything wrong, we don't need to hide what happened!"

"Marc, it's just some forms. *De perdidos, al río.* You say we lose nothing, have nothing to lose. Whatever we say the lawyers will want more. So things go quicker if we don't tell them too much detail at first. Keep it simple. We get the legal business done and we will look after Pete's family, trust me."

"What does that mean? It won't be down to you or me, Enrique. This is exactly how the lawyers hide things, so the company can wriggle out of any liability."

A hard edge appeared in his voice. "Yes, it's not down to you, or me. We just got to do the paperwork and then we get back to our job. You need to sign these."

"There's not half of what happened in here. I'm not putting my name to some cover story written for me by someone who wasn't there."

"So, no problem, I wrote it. Just fucking sign the papers Marc. Bring them to work tomorrow." He tapped the papers on the table with a stubby finger, fixed me with a hard stare under a frown which doubled the number of lines on his forehead, and then stood up to leave.

"Enrique … Pete was my friend, my buddy. He was someone I looked up to. I met his wife, his family, they're my friends. I can't just …" I never finished the sentence.

"He was my friend too, Marc. There's nothing we can do. I will see you at work tomorrow."

I had scarcely given vent to my anger and was left in such a state of agitation that I didn't know what to do with myself. I could've thumped the wall if that were my thing. I tried it anyway, but it just hurt. What was that stupid saying he tossed at me? He meant we had nothing to lose by trying it on.

The papers stared up at me, blandly, from the table. The space for my signature was conspicuously white. It wasn't going to go down well tomorrow if I didn't take something in with me. Still worse was the overwhelming sense of dread

19

I now felt at the idea of going back into the water. For me, suddenly, danger lay hidden within the gloom, instead of undiscovered secrets. It didn't seem like freedom any more, but had become a trap instead. The very idea of returning to the place of death made my guts coil and I felt sick.

I was clear on one thing however. Enrique's draft statement missed out far too much detail. Maybe it made no difference to the result, but maybe we'd made some procedural errors. With hindsight, I saw it was possible to ask some awkward questions about our planning. I sat down to write a more detailed statement about the preceding 24 hours, but my mind wandered.

I was wondering about Pete's wife Amy, whether she even knew yet. I hadn't thought to ask Enrique about it, but I suppose it went through our agency. I had no idea how to get in touch with her myself. Was it appropriate? Sure it was, but how? Not knowing of a better or easier way to do it from the far side of the world, I found her on Facebook and sent her a friend request. I would have to wait and see, although I could write to her as well. I could remember the street name, if not their house number. Then I wondered who else I could message and I looked at my list of friends. But I realised with no great surprise that there was no-one any more. I'd drifted apart from them all.

ɣ

Next day was a showdown with Enrique that we both could have done without. I hadn't finished my own statement and I refused to sign the papers which he'd provided, so we rowed about it, and I was sent off site. But the real truth was, I was afraid of going in the water. I was so mad at him that I couldn't explain it to him, but I just wasn't ready to carry on.

I couldn't find the words to admit it while maintaining my sense of moral superiority over him, so picking a fight over the legal business was the easy way out.

That was the last time I saw Enrique, although I hung around the town for a few weeks longer, for the sake of Pete and my renewed relationship with Milena. I didn't regret the fight, because he was wrong and he knew it. But I'll always regret that I lied to him. I was too weak to admit I had a problem. I sometimes wonder if he saw through the smokescreen anyway. He was really such a nice guy underneath it all, and perceptive. He understood me more than he let on. Maybe he was just playing his part in the charade.

In Memoriam

Winter assaulted me with a Baltic chill as soon as I arrived back in England.

I had planned to arrive the day before Pete's memorial service, but between a flight delay and a mix-up with the car hire, I only just made it to the service, arriving a little late, and having to sneak in at the back. I was able to spot the other divers easily without introductions. Several of them I knew, including some who were on special leave. And as for the others, well we shared certain characteristics: we were fit, well-weathered and in some cases a little scarred. There was also an almost tangible connection between the members of this group – something about the understanding and respect between those who share and deal with danger together. It was expressed in a touch, a nod, or a glance held for a moment longer than would be exchanged otherwise. Pete was a popular guy but I was surprised how many of his colleagues had taken time out and made the trek to see him off.

Divers apart, Pete had a big family and it seemed the whole village had turned out, so the church was well filled. After the service, we all spilled out into the churchyard, where we were met by a biting wind which curled cruelly around the corners of the church. There was no warmth from the leaden sky and no shelter under the bare trees. The Cotswolds stone seemed to have been drained of all its honey-cream colour, leaving behind only dismal grey. A few crocuses lay forlornly in the grass, battered and broken, having come up too soon and, discovering their mistake, found themselves unable to go back. I knew the feeling. I turned up the collar of my coat and buried my hands in my pockets.

I felt awkward in the circumstances and was standing slightly apart from the group when one of the other divers came up to me: John. Like me, his deep tan made him stand out among most of the other mourners who were pallid at the end of winter. It was the first time we'd spoken since the incident. He gripped my shoulder with a gloved hand.

"Marc, in case we don't speak for a while, I just wanted to say I'm sorry about Pete but I'm glad at least you're still with us. Terrible thing. It hardly bears thinking about."

"Thanks," I replied. "I've probably been thinking about it too much. Did you see Pete had a wife and son? Charlie's only five. And she's pregnant too. I must've forgotten."

"Be careful what you say, she might just have a weight problem. Mind you, she does look good in black. Pete was a lucky dog."

Signs of our diverging trains of thought immediately began to appear. "Children don't process grief in the same way that adults do. It could be the start of a long journey for him," I said.

John: "Like you say, it's best not to think about it too hard."

"It was going to be me down there that day, did you know? Then we swapped over at the last minute. It was meant to be me. Maybe it would have been better like that. Me instead of Pete," It was a pointless thing to say, I knew. I just wished events had gone differently. That it hadn't been me who was

23

responsible. If it had been me who died, who would have missed me, in any case? Everything was wrong about it.

"There's no point going down that road, Marc," John said. "You shouldn't blame yourself. You did everything you could. Anything more and it could have been you both who died, from what I heard. Isn't that right?"

"I'll tell you about it another time," I said. I should have known he wasn't the right guy to try to have this conversation with. A good mate, but a bit too blokey for this kind of territory. Neither did it seem like the occasion for it, on reflection. It was a day for Pete, not me. I'd mainly succeeded in embarrassing John. We were friendly, but not friends and I think that went for the other divers who were there too. I felt like talking to someone about the flashbacks, the disturbing dreams and the fact that I couldn't think about diving again. But I couldn't think who that might be. Pete would have been great. Maybe my brother would extend himself beyond the usual.

"What's your plan – when are you flying back?" John asked, seeing the opportunity to change the subject.

"I'm not. I was almost at the end of my contract so we agreed to end it early. I need some time to get over the whole thing, think about my future, you know."

"You know what they say about falling off a horse…"

"Sure, I know. But before I do anything else I'm planning to make a social call on my brother. I gather that he's got a fancy new pad and a girl to go with it."

John smiled and said a quick farewell, then we shook hands and he was off, heading towards some of his old contacts. Even while we'd talked I'd begun to feel disconnected from the scene. I felt as if I were standing behind myself, watching from a distance, detached from my body. That's how the flashbacks often started. And for a moment I was there in the water again, peering through the dark green water looking for Pete, paying out a new safety line into the gloom, trying to stay clear of the current. My heart in my throat. Powerless. Useless.

♈

I came to. Someone else was talking to me. It was Pete's widow, Amy, rather pink around her eyes.

"Marc, thank you so much for coming," she sniffed.

"Hi Amy, I'm so sorry for what happened. I wish there was anything I could have done to change it." I grasped her hands in mine. Hers were cold and bare, like the feeling of damp perspiration on my brow, my reaction to the flashback. I was still trying to shake my mind free of its after-effects.

"You've been a great help and I appreciate you bringing his ashes back," she said. "You've had a difficult journey."

"I'm really sorry for the last-minute delay. I've got them in the car, I'll fetch them in a moment."

"It's not a great situation." She looked down at her swelling tummy, upon which she now rested her hand. She didn't seem to have noticed the chill.

"Is the company being more co-operative over the insurance now? You know I'm happy to help as much as possible, if there's anything more I can do," I said.

"They were very obstructive, as you know, and all the papers were in Spanish, but the information you provided made a difference. The law firm says they're expecting a settlement offer, eventually, which will be good. I'm just looking forward to drawing a line under it all and moving on."

My brain hadn't been functioning quite right lately, in all sorts of ways, and I was now mildly shocked by my instant and growing sexual arousal in her presence. No doubt she stirred my inner caveman, who happened to see pregnant women as a fertility symbol. But there couldn't have been a more inappropriate time or place for it. Perhaps John's thought process wasn't so different from mine. I needed to get a grip on myself, to get back to here and now. I dug my nails into my palms.

My relationship with Milena had become intensely sexual in the final few weeks before coming home, a month lost in a sensual fusion between us. The diversion, gratification and sense of well-being which followed our frequent coupling was like a drug to me, a palliative which got me through the difficult business of acting on Pete and Amy's behalf. I had become her man on the ground, the one able to talk to the authorities for her, clearing his flat, sending his belongings home and eventually reclaiming Pete's remains.

Sex released endorphins, I'd read, which were the thing that gave you the euphoric sense. The sensation numbed my feelings of guilt about the accident and I couldn't get enough of it. I don't know what Milena's motivation was, escapism maybe, but she was a very willing accomplice. Now I hadn't seen her for 48 hours, which seemed like an immense amount of time without her around, and I was feeling very cold turkey.

"If there's anything more I can do ..." I stuttered. Despite willing myself to be good, there was still some intended ambiguity in my offer.

"No. Well yes in fact, tell me something. Do you think he was in pain? When he drowned, I mean. You were there, you must know."

"I don't think it's like that. In some ways it's quite peaceful, people say. And he wasn't the kind of guy to get into a blind panic or anything. He was always very composed if he found himself in a tight corner. He had a massive amount of self-control."

"I'm sorry, I didn't mean to be morbid," she said. "I just wanted to know. It'll all come up again at the coroner's inquest, I suppose."

I mumbled a few words in reply, not wanting to prolong the discussion for fear of spilling too many details and implanting an unpleasant image in her mind.

"By the way, I want you to have this," she added, pulling Pete's orange-faced watch out from her pocket. "It was a real gadget of his, I'm sure he'd love it to go to you, his friend."

"No really, I couldn't," I said. "Don't you want to keep it?"

"It's a diver's watch. Use it for what it's meant to do and remember Pete by it. Here." She pushed it into my hand. "Don't argue with me."

Reluctantly, I accepted. The cold wind dug deeper and she gave a shiver, looking around for her son. I realised I had better get on with the business part.

"Wait here, I'll get Pete's ashes for you."

Without realising it I'd tensed up and my chest had been tight while we talked. As I started back to the car I was breathless. I'd evaded answering her question properly too. Pete had asphyxiated, hadn't he? A different thing, but not something I wanted to go into with her, especially not here, not today. I remembered his face when Victor pulled his helmet off. It was just slack and unconscious, giving away nothing of what he'd felt at the end.

For all the scrapes I'd ever been in, or around, before Pete died I'd never considered the reality of drowning or asphyxiating or if it would actually be a painful end. I knew about the risks, obviously managing and avoiding risks was built into my working routine. But not how it would feel when things went wrong. I'd seen no clues etched onto Pete's face when we pulled him out.

I picked up the carrier bag containing the box of Pete's ashes and made my way back to the picturesque church in less of a hurry than I had been earlier. It was pretty in its traditional way, with its squat and somewhat oversized tower. The sense of arriving again made me realise that Pete had succeeded in being late for his own funeral, with a little help from me. He'd have seen the humour in that.

I found Amy and handed over the bag to her, wishing it could have been somewhere more private and more timely. She had underestimated how heavy it was. Her arm dropped as she took it from me. She gasped faintly under the unexpected weight and her emotions welled up again. She bit her lip and gave me a look through tear-filled eyes but was unable to speak for a moment. I could sense that she wanted to get away. I said so long and began to make my excuses, edging backwards.

"Thank you for everything, in case I didn't say," she said, tearfully, and not quite in her senses. She turned away, bag in hand, and walked back to her family who were now gravitating towards the car park.

Talking to her and to John had at least made me decide one thing. There was no way I was going on to the reception. My business was done and I didn't want to risk being cornered by anyone else asking for details about the incident, or asking me what I was doing next. I said a muted cheerio to the lads and wandered back to my hire car.

I climbed in, started the engine and turned the heater up to maximum. I wasn't going to take my overcoat off until the car warmed up. While I waited, I thumbed Pete's watch, musing over what to do with it.

Damn the bloody watch, I thought. I didn't want to

consider when or even whether I would dive again, but now I had acquired another diver's watch, one that held a bad association, one of the worst kind like an ill omen or an evil eye. I would pass it on as soon as I could. It was a collector's item, he always told me. If I could get a few quid for it, it might help to postpone a difficult decision about returning to work for another few days.

I twisted the dial in the same way as I'd seen him do on the last day – the last moment indeed that I'd seen him alive, taking my place on the dive. The moment returned to me and I realised that maybe this watch had come to me for a reason. It was a connection to that moment, as if his ghost had resurfaced and come to remind me. It was a token of my guilt, for me to bear like the mark of Cain. So with a sigh of resignation, I slipped off my trusty Seiko and replaced it with Pete's Doxa.

Then the warmth and the effects of jet lag combined and I fell into a deep sleep in the driver's seat, which lasted for half the afternoon.

My Brother

After I woke, I made the short drive to the town where my brother Magnus now lived. He'd moved out of the city quite recently to a spa town of the Regency era, which was full of remnants from the more elegant age.

His house was, as promised, no disappointment. An ornate wrought iron veranda stretched along the whole of the terrace, and provided a splendid focal point to the otherwise plain frontage. It was reached from the road through a small neatly kept box parterre garden. It was all very classy, a city-dweller's dream. It came to me that academics were better-paid than I'd supposed, unless his new girlfriend was loaded. Maybe he'd simply done some of his clever tricks with numbers.

It was a while after I knocked that he answered the door, and he was out of breath. "Marcus, it's great to see you." He stepped out and we embraced. I noticed that his clothes were looking pretty sharp.

"Sorry for the wait – my study's on the top floor," he said. "Anyway, hi! Are those your only bags? I'll take them. Did you manage to park somewhere?"

I followed him into the hall, whose wooden floorboards lent a hard-edged sound to the bumps and knocks of set down luggage and discarded shoes. It was a step back in time with its classic staircase and stained glass window at the half landing and the cool, dark, well-ventilated atmosphere of an unheated room reminded me of my childhood. The living room on the other hand was warm and carpeted and had been knocked into one with the kitchen and so stretched all the way from the front to the back of the house. As a consequence it was filled with light, even on a dull day like today. It was freshly decorated and looked ready for an *Ideal Home* photo shoot.

"Wow, it's fantastic isn't it? You've come a long way since your little flat in Edinburgh," I said.

"I've got to give credit to Izzy for the tasteful decor," said Magnus, as he put the kettle on. "I'm sorry she's out at the moment, but she'll be back from work soon."

I plopped myself onto a comfy sofa and began to absorb the details of the decorations. Magnus and I had grown up in a small town, in a Georgian house which was similarly beautifully decorated and furnished, reflecting our parents' tastes and ambition for themselves and us, so I couldn't help but admire it and consider that as ever, it looked like Magnus was the one who was carrying the baton of the family's aspirations. I wasn't carping, I was glad to see him doing well. And I could see that Izzy had a genuine flair for decoration, like my mother once had. She'd been sensitive to the period details. For the neat and orderly arrangement of the furniture and fittings, slightly sparse, I could imagine Magnus had more of a hand in it than he admitted.

"Thanks for putting me up till I get my own flat back. I hadn't expected to be back in the country so soon," I told him. I'd only shared the bare bones of recent events with him.

"I'll show you your room in a minute when you've drunk this," he said, coming through, handing me my tea with a shortbread, on the best china. "I envy you your tan. I suppose it's the privilege of manual workers to stay fit and good-looking."

So, it had lasted just over five minutes. The dig was probably felt more keenly than it had been intended, but it was wholly expected. My family's hang-up about their non-professional youngest member was always lurking somewhere just beneath the surface and never took long to emerge. Naturally I wasn't going to let him get away with it that easily, I had to pay him back in kind.

"You've put on weight, bro," I replied. "And what's with this beard? Are you too busy to shave now you're commuting?"

"Look at it this way," he said. "It's weather-resistant if nothing else. As you've noticed it's been a cold winter and it doesn't seem to want to end. Besides, Izzy thinks if I look more like a maths professor that'll help move my career along."

I assumed that was a joke. "I suppose it does make you look older than me, as you should, despite your softy indoor lifestyle. It might benefit from a trim, next time you're doing the box hedge. What does Izzy do, apart from interior decoration?"

"Oh, she's a security analyst, something like that. She doesn't talk too much about it, obviously. They like to keep it all quite Secret Squirrel. It's all part of their game. You'd better keep that information to yourself, if you don't mind. She can be frightfully sensitive."

"So I guess that's how you met? Same sort of business as you're in?" I was a bit vague about what Magnus did nowadays but I was pretty sure that cryptography was still at the heart of it and he'd always had lots of connections with the industry.

His face creased briefly into a frown. "I don't work for the government people, you know. I don't trust any of them, for a start. They've even recruited within our department at the university, as far as I can tell. There's no getting away from them, or the feeling of them being nearby."

"You must get used to it in your type of work," I said

"The problem is they're too damn sure of themselves. They assume that their world is on the side of right and can't understand why the rest of us don't believe it. In truth they all fight and bitch between themselves like petty parishioners. It boils down to personal empires, self-promotion and power-seeking." He spat his p's out with some vehemence.

I could see he was getting onto an old hobby horse of his, but I was enjoying it too much to let him stop.

"Aren't they trying to stop the bad guys from blowing us up or stealing our state secrets or whatever?" I asked.

"Of course they are, that's their job. If they didn't do that then they wouldn't get away with all the other stuff. They do whatever they like, until they get caught."

I'd had my fun and it was time to do a handbrake turn. "But Izzy's different?" I asked.

"Yes, of course. She sees through the hypocrisy and the paternalism. I've been working on some pretty radical stuff lately, and there the establishment dead-hand isn't in everyone's best interests. She gets that. I'll tell you about it later, maybe. Wait till you've met her first, though."

I knew better than to encourage him too much once he got onto politics, and he knew better than to try to explain the technical details about what he did, although it seemed he was going to give it a try.

"Were you planning to go up to see Dad at some point?" he asked, tugging his beard lightly.

"I should, I suppose. There's not much joy in it, as the

33

errant offspring from his point of view. He'd much rather see you or sis. I'm sure I'll get the lecture about getting a proper career or settling down or some such."

"Well do, if you can bring yourself to do it. He's had the stuffing knocked out of him since Mum died. He wants to see you. I did mention the reason why you were back early, by the way."

"I'll see if I can get there and back on the overnight train," I conceded. "I'll call this stage one acclimatisation before I go the whole hog and let the Caledonian weather leach out what's left of my tan."

It was strange and surprising how and when the flashbacks came on. The triggers were unconscious. Maybe it was an echo from this afternoon's service, or the mention of our Mum's recent departure, but without warning, the chilly sense of helplessness returned to me as on the day when Pete died, followed by a tide of guilt. I was out of time for a few moments before I heard Magnus saying "Are you OK? You seem like you're miles away."

"Sure, I'm sorry," I said with a shiver. "The accident I mentioned, it's affected me. Pete's funeral, you know. I feel responsible for the whole thing. And still not got used to Mum having died either. It's still all a bit unsettling and I'm finding it hard to shake off."

I'd long since learned to understate my personal issues when talking to my family, for one reason or another. I'd been worrying about explaining the circumstances of the accident to my father, and how that led to the sudden conclusion of my contract, because I was certain that he'd be vindicated in his rather dim view of my career choice, just when I could use some support. Neither of my parents had reconciled themselves to it. They didn't appreciate the skills or the discipline. To them it was just a practical vocation, unlike the professional careers that my brother and sister had followed. After several disagreements I'd learned to avoid fighting them over it, and avoiding them altogether was the easiest way about it when I worked away for months on end.

"It must be alarming to confront your mortality at those close quarters. It shakes you up a bit I suppose," Magnus said. It was a good effort for him. He didn't really look at the world from other people's points of view. My elder brother was smart and logical, but didn't – wouldn't ever – really consider other people's feelings so automatically as the rest of us did. He was probably "on the spectrum" as people like to say, which was not that unusual in the academic world. So despite his acute intellect which set him apart from us mere mortals he was still clueless about some very ordinary things, and I loved him more for having any weakness at all. Ironically, it was his difficulty empathising that brought us closer together.

"Yes," I replied. "There's the horror of it, and the pain and the guilt. It might take some getting over, if that doesn't sound like me being a softy. But nothing that a good cup of tea couldn't help. That was more than welcome, thank you."

"Would you like to see your room?" he asked, looking at the floor.

♈

I'd changed out of my funeral suit by the time I came down again, and I could hear talking in the living room. Magnus and the woman he was talking to both turned around as I entered. She was as beautiful as anyone I had ever met. She was dressed immaculately in fresh sports gear and had the glow of someone who had come straight from the gym.

"Marcus, I'm sorry I wasn't here to greet you," she said,

with a welcoming smile. She was tall and slender and she bore herself gracefully. Maybe it was the easy economy of her movements, maybe it was because her footsteps fell silently as she crossed the room, or maybe it was because, despite her cordiality, her eyes were quite cold, but something made me think of a tigress, the way a fawn might. We kissed on the cheek. She smelt lightly of roses.

"I'm Isidora, I'm sure you've guessed. But call me Izzy, everyone does."

I had meant to suggest she called me Marc, but somehow that never worked in my family, and I sensed she would prefer the upmarket version, so I let it go.

"I love what you've done to this place."

"Thank you, I'm glad you like it, it was a lot of fun, even if I ruined my nails doing it. I'm glad it's finished so we can enjoy it. But just look at the two of you, you're so alike, you're almost twins," she said, standing back and looking between us delightedly. "Magnus, you are going to lose some weight this year." He grinned sheepishly.

"Darling, you'll think me terribly rude," she turned to him, "but I've said I'd go and see a girlfriend this evening, and I still need a shower and to get changed. Why don't you and Marcus go out tonight and get yourself some dinner and a drink? Marcus, there's plenty of time for us to get to know each other, I'm so looking forward to it. You must stay as long as you like." She looked me up and down. "Maybe you'd like someone to take you down to the shops this weekend and help you choose some new clothes?"

Ouch, I thought. But she was right, I needed to sort out my gear, and despite her direct approach she sounded genuine. From the way Magnus was dressed, nothing like his usual scruffy self, I guessed this was another area where she liked to apply her good taste, which was a chance I'd be a fool to ignore. I was curious to find out more about this woman who had given my brother's little bit of the world such a radical makeover. Most of all, I couldn't understand how he'd succeeded in making such a sensational catch as her. Looking back, I've often remembered that moment and I can see I was smitten by her before she'd finished crossing the room. She seemed completely out of his league. Maybe I'd failed to see what league he was playing in, but evidently he was on a roll.

"Thank you, that would be great. But only so long as Magnus doesn't mind and can spare you," I said, and so the contract was sealed.

Dining Out

We were spoiled for choice for dining out, but Magnus had a new restaurant he wanted to try, only walking distance away. In contrast to the cold damp outside, the ambiance inside it was warm and cosy and there was a relaxed murmur of conversation and the clink of cutlery on china in the background as the tables began to fill. The service was informal but good and we settled into the evening over a starter washed down with a bottle of Esencia Divina. The eating experience was something I enjoyed about being home, and it was relaxing to be sharing it on my own with Magnus.

"When are you getting your flat back?" he asked.

"The tenants are in there till the end of the month, but they've asked if they can extend it for another six."

"That would suit you wouldn't it? You're not normally back in England long enough to move in."

"I'm not decided. I'm wondering about training to work top-side. A bit of career development."

"I thought you were born to be a fish."

"Yes, but I've lost my confidence since the accident, you see. I can't rationalise it, it's instinctive." I put my fork down, momentarily put off my food.

"You've always followed your instincts on things, maybe

a change will be a good thing. I wouldn't try to account for it. People aren't rational, are they?"

"Yourself excepted."

"I can be as irrational as the rest of you," he said, defensively.

"You seem to have life very nicely organised for an irrational person. I mean that in the nicest possible way, bro. You'd be surprised how chaotic the rest of our lives are."

"Are you confusing order with rationality?" he asked, and I laughed because it was a classic Magnus point of detail. "You know, that's the first time you've laughed since you got here," he said. "Good food and good wine make powerful medicine."

Bolstered by the evidence of his good advice, we opened a bottle of Morgon Cru Beaujolais with the main course. A few quiet moments followed, the good sort of lull which comes with paying attention to new drinks and a fresh plate of food. In the pause, Magnus had been musing over something else.

"There are a lot of problems where there isn't a right or final answer, just different levels of goodness." he began. "Take what I'm doing at the moment. The work's incomplete, but it's very promising. It would cause a real furore if it got into the public domain, but it would also be bad for it not to."

"Why wouldn't it, if it's so important?"

"There are people who might want to suppress it – stop me from developing it, or at least restrict me from talking about it openly. Not even within academic circles. Like I say, the work's incomplete. Did I say that I'm working out my notice with the department by the way?"

"What? Hell, no you certainly didn't. Is it connected? Who are you going to work for next?"

"I'm still in talks. There are a couple of very good prospects. I'll have proper support and more control over how and when I publish."

"That's great. I hope you don't have to move just when you've sorted out your house so nicely," I said.

"It's a problem of scale," he continued, oblivious to my comment. "There could be major global consequences out of this. Major." Magnus looked me in the eye, unusual for him, and, unusually also for me, I was stuck for words.

He dropped his voice and leaned across the table towards me. "What I'm saying is, think about when you connect to your bank's website, or a shopping site, or even your blessed social media, and you see that little padlock thing that says you're safe and secure? Well suppose you couldn't trust it any more. You couldn't be 100% sure it was private between you and your bank, and your bank couldn't be sure that you were you? Then the whole shooting match falls down."

He sat back waiting for a response, while I struggled to absorb what he just told me. "You mean you've hacked the whole Internet?"

"Could upset things quite a bit, couldn't it?" he said.

"I think I know what the right answer is then," I said. "Stop poking your stick down that hole before something jumps out and bites you."

"There were some challenges which were made public. I've solved some of those but no-one knows yet except for you and Izzy," he said. "It should be enough to spread some panic, but the thing is I'm sure I'm on the verge of taking down the rest," he said. "So really it's too late to go back now."

With that off his chest, and me too dumbstruck to ask any questions, Magnus didn't return to the subject until we were walking home through the High Street.

"See what a hole this place is turning into, all charity shops, pound shops, betting shops and voids," he said rather too loudly, the drink having made him vociferous.

"It seems to be quite nice as shopping centres go, but I kind of get your point," I replied. "Online shopping and everything kills the community."

"Just a few lonely souls locked into their mobile phones, reading nonsense dished out to them because some bot decided that's the kind of drivel that they like."

"Obviously there's nobody out, the weather's awful and it's bloody night time," I said with a shiver. It was funny, the alcohol was really bringing him out of himself. He needed it to let off some steam as much as I needed it to dull my senses.

Not far from home, we passed a pub with a double-fronted facade, ornately decorated with pilasters and with a covered passageway at the side which led through to a cobbled courtyard at the back. I supposed it had once been a coach house. I looked in through a sash window to the bar. The interior was all dark wood and red velvet. Its golden lights were inviting and, as a reveller emerged through the narrow front entrance, the cheery sound of laughter and a blast of its warm beery atmosphere escaped through the door behind him.

"Is this your local?" I asked.

"They serve good ale here," Magnus replied, and we took a sharp left into the warm and jolly fug.

Over several pints I sat and listened while Magnus expanded on the things that worried him. His invention, if I understood him right, was most likely to be placed under the category of "too dangerous to let into the public domain" on account of all the economic damage and security risks, but as he saw it, the government would be only too pleased to use it to listen into the Internet "safe places" that the bad guys used, and incidentally see what the rest of us were up to as well.

"I don't entirely see what's wrong with that," I proffered. "I mean, we need to stop the bad guys and if you've done nothing wrong then you've got nothing to hide, have you?"

That lit the blue touch paper. He'd been thinking about it a lot: the risks of unlimited mass surveillance weighed heavily on him, shortly followed by the loss of control of personal data which we were collectively yielding up to the near-unaccountable global corporations. I could see why he didn't want to make things worse than they already were.

He had other concerns besides. The Internet hierarchies of power turned national governments into clients of those same global corporations. I got that. International finance was transferring risk onto governments and private citizens. I think I got that too, except money was never my strong point.

But the more the tirade of gloomy predictions showered down on me, the more hopeless it all seemed and the less I cared. We were fairly drunk and his words seemed to be getting mixed up. Either his mouth wasn't working properly, or my ears, or my brain, or all three, I wasn't sure. But it was a sign we were making the right kind of progress. He could have said anything he liked and I'd have agreed with it. I kept the drinks flowing and offered him no further encouragement towards the subject.

Eventually, he too was overtaken by the drug effects of overwhelming alcohol intake, and he eased up at last. We talked, in descending order of intellectual effort, about betting strategies for the upcoming races, our university days and girlfriends past.

♈

If the aim of our evening had been to relive or outdo some of our adolescent excesses, then Magnus scored full marks, leaving me standing as you might say. Not that I was very far behind him. The quarter-mile walk home followed a longer and more meandering path than usual.

When we got back, I frisked him for his keys and in the time it took me to open the door, he had fallen asleep on the step. I hauled him straight upstairs and popped him onto his bed. There was no sign of Izzy, so I pulled off his shoes and coat and covered him over with the quilt. He was out for the count. I hadn't seen him like it since we were sneaking home, trying not to wake up Mum and Dad.

For myself, I had by then achieved that legendary state of drunkenness which was so ingrained that it transcended the merely physical. Indeed it seemed that my motor skills had returned to me just at the point when my psyche had descended into that primal and dangerous state where I could focus my attention with great intention at the cost of extreme subjectivity.

I wandered back to the kitchen to look for a nightcap, to ensure my own complete oblivion.

The lights were on and there was Izzy, looking like she herself was about to turn in. Even now, she looked ready for a nightwear photoshoot, in a creamy satin night shirt, her complexion quite natural, her hair tucked up tightly, but the harsh formality softened by a single tress which had fallen loose.

"Did you lads have a good night out?" she asked, maybe a little too casually.

"Yes, Magnus is off with the fairies already." My tongue had gone lazy and as if from a distant place I could hear my speech was slurred.

She snorted with mild disgust. "Well I haven't had a drink

yet. Are you up for another? You don't look too much the worse for wear."

This made me less sure about her powers of observation, but her offer fitted my plan. I focused on regaining control of my speech. "A whisky if you have one please," I said, falling back on the sofa.

She stretched up, reaching for two glasses while I watched her night shirt rise up, fascinated, anticipating a glance of her trim buttocks. Sure, it was a bad idea to indulge my imagination this way, but the drink had made me careless and her very presence was promoting good feelings in me. In any case, I discovered that her modesty was protected by grey cotton panties.

"So what exactly have you done to your brother?" she asked, in a slightly school ma'am tone.

"He's OK. I think he's wound up about his work. Do you talk about it with him? Anyhow, at least it's off his mind now." Fantastic effort at coherent speech, keep it up, I thought to myself. I hoped it came out quite as well as I heard it.

"Of course I know about it, he tells me everything," she said. "What did he say to you? Never mind, just keep it to yourself or you'll call down more grief than you ever knew existed."

"Anyhow, tomorrow he'll be able to worry about his headache instead. You might find he's hard to wake," I said.

Her voice softened. "Is he definitely OK, I mean he's not going to sick himself to death in his sleep or anything?"

"He's fine. I propped him up sideways."

She grimaced and then ducked down to look in the cupboard, momentarily disappearing from view before reappearing with a bottle of my favourite amber liquid in her hands. "You're in luck. We happen to have this fantastic

Ardberg on the go. By the way, do you have any idea how you pronounce *Uigeadail*?" She made a comical mouthful of it, saying it hopelessly wrong and we both laughed.

She filled both glasses straight up, and didn't ask me if I wanted ice or water. I tried to remember the proverb which went something like "of the two things a Scotsman likes naked, one of them is malt whisky" and I all but said it out loud.

Placing her drink on the coffee table, she knelt on the sofa and reached across me, aiming to put my drink on the far side. In the process, the neck of her night shirt fell open to allow a glimpse of her small breasts, hanging temptingly, soft and shapely. It seemed almost inadvertent, but the temptation was too great. My hand went up, meeting her hip, touching the part where her pelvic bone protruded sharply.

She gave a gleeful cackle and tumbled across me, landing on her back on the sofa, her legs across mine. "That's quite ticklish," she said, grinning playfully, a hand on a button of her shirt. A long pause followed. It seemed obvious that she knew what I was thinking. She was watching me quite carefully, waiting to see what I did next. I twisted towards her. She smelled as fragrant as before. I must have reeked of beer, but she wasn't complaining. She tipped her head back slightly, still watching me coolly as I leaned over and pressed my lips to hers.

Her hands went to my chest, unbuttoning my shirt, beginning to explore the muscular torso inside it. "My God, you're made of wood!" she exclaimed, and began alternately to bite and to kiss my lips, then my body, gently, while we disrobed each other efficiently, enthusiastically. Then we made delicious passionate love, the fluidity of the sensual experience all the more dreamlike for my giddy mental state.

Once we were both satisfied, I lay cradled by her side, my

head spinning from the drink and the excitement, almost ready to slumber. The first pangs of guilt, set aside during our ardour, momentarily surfaced before I pushed them down again.

Izzy, on the other hand, was sanguine. "That was pretty good, for a first time," she said, fondling my scalp, twirling a lock of my hair with one of her elegant fingers. I understood then, if not already, that it may not be the last. She had me in her power and I didn't see how I would be able to resist her. I made to get up and tidy my cast-off clothes.

"You are still going to stay for a while, aren't you?" she asked. I acquiesced. "Good. But now I suppose it's time we both got our beauty sleep. Work tomorrow, for some of us." She skipped off, so prim and proper, and without another word she was gone, leaving her Scotch scarcely touched.

I remembered the untried glass of whisky behind me by the sofa and gulped it down. It was good, she hadn't lied, so I finished hers off as well. I straightened myself up and wove an unsteady path up to my bedroom, lost in the alcoholic fog which promised complete unconsciousness, but which had in the meantime blunted both my reasoning and my conscience.

The Morning After

There was a large glass of water by my bedside with a well-travelled, slightly discoloured packet of Alka-Seltzer and a note from Magnus which read *Ignore the Use By date on this packet, you are in no state to quibble.* I checked through bleary eyes and the box was at least ten years old.

Fortunately for my hangover, the house was quiet and dark. The only sign of life downstairs was a lukewarm teapot, and I guessed the others were up and out. I made myself another brew which was when I found a note by the fridge, with a front door key on it.

Marcus – we're both at work. Didn't like to disturb the sleep that knits up the ravelled sleeve of care. See you later love Izzy x. P.S. Can you get the items below from the shops for supper tonight?

A vision of the three of us sitting at the dinner table that night, she and I concealing our infidelity, was the first sober thought where I'd considered what we might have started the night before. How could I have done that? And to my own brother. I closed my eyes, needing to shut out the world while a tide of guilt and self-loathing swept over me. What had I done? This wasn't me at all.

Yet, though I was regretful and feeling ashamed, in my heart of hearts I was not wholly contrite. It was a mistake, sure, but one caused by drink and my overwhelming urges following my abrupt separation from Milena. We could bury the whole thing, surely, if we kept cool heads and hearts adamant, and then it wouldn't matter. Saturday would be the right moment to talk about it, when we went shopping together. A chance for a private word, in a public space.

And yet a taboo had been broken, a bridge crossed, and the question I couldn't answer was how to resist her, if she offered me again the thing I craved for most desperately.

As I gradually rehydrated, and my physical being began to recover from last night's excesses, I heard a knock at the front door. I answered it to a woman in jeans and a smart leather jacket, framed by bright sunlight. The shock of daylight stunned me momentarily, and she breezed straight past me into the house, like she owned the place.

"Hi Magnus, you lost the beard I see. It's a definite improvement," she said, heading towards the living room. I remained looking out of the front door, surprised by how much the weather had turned around since yesterday. The sun was out and there was a hint of warmth for the first time since I'd arrived in England, even if the air was still cool. The birds had noticed it too – the front garden was filled with song. The capricious spring had begun to show itself at last. I followed her into the house and found her pulling open the curtains. Light flooded in.

"Err, I'm his brother, Marc. Are you a friend of Izzy's?"

"Wow, are you twins or something? I thought you'd lost some weight." Her accent was American, west coast, but softened maybe by living abroad for some time.

"I'm not actually, but don't worry, everyone says that. Who are you?"

"I'm so sorry. Here's me making myself at home and you don't know me from Eve. I'm Persi." She offered her hand

and flashed me a dazzling smile. Perfect teeth. "I've come to see Izzy. Is she in?" Behind her animated expression, her voice was level, metered, evenly composed and she had a steady gaze which hardly left me. I had the feeling of being sized up by someone both vibrant and mature beyond her years.

"She's at work. I haven't seen either of them this morning."

"OK, let me just send her a message then." She jumped up to sit on the kitchen counter, pushed her perfectly conditioned hair back behind her ear and retrieved her phone from inside her jacket. For a few seconds while she tapped the screen I was able to admire both her natural curves, which were enticing, and her tailoring, which looked expensive. Another piece of Magnus' life which made mine look so sad.

She looked up again, smiling eyes twinkling from the reflected light of the front window. "So whaddayou do, Marc? Are you a maths professor too? You look like you've been somewhere sunny lately."

"I try to keep up with him a bit, but it's way too deep for me. I'm a diver. Commercial stuff. I'm just here paying social calls while I'm between contracts, thinking what to do next."

"God, I love diving. I've done scuba a few times when I've been on vacation. How did you get into it?"

"Through the university diving club. Before that I was always a swimmer, as far back as I can remember. Felt I was in my element." She was easy to talk to, and I could tell she liked listening. Remembering how I used to feel about diving until so very recently, I felt a twinge of regret at something dear to me, my life's passion, now spoiled by the dreadful association. My voice trailed off and I hovered at the edge of introspection, dark clouds gathering.

As if sensing the change of mood, Persi now pulled a piece of fruit from the bag she'd brought in with her. A pomegranate.

"Have you got a plate, something I can cut this over?" she asked. "They're so delicious and I missed breakfast. I simply must share one with you."

"Are they any good for hangovers?" I asked.

She shrugged. "Call it an experiment. You tell me."

I fetched what she needed and she scored the tough outer skin before breaking it apart into quarters, handing one to me. I folded back my segment and began nibbling off the juicy bittersweet crimson seeds. Quickly the red juice began to run down my chin and made my fingers sticky. A seed popped out and bounced across the floor under her feet. She laughed and while I bobbed down to retrieve it, I noticed how she carefully slid her legs together, as if she saw my next thought before I did. I suppose the pomegranates were a little suggestive in that way.

She asked a bit more about my upbringing with Magnus in Perthshire while we ate. Before we had finished she was in the same sticky state as I was and I grabbed some kitchen towel to clean us both up. The distraction had relieved my tension somewhat. I felt refreshed and yes, a little less hungover too.

Then she somehow steered the conversation back to my work, and suddenly words came streaming out of me: "You see, there was an accident at work last month. The diver I was working with was killed. I was down there, trying to rescue him but I couldn't get to him in time. Since then it's like I can't get away from the whole nightmare. The episode keeps coming back to me. And the worst thing is it was my fault he was down there to begin with. I'll never forgive myself."

"Have you spoken to anyone else about this, I mean about your flashbacks and so on?" she asked.

"No, there isn't anyone. It's not an easy thing to talk about."

"I see that. It's painful and distressing and still quite recent, you say."

"I should have been able to do something, anything. But there was nothing I could do."

"It's understandable you feeling that way, you feel grief, naturally, but you've had a traumatic experience too. It sounds like what people used to call survivor guilt. A lot of people don't see how deep it goes. It's ingrained in your unconscious so it's hard for them to comprehend." Her perception was so acute, I wondered if she had been through something similar. It was hard to imagine, she seemed too … innocent.

Her phone began to buzz, and she picked it up. "Izzy, where are you? I'm at your place talking to Marc. Yeah. Do you want to meet up there then? OK."

She hung up and jumped down from the counter. "Marc, I've got to go now, but maybe you want to talk again? Here's my number." She took my hand and wrote on it with a biro. She had a firm grip and I noticed her slender fingers were stained red. Standing beside her I could smell the sweet scent of her unperfumed skin. Then she detected something a little too close about my attention and looked up, slightly embarrassed.

"You know if those traumatic feelings don't start to wear off, then you should really see someone on a professional basis," she said. "Give it a little time, but sharing it is a good thing. You have to take help from wherever you can find it." And with that, she said she would visit the bathroom before letting herself out, and then she was gone.

51

As I heard her leaving, I realised that apart from being hungover and unshaven I was still only wearing a t-shirt and my underpants. And I never asked her a thing about herself. I must have made a poor impression.

But for all that, I was now awake, my mind freshened and I was ready to start the day. I'd had it in mind to contact Amy, and so I sent her a message:

Hope you're OK. Would you like to meet sometime?
Marc

Her text came straight back:

Lovely. Dropping Charlie off with parents, back in an
hour. See you

She caught me out with that. I'd expected to be put off a little, and to boot she was over half an hour's drive from here. But then, what else was there in my busy diary? I ran upstairs to get ready.

$$\Upsilon$$

The day had gone on getting warmer and the sun streaming in through the window from behind her lit Amy's hair like a golden halo. Her skin glowed with the flush of pregnancy, and she spoke with the serenity of an angel.

"You see, I've been used to Pete being away for months at a time," she said. "It's made it harder for me to assimilate the fact of his having died."

"That makes sense," I said. "I suppose having his ashes doesn't help move things along much for you either." I'd noticed the box with his ashes was still in its carrier bag, lying neglected beside their TV in the toy-filled living room.

"More than you'd think. But time does its job too," she said. "It's easier to think about him now. Actually, I think about him nearly all the time. The other mums at the school gate think I'm depressed, but it's not really like that, more that I need time to reflect. It's made me a bit anti-social. I suppose that passes with time as well, but I'm not really ready to start over yet."

Recognising her inching towards her spiritual inner peace had in itself a calming effect on me, and I began to see that her character had strengthened and grown immensely since we'd last met a year or two ago.

"When's the baby due?" I asked. I could see the slight movement under her skin as it moved an arm or a leg around. Her own exposed tummy button had popped inside out.

"Only another eleven weeks to go," she said. "My mum's going to come and stay for the first fortnight. It's a girl, by the way. I'm calling her Petra."

"You look radiant."

"Thank you," she said, with a faraway smile. "That's better than I was feeling. I've been quite lonely, I'm glad you came to see me." She leant across to kiss me and her naked breasts brushed against my chest.

"Pete was so lucky to have you," I said.

She rolled onto her back on the bed and exhaled, taking on more the appearance of a beached whale. "I'm not looking for a relationship right now, you know. And besides, I think you have your own issues to work through."

"Yes, I do," I said, getting up to look out of the window onto the road.

I held a pillow up to avoid exposing myself, but I needn't have bothered. The road through the quiet little village on a Friday was deserted, and the only sound was the hum of a tractor working the field behind the house. It was a beautiful part of the countryside.

"Pete was my helmsman, in a way," I said. "I've never had what you'd call a career, but I got used to following him

53

around on different contracts. He made it easy. I'm not sure what I should do to fill the gap he's left."

"He said that about you," she said. "He felt a bit guilty, thought you should probably wear more responsibility than you did as his buddy. You should think about that now."

"Well I don't think my future's in diving anymore," I said. "I don't feel the same after what happened."

"I can't picture him saying the same thing, if the roles were reversed," she said, tartly. "He was a diver through and through. I thought you were too."

She was struggling a little to get her feet off the bed, and I gave her my hand to pull herself up. She immediately began stooping to pick up our clothes, which were strewn across the floor. I ran to help her, and we began to dress ourselves. Then we faced each other, fully clothed once again, and I stroked her shoulder, smoothing out a fold in her shirt, knowing what I wanted to say, but unsure how to put it into words.

"Is this what's called a pregnant pause?" she asked.

"I could look after you," I said.

She didn't seem surprised, only she took me in her arms and said: "It's a sweet offer, thank you. But you know I can't give Pete back to you, and you can't take his place for me either." Then she remembered something else. "Petra needs godparents, Pete was going to ask you."

"Yes, of course, that'd be great," I said, and I meant it. "Charlie too, if it's not too late."

"She'll never know her dad, and Charlie won't remember him. I wish I could change that."

"I'll never forgive myself," I said.

"You'll be a link to their father for them, but you need to be yourself again. It'll be all right, you know. Time heals all wounds," she said, with conviction.

We worked our way back downstairs and reviewed the half-drunk tea and uneaten biscuits, which we'd abandoned soon after my arrival.

"Thanks again for coming to see me. It was ... therapeutic," she said. I gave her a sideways glance and she started to giggle. "You'll come and see me again, won't you? Not too soon though," she said.

"Of course," I said, "but why don't you let me do a few jobs for you while I'm here? I have many uses, you know."

She gave me a look as if to say how long have you got, and said: "I could make a list, and if you don't mind I'd quite like to put my feet up for a snooze."

♈

It was late in the day when Amy's mum dropped Charlie home, and I took my leave soon afterwards, catching the end of the rush hour. I didn't mind the journey being longer as I was no more anxious to arrive at my destination than I had been to leave Amy's. Driving, with its regular mental diversions, did at least occupy enough of my mind to stop me from falling into some dark space.

I was musing over the remarkable succession of feminine encounters I'd enjoyed since yesterday, beginning with Amy, who I had by now elevated to Madonna-like status, to the sweet, warm Persi, and the irresistible Izzy. I was sure it couldn't last, but for now I felt like a junkie who'd been let loose in a pharmacy.

Of course, there was a price to pay, and I began to anticipate the impending awkwardness of dinner tonight. I was wondering who would get back to the house first and whether, if it were Izzy, I should try to have a serious talk with her before Magnus returned.

But in the end, it didn't play out at all as I had expected. Magnus came home first, but not alone.

"Hey Marcus, this is Mimi, my colleague from work. She's staying for dinner tonight."

Everything I'd anticipated about the evening was suddenly cancelled with the arrival of the unexpected guest. Mimi was a petite lady, very clever, demure and attentive. I soon discovered she was interested in number theory and a martial art called *Silat*. These two things only, neither of which meant anything to me, that I could think of, especially number theory. Bloody hell, that sounded evil. My claim to have kept up a bit with what Magnus did was in tatters in the space of two minutes. We moved onto martial arts. Had I seen the film *The Raid*, she asked. I had, by good fortune, and I recalled the image of an unstoppable miniature maniacal killer, who pursued his art by breaking people's necks bare-handed. The thought of it didn't draw me any closer to her.

Izzy arrived a little later and I slid off to talk to Magnus in the kitchen area.

"Bro, are you trying to set me up with this lady?" I asked. "If so, then it's not going well, I'm afraid."

He paused from preparing food and wiped his eyes with a sleeve. "Sure we are. It was Izzy's idea, this morning. Mimi's a high achiever, very talented in the things she does. Did you know she practices swinging a machete at people for a hobby? I'm not sure what happened to her last boyfriend," he said with a smirk. "Perhaps I should get her to chop these onions."

"Is that what she's always like? Izzy, I mean."

"Oh yes. She's a non-stop typhoon. A life force, hardly sleeps even. She insisted we get straight to work on you. She says you're in need of a strong woman."

That struck me as funny, given all that had happened in the last 24 hours. "Do you happen to know any women who *aren't* strong?" I asked.

"What do you mean?"

"Persi called today."

"Persephone?" He looked up, surprised. "What did she want?"

"She was calling on Izzy. We had a bit of a chat."

He looked puzzled. "But Izzy was at work, wasn't she?"

"I believe so, yes. She didn't stay long, unfortunately."

"Why unfortunately?"

"She was really nice. We could've talked all day."

I looked over towards Izzy and Mimi who were talking and giggling in the living room. Mimi was showing her some moves. They had a rolling pin out from the kitchen and were swinging it round at each other's heads. I wondered what game she, Izzy, was playing. Was I being put in my place, told to keep my distance? Was she creating a social barrier to dispel any risk of my revealing something personal over dinner? Was she building a cover story about setting me up with someone else in order to allay other suspicions?

As soon as Magnus had the pots on to boil, Izzy dragged us over to help with the martial arts practice. As far as I could divine, this was intended to be an ice-breaker on behalf of myself and Mimi although she, Izzy, could cross the floor in the blink of an eyelid and she seemed to be the one with the greatest talent for finding herself in my arms. She never missed a chance, and I wondered why the others didn't seem to notice the way she pressed herself on me.

Mimi ran us through face and neck strikes, eye-jabs, knees to the groin and raking your shoe down someone's shin. She wasn't so big on the machetes part – despite every encouragement from Izzy – her interest was in urban self-

57

defence and she wouldn't carry a blade if it were legal, she assured us.

Magnus seemed blind to Izzy's manoeuvres and dinner went off cheerfully enough. He and I were steering clear of the drink and I tried my honest best to find something in common with Mimi, who, having established comprehensively that I wasn't able to talk about number theory, interrogated me about diving technicalities instead, while I tried to change the subject to anything but.

After a few further attempts in vain to find anything else we had in common, she and I both retreated and regrouped within our respective gender groups. In truth, despite the intimidating amount of conversation we'd had about extreme physical violence, I realised that Mimi was otherwise perfectly normal, and I wondered why I couldn't generate an interest in a normal uncomplicated person. In the end I just put it down to too many new women in one day, and a dose of jet lag. When the evening broke up, and a taxi had taken Mimi away, we quickly sloped off to our beds without a debrief.

The next day would be Saturday, which meant shopping with Izzy, which meant a chance to straighten out things between us. The problem with that was, although I knew what I should do, I was still ambivalent about it. Adding to my uncertainty, I was more and more certain that she knew exactly what she wanted, would have some kind of plan which fitted everything that happened. Hadn't she manipulated everything the way she wanted this evening? Would she play along tomorrow? At least we would be able to have a discreet talk and it being in public might be a good thing. Unless she had secretly invited a surprise guest to tag along and mess up the script again.

Acquisition

A slow start to the day always suited me at the weekend. I'd slept fitfully and woken early, feeling drained but determined to keep my troubles to myself. I put on some of my smarter gear to set the bar high, and went downstairs with the intention of gaining a head start. The antique wooden stairway creaked, but otherwise the house was silent.

Then, as I passed through the hall, Magnus came in through the front door carrying the newspaper and bringing in a blast of cold air. I offered to lay the table and he settled down to read the sports section. I leafed through the magazine until the kettle boiled and the toast popped up. We shared breakfast without much conversation, enjoying instead a traditional homely peace, where the only noises were the occasional shaking out of a paper, the clunk of coffee cups on the table and the crunch of Dundee orange marmalade on toast. After the last few days of manic activity, it was a huge relief.

By the time Izzy appeared, I was halfway through the review section. It was mid-morning, so much for her hardly sleeping. As soon as she made her entrance, the level of activity in the room switched up several notches from soporific dozy calm and we were caught in a flurry of activity, and the rustle of newspapers being folded away like leaves blown by a rising equinoctial wind. Her breakfast seemed to consist entirely in a glass of fruit juice and she buzzed rapidly in and out of the hall, making preparations to leave. I noticed that she wasn't wearing makeup, in fact she hadn't done since I'd met her, or if she ever did then it was pared back to a minimum. She didn't need it in any case. She didn't seem to like heels either, maybe because she was tall. For all that she was immaculately presented and tightly done up for warmth.

"Chop-chop sweetie, it's time to go. Busy day ahead of us," she said to me, seeming to notice me for the first time, and giving me a brief but charming smile. "If you're wearing anything that you might want to bring back with you, then I suggest you consider changing into something else, as a precaution."

Here we go, I thought. I dashed upstairs to change, leaving her giving Magnus a cuddle. In that moment they were completely absorbed in each other, eye-to-eye and nose-to-nose by the breakfast table. He and she surrounded themselves with an invisible bubble of love and intimacy as she took her leave of him.

♈

Buying clothes had never been so quick, easy or, I should say, so expensive. The January sales were a faded memory and style and quality, not price, were the determining factors. Quantity was also a requirement.

Like a well-executed military raid, we advanced briskly into town and were in and out of each shop in short order, picking up everything along the way – shoes, trousers, shirts, sweaters, jackets and underwear. To lighten the load as we went along we left behind my old trainers and some of the clothes I'd set out in. The new stuff fitted me better and I felt comfy wearing it, even the man-bag, which was pretty darned useful, especially when changing clothes at the rate I was. Happily for any sensitivities I had about my image, it was undeniably masculine, in the style of Indiana Jones, if not yet so worn. I could begin to see most of my old wardrobe (since when did I start thinking of it as a "wardrobe"?) being slung out or downgraded to work-only. She even tried to buy me a new watch to replace the orange-faced Doxa, which was the only time I resisted.

Only on one occasion did she pick something up that she liked, and ask me my opinion. It was nice to pause to admire her and pay her a compliment, for a brief flirtatious moment. Her eyes glittered with enjoyment.

It was amazing what could be achieved in a couple of hours, and yet it had been so intensive and business-like. I was glad to have dissipated the morning so enjoyably, and it had lifted me out of my listlessness, but I was disappointed that we hadn't managed to talk at all about personal matters. It was well into lunchtime when she finally announced, and I heartily agreed, that we were finished. To reward ourselves, she told me, she had reserved a table for lunch nearby.

At last, we could draw breath. We had only to walk a few metres before we came upon a magnificent Palladian-style edifice, the most spacious and swanky hotel in town, which smelled of privilege and exclusivity. In my new outfit, I didn't feel a bit out of place. We walked into the reception looking like the perfect couple. Izzy announced our arrival and asked them to take care of the copious quantity of shopping bags which disappeared magically while we were led to a table in the intimate surroundings of the richly upholstered lounge bar.

61

♈

Our drinks were brought to the table, and canapés on a silver platter. There were couples eating lunch at tables on either side of us, all looking our way, and I realised that wherever she went, she would draw people's attention. I felt too self-conscious to launch into the things I really wanted to talk about, in case we were overheard. I still needed more time to work myself up to it.

"Did Persi manage to catch up with you yesterday, in the end?" I asked.

"We had a coffee," she said.

"I never found out what she does …"

"She's a woman of many talents, if she had the ambition to put them to use. Why she thought I would be free for coffee on a workday eludes me, except that she's so free and easy about that kind of thing. She must have a private income. What did you and she talk about?"

"About what I do, mostly," I said. "She mistook me for Magnus."

"She didn't ask about his work by any chance, did she?"

"Not that I remember. No, I'm sure of it. That can be all his party."

"It's better if it doesn't leak out, you know, it could spoil the show. We want recognition – for him – out of the stuff he's working on."

"You mean public recognition? He seems worried that it'll all be hushed up and kept out of the public eye."

"He's told you far too much already. I can't discuss details with you, especially not here, but the whole hush-hush thing would deny him the rewards and career progression he deserves. We're looking to find the right partner for him to work with. He needs an organisation with the balls to back him up and the clout to make the most of his talents. A real top-tier institution. We won't find that here in the provinces, maybe not in the UK at all."

I supposed from this that she still saw herself very much as part of Team Magnus when he reaped his reward, and I also recognised ruthless ambition. "That doesn't exactly sound like a loyal servant of the state," I commented.

She shot me a filthy glance and checked that the diners at the other tables were engaged talking to each other. "What I – what we're doing is for Magnus. And as I understand your other suggestion, then I can neither confirm nor deny my employment status. I'm definitely not talking to you about it."

The sudden change in her manner was unnerving. I'd upset her and I was annoyed with myself for having done so. I didn't pursue the subject further. I guess Magnus had told me that it was off limits.

"I suppose what I should have said is there's so much about you that I don't understand," I said, trying to recover the situation. "You're still an enigma to me. I'm guessing things about you because I know almost nothing except what I can see, and that you're smart and have developed tastes. Please, tell me something about yourself."

"What else would anyone want to know?" she asked. "My father was a superintendent in the Hong Kong police, so I went to various boarding schools from very early on. I didn't stay at any of them for very long. I did some travelling when I left school: South East Asia, the Americas. Then I started work. I met Magnus last year. There you have it."

"Do your parents still live in Hong Kong?"

"My father left the force a few years ago but he still has a business there, as far as I'm aware. We're not really in touch.

I'd rather not talk about him. My mother committed suicide when I was a teenager."

"That's awful, I'm so sorry."

"People say that, but she'd tried before so it wasn't such a surprise when she succeeded. Anyway I'd learned to be independent by then, I could be my own mamma."

Her resilience was amazing to me, but she seemed happy enough talking about herself, so I carried on, cautiously. "I'm scared to ask now. Do you have any other family?"

"No doubt some will turn up if I ever get to be rich and famous."

"It wouldn't surprise me if you did either," I commented. "You seem to want it, and you are exceptional."

As time passed, the other couples left their tables and we had some more space around us, and the parade of tasty morsels delivered to the table between us began to reach its end. There was our personal matter to talk about and finally I took a deep breath and broached the subject.

"About you and me, the other night ..." I began.

"I was wondering whether you'd forgotten it, in your haze."

"I'd hardly be likely to forget that."

"You know just what to say to a girl. What about it anyway?" she asked, sipping her Martini.

"Well, what about Magnus?"

"Oh, don't worry about him. He doesn't need to know."

"I mean, maybe we shouldn't ..." I'd never been so tongue-tied.

"Do it again?" She asked bluntly. Then she leant forward quizzically, confidentially, her gaze fixing mine and there was a thrill in her voice. "I know you want me, and I swear I'll make you want me more yet."

I was compromised, speechless, transfixed.

"I meant to say," she continued, playfully now, "I booked a room for us, upstairs. We need to go up there to collect our bags in any case, when you've finished lunch."

Checkmate. I was so astonished that I laughed to relieve the tension. The rush of excitement wiped all other thoughts and ideas from my mind. I scraped my chair back to stand up and follow her, my half-eaten vol-au-vent left forgotten on my plate as she led me out.

We ascended the stairs slowly to the second floor, she leading one step ahead and occasionally looking over her shoulder, checking me, delighting in extending the anticipation. Her hand rested lightly on the elaborate balustrade which wound up the stairwell, elegantly framing her, a vision contrived to mirror her artifice.

I'm not sure when she had picked up the key but she led us straight to the room. It was airy, with a large four-poster bed and full-length windows which could open onto a veranda. A faint hum from the traffic below permeated the traditional glazing.

"Do you like it?" she asked, knowing an answer wasn't needed. The room was only a setting: she was the jewel. Her smile reached from ear to ear as she peeled off her jacket. My blood was racing. I put my arms around her. Hers reached up around my neck, and we sank down onto the covers together.

♈

Sometime later that afternoon, we lay apart, facing each other, my hand on her waist, her head propped against her elbow, both of us relaxing in the afterglow.

What had happened to that talk we were going to have? My plan had gone straight out of the window, a victim of its own insincerity. She had transported me, lifted me up and I saw in her now an easy escape from the darkness and pain which always lurked so close behind me. She had that effect, like Milena, but different. She was the cocaine to Milena's opium, a stimulating rush rather than a mystical sedative, but more dangerous and addictive. And I had become like a drug addict, stealing from his family to feed his habit.

"We probably ought to get back soon," she said after a few minutes. "I might have to think of a reason why a humble shopping trip took us quite so long. Maybe you're just a slow shopper. Just go along with whatever I say."

She rolled over to kiss me and I held onto her for a while, willing the moment to go on, then she prised herself away from my grip, stood up and began gathering up her clothes. "It won't always be as easy as this. Don't be impatient, though. Let me see about arrangements."

"Sure, whatever," I said, feeling a new kind of guilt, but also relief that she would let the responsibility lie on her shoulders. But then as I cogitated I realised she was talking about future arrangements, stretching beyond today or even tomorrow. That was far beyond the limit of my thinking lately, and I felt the need to clarify her intentions. Besides, the question was burning inside me.

"Is there something serious going on between us?" I asked. "I mean, where is this leading?"

"Sweetie, adorable as you are and compelling as the idea might be, it's not great timing what with Magnus on the career opportunity of his lifetime. Don't get your hopes up. It wouldn't be fair to upset him when he's working on something so important."

"What does fair mean in this context?" I asked.

"It means you have to take what's on offer and not make things awkward. Let things be as they are."

So it was just an affair to her, nothing more. Part of it suited me, and part of it was killing me.

"I'm not sure I can. Deceive him like this, it's unbearable."

"So, you shouldn't be playing this game."

"It's not a game for me."

She pushed me back down on the covers and leaned over me again. "You're getting serious over me," she cooed, gently, her sweet breath kissing my face.

"I can't control my feelings," I said. "And I don't know if I could give you up."

She pouted and went on: "You're out of your depth already, but don't worry, baby, it's all going to be fine. Mummy's going to sort everything out."

I twitched involuntarily and slid away from her. The way she watched me so closely as she did, half-smiling, I saw her pitiless eyes mocking me, waiting again to see what I would do. I jumped up, furious, and started collecting my clothes. She was quite unruffled, she just arched over on her back, her long body drawn out across the bed, fantastic in its naked perfection as she looked at me from upside down and laughed.

"Ah come on, don't be so sensitive. I was just teasing you," she said.

"Don't push your luck," I answered gruffly.

She reached up for my hand. "I must say I like that about you," she said.

"What?"

"You getting all emotional over me," she said in a girlish way, as if she needed some reassurance that she mattered to me.

I relaxed a little, then she told me, in a matter-of-fact way: "You'll want a quick shower before you get dressed. You've probably got my perfume all over you."

I retreated into the bathroom and by the time I came back out, she was dressed, tightly done up as before, and putting up her hair, with her back to me. I started pulling my clothes back on. We were back to the business of routine deceit again, even between ourselves. A space reappeared between us as if nothing had happened.

I saw her face in the mirror as without looking round she said: "By the way, would you mind paying for the room on your card? Just to avoid any accidental disclosures. And if anyone asks, even though I don't see why they should, just tell them that we had a family emergency – a poorly aunt in Peebles – and we're having to cut short our stopover. Anyway, it's time to go now. Chop-chop."

♈

On the walk back, she returned to a question that had come up during our morning's shopping.

"How come you're so attached to that orange watch of yours?" she asked.

"It was Pete's," I said.

"Your diver friend who died, Magnus told me about him," she said. "I suppose you should honour your friends, of course, even the dead ones." She recited it like a mantra, or something that she'd read.

"It reminds me that we traded our lives on that day, however unintentionally. I have to carry the guilt for that, like this watch. It's a symbol."

"That's the bit I don't get," she said. "Someone had to die that day. You were lucky, he wasn't. It could just as easily have been the other way round. That's nothing to feel guilty about."

68

"Nobody had to die, we screwed up. But that's not really the point. I just can't help feeling responsible that it was him instead of me."

"Of course you can," she snapped. "Do you think he'd have wanted you to get all hung up over it? You sound like such a loser when you talk like that. There's something abnormal and very unattractive about it, and it doesn't suit you one bit."

"So it's something you don't understand," I said. "Maybe there's no point us talking about it."

But she was going to have the last word. "You should do it right, for everyone's sake," she went on. "If you're going to wear it then you should do it to honour him, not as a way of punishing yourself."

She didn't make me feel any better, rather the opposite. She didn't understand where I was coming from at all. I thought I had gained not much more understanding of her either, except that maybe an emotionally damaged childhood accounted for her being the way she was.

It seemed to me that having broken through the boundaries of common decency with our relationship, we, or rather she had set some new ones, such as the limit of how far our affair was allowed to go, and who was in charge. And the things we should and shouldn't talk about, even if those limits were ones we would both breach.

I wished she'd been a bit more sympathetic towards my personal issues, but I had begun to see what she was like: when she wasn't being completely charming and seductive, she was hitting you over the head with a cudgel.

The Castle

Magnus and Izzy went out together the following day, abandoning me to my own devices. Except for when they retired to their bedroom, Magnus had seen less of her than I had over the last few days, so it made sense. I could hardly complain.

Izzy reminded me of a girlfriend that Magnus and I shared when we were growing up. We'd spent a lot of time together in those summer holidays as a threesome, but she was attentive to spending time with each of us on our own and while she and I had engaged in fumbling and petting, I naively supposed that she wasn't also experimenting on Magnus. So it had been quite a shock when I came across him with Davina, them both semi-naked in our garden shed on a hot day in August. I stopped seeing her after that, and we brothers were rather cool towards each other for a while afterwards. So it seemed our past rhymed with our present and I felt a little less sorry for him after I remembered it, even if I was conscious of trying to justify myself unreasonably.

I'd discovered that I was no longer good company for myself as I was liable to slip into introspection and fall prey to the bad thoughts. The only ways I had found out of this seemed to be predicated on diverting myself through human company with good conversation, or something even more stimulating, or getting blind drunk, or a combination of these things. Once upon a time I would have settled down and read a book, and indeed I had started Izzy's well-thumbed copy of *Vanity Fair*, but my concentration was wandering. I became restless and, it being a little early to start drinking, I felt the pressing need to conjure up another human to sustain me. So after I'd watched Magnus and Izzy's car turn off at the end of the road, and stared into space for a while, I texted Persi.

Would really like to meet up. When are you around?

A few minutes later she replied:

Busy today, sorry. Free tomorrow. Could pick you up after the rush and go somewhere.

Of course, that was a big disappointment:

Fantastic, I'll look forward to seeing you.

A long empty day stretched ahead of me and after a microsecond spent wondering whether to call Mimi, I moved swiftly on, figuring that I had to try something new. The best thing to avoid stillness was a heavy-duty training session, so I went out for a run in the soft drizzle, glad that I had retained at least a pair of trainers and a tracksuit after the shopping trip. Then, with apologies to the French-style period furniture, I had a no-equipment workout in the living room when I got back. It didn't make the endorphins flow in quite the way that sex could, but it certainly helped, and so I got through half the day.

I got through the rest of it with alternating between reading and watching *Judge Judy,* and going out to restock the ever-dwindling supplies of beer. Between Becky, Judy and Stella, I felt I had no lack of strong women around me.

♈

The working week began again, for everyone except myself and Persi. Magnus was working at home until lunchtime, and disappeared into his study. From the front window I watched Izzy setting off in her spritely little Audi, which looked all the more tidy when compared with a neighbour's dowdy blue box-shaped Volvo which lurched off at the same time as her. Normal lives were all about the routine, I supposed. The same people, the same cars came and went at the same times every day, while I spectated.

The number of parking spaces went on growing until Persi arrived and pulled into one of them with a sporty little BMW. She'd brought the sun with her again, and the top was down. I met her at the door, we greeted each other with a peck on the cheek, and I caught her sweet scent again. She didn't come inside further than the hall.

"Hi Marc, you look like you've had a Magnus-style makeover. Much more presentable with your pants on," she said with a touch of irony. "Here's the plan. There's a castle near here worth a visit. I'll drive. We could make a morning of it and have lunch, if you'd like that."

I grabbed my coat and followed her out to her car. Only mildly understated and very stylish, it suited her, and she liked to use its power as she confidently whizzed through the tail-end of the rush hour traffic. I began to see there was a little more cut-and-thrust about her than I'd imagined.

"Are you not working currently?" I asked. "What exactly is it you do?"

"Just temping here and there," she said. "I like the flexibility. Things are a bit quiet at the moment. It can be like that."

"I'm guessing from your accent that you're from the west coast, maybe."

"Very good. I'm originally from San Francisco."

72

"So what brought you to England?"

"I'm from a forces family. My dad had a lot of postings in Europe so I kind of got to like the place. It's more my home than the States is now, really. Anyway, how about you? How are you managing?" she looked across at me.

"I'm OK. Well, not that great, you know, like I said everything's a bit pear-shaped. But I'm very glad to see you in any case. I like talking to you. You bring a bit of light into my life, literally," I said, waving my arms towards the sun.

She smiled and gave me a quizzical sideways glance. It was a meaningful look, but I didn't fully understand. But I hadn't finished asking her about herself yet.

"I still haven't found out how you know Izzy."

"Through Magnus, actually," she replied. "I don't remember exactly. There was a social occasion. She's gorgeous, isn't she?" She pushed her hair back behind her ear and looked again to see how I reacted. I felt so self-conscious that she might have read my thoughts and heard "the woman of all my fantasies" as clearly as if I'd said it. I gave the most non-committal shrug I could.

"I'm a bit jealous, if I'm honest," she said. "I feel better when I remind myself how the end of her nose moves when she's talking. Is that too wicked of me?"

That was quite funny, when I thought about it, but Persi didn't seem the insecure type. "You've no need to worry on that score, you're perfect just as you are," I said, not just to make her feel better.

The compliment was accepted and she continued: "I've not talked to him about his work lately, has he progressed it far?"

"He's very engaged with it right now, I think he's enjoying himself," I answered, saying as little as possible but wondering also whether there would be a follow-up question.

"He was talking about looking for new research partners. How's that going?"

At the back of my mind an amber warning light glowed dimly. Izzy had said something. What was she fishing for?

"He hasn't mentioned anything like that to me," I said, which was scarcely true. I had a suspicion that I was being gently pumped for information and I wanted to test her. "Do you know much about what he does?"

"Me? I can't even do the killer Sudoku," she replied. "I'd say it was all Greek to me, but maybe you guessed my ancestry as well as my accent." She put her foot down to overtake a dawdling car. "But I have a friend of a friend who knows some people it might be worth him talking to."

Although that seemed like a fair offer, if tenuous, I now had a reason to question her motives in taking an interest in me. But it was only my supposition and she didn't push the point. It was still a pleasure to go around the castle with her. She took my arm and she looked more than decorative. She listened well and she knew her history too. Her father had been stationed in a USAF base in the east and she told me she'd visited the burial sites of Henry VIII and four of his wives: Catherine of Aragon in Peterborough, Jane Seymour in Windsor (beside Henry) and Anne Boleyn and Catherine Howard at the Tower. We were both fans of *Wolf Hall* and its sequel, it soon transpired.

For this reason we began our exploration of the castle by visiting the church, where there was a canopied marble tomb of Katherine, Henry's last wife. The deathly cold white alabaster flattered her, even if she did have quite a large nose. I wondered if it had moved when she talked. She looked young and serene, at prayer. How old had she been when she died?

Persi scanned the guidebook. "She married Henry mostly out of religious duty. But she really had a thing for Jane Seymour's brother, Thomas. They were back together less than a month after Henry died and they got married in secret pretty soon after that," she told me. "She was catching up with Henry's score, since Thomas Seymour was her fourth husband, although she died a few days after having their first child, in her mid-thirties. She was so young for all that to have happened in her life."

A memory triggered. "Thomas Seymour – was he the one who had the thing with teenage Elizabeth I? There was a ripping yarn about him cutting her gown to shreds and there were romps and cuddles in her bed chamber. Was that after he married Katherine?" I asked. "If so he would have been Elizabeth's step-father when he did all that."

"Shocking, even by today's standards," Persi said, although she looked like she was enjoying being scandalised. "Apparently it cost him his head later on. Going by what it says here, he seemed to be running around following his codpiece wherever it led him. Elizabeth called him 'a man of much wit and very little judgement'. That's neat, I like that."

I had begun to feel uncomfortable about the conversation. The parallels with me being led by the codpiece into a familial love triangle were too close for comfort, and my face burned with embarrassment, not for the first time today.

She looked at me enquiringly. "You're not what I imagined the average diver to be like," she said.

"There are much smarter divers than me," I replied, hoping that I had understood her meaning correctly.

"I mean your interests are not so down-to-earth as I supposed," she said. "You like history and literature."

"You mean the bookish tendency," I said, catching her

75

meaning at last. "That's my parents' legacy, but it's not really me. I'm the errant adventurer of my family. I just haven't managed to shed the other traits entirely."

♈

Our day together stretched out, the castle proved to be a picturesque mixture of ruin and restoration, and we were relaxed in each other's company. The appeal of the royal scandal hadn't been lost on the owners, who supplied the complete details.

We took our time over lunch before walking round the gardens. We were sat gazing into a piece of the original moat whose murky waters could have been a foot or a mile deep, when she picked up another loose end.

"When you said you were thinking what you'd do next, did you mean you were thinking about a career change?"

"I'm not sure how that's going to happen in reality, but I really don't feel like going back in the water."

"You mean like hydro… aquaphobia?" she asked.

"Something like that, to add to everything else," I said.

"You sure have a lot of complications in your life."

"If only that was the end of it."

She thought for a moment and then asked: "Relationships?"

"Thomas Seymour would have been proud of me," I said.

She pulled a face. I realised that morsel fell into both categories of too much and not enough information at the same time. I sought to make amends. "I mean since the accident I've tried every way to numb the pain and guilt, and sex is one of those ways, and then I met someone … got involved with them deeper than I should, and let my feelings run away with me."

It felt weird talking to her like this, a comparative stranger, but she was such a good listener, she made it too easy.

"You shouldn't be afraid to fall in love," she said.

"That depends on who it's with."

It didn't help, I'd only added fuel to the fire. And maybe it wasn't the kind of thing you shared with a glamorous companion on your day out together. I wasn't usually so insensitive. Now she was machinating, and although we continued our tour of the grounds, the conversation was a little forced afterwards and we didn't link arms again. I wished I'd kept my mouth shut.

We headed back before the evening rush started and she drove hard and fast, concentrating on the winding road. We didn't speak until she dropped me off at the end. Then before I got out she said: "I'm really sorry for your situation Marc, and I'm trying not to sound judgemental. You seem like someone in need of friends, and they're all around you if you want them. I've known people who reached rock bottom. That's not you, but I wonder if you're still on your way down. It seems like you want to talk, but also you're holding out on me, so maybe you're not ready to be helped."

"You're right, as ever," I said. "I don't know how I've got into this position but it's too much for me to admit to. I've got to spare you the details, but it's like I'm so deep in this mire that it's easier to go on alone than to try to go back."

She looked perplexed, but had nothing to add to what she'd said already.

"Just let me say," I added. "I've never found anyone who I can talk to like you. You're so kind and thoughtful and I'm sorry to burden you with my problems. I really am. I hope I haven't ruined your day."

She made out that she was fine about it, and the parting kiss on the cheek was as pleasing and unhurried as ever, but she didn't want to come in for a drink, despite my earnest attempts to persuade her. At least we agreed we'd meet up again soon, without talking about the specifics. I thanked her for the day out and let myself out of her car.

And so even though it had been a beautiful day out, I wound up feeling blue, for which I could only blame my big mouth, and the problems which were of my own making.

When I walked into the house, I found that Izzy was already home, sitting in the living room drinking a glass of wine and browsing through a furniture catalogue, poised as elegantly as if she was appearing in one herself. She gave me her sweetest smile and asked about my day, although she didn't seem at all interested in the answer.

"We've got an hour, if you're in the mood," she said with an arched eyebrow, as if my answer were in any doubt. She looked at her watch and sprang up, leading the way up to my bedroom, with me catching up from behind, trusting her to make me feel right again.

A Tail

It was one of those occasions when I'd seen something and at the same time not noticed it. There was no reason why the neighbour in his Volvo shouldn't come and go as often as he liked. It was just that they were always on the move whenever Magnus or Izzy took their car out, but I never saw the neighbours getting into or out of their vehicle. Then, having seen it and not noticed it, I did at last register that they weren't following the script. But still I dismissed it, because I had enough to think about. It was none of my business, even though something about it struck me as odd.

It was Tuesday when it happened again, and now I didn't dismiss it so quickly. Magnus and Izzy set off to work together, him dropping her off on route to his university. I liked to watch the world going by through the imperfections of the wavy antique glass panes of their front window. The way it distorted shapes and movement was like looking through the surface of a pool. My childish fascination with the illusion never faded and I looked up and down the street to exaggerate the effect. I could see the Volvo was one space closer than usual and the driver, male, bejowled, was already sitting in his car when they went out. He belted up as they walked to their car and he set off soon after them.

A silly thought came to me, then after a moment I laughed

at myself. Maybe my imagination was as warped as the glass. Nobody actually tailed one car from another these days, did they? And they (whoever "they" might be) were much smarter than that. They switched cars or just bugged your car or your mobile phone, or tracked you from a helicopter or a satellite or something. Of course nobody did those things in real life, and even if they did, then it happened much less often than fancy led us to believe.

Nobody did that unless it were for some cheap and mundane type of case like health insurance fraud or a domestic infidelity suit. I'd known someone who did that for a while. So there was a thought. The cogs began to spin. Could it be Magnus? Would he actually do something like that? To his own girlfriend, or brother? Hell's bells, I only arrived here less than a week ago, it couldn't be on my account, could it? It was worse than preposterous, it made no sense at all and I was sorry for suspecting him. It was just very hard to put the thought away, and as I tried to think of alternative explanations, the number of possibilities began steadily to multiply in my head.

There were other reasons someone could be watching him or her, but that didn't stop them from finding out about me and her. I could be uncovered because I was caught up in the wrong conspiracy. Never mind my guilty conscience, suddenly that bothered me a lot less than the fear of being found out.

I soon resolved that I had no choice but to follow the tail, to find out for sure, and in all likelihood put the idea to rest. It would have to be the next day at the earliest, depending on Magnus and Izzy's plans. The need to know gnawed at me through the whole long miserable day.

That evening, when we were together again under the same roof, I began to find that my contingent suspicions were adding imagined motives to everything either of them said. Magnus suggested again that I should visit my father. Did he want to get rid of me, and was that because he knew something? Izzy was asking Magnus a few too many questions about his day at work. Could she be checking up on him for some reason?

I did, however, learn that their plans for going out tomorrow were much the same as today's and so I noted to myself that it would be a chance to execute my plan, and as a pretext for leaving early I said that I was going to visit Amy again.

On the whole, it added up to another uncomfortable evening, and the idea of a trip to see my father did begin to feel less of a drag by comparison.

♈

I pulled abruptly out into the traffic and the car behind me braked sharply, stalled, flashed his headlights in rebuke and blew his horn at me.

It was the next day, and I'd been ready and waiting around the corner from the house in my plain silver hire car long before I saw Magnus and Izzy go past in their little black Audi. Sure enough, the Volvo had followed them out again and set off in the same direction. I signalled, let one car get between us and then pulled out determinedly, keen not to lose sight of him.

The driver of the car I'd pulled out in front of hadn't finished making his point yet, and waved his arms around and voiced some rude language in my direction. He was so uncouth that I lost all sympathy. It was nice to think I'd helped get his day off to such a good start.

I knew where the Audi would be going, I thought, but not

how the Volvo would track them. Magnus and Izzy were nearly out of sight for me, but I couldn't afford to lose sight of my mark. The guy's driving seemed pretty relaxed however, and at the point when he stopped for an amber traffic light, seeing the black Audi putting distance between us from the far side of the junction, I began to believe the problem was my overactive imagination.

On my way out half an hour earlier, I'd wandered up the road and discreetly confirmed that the Volvo was in its usual starting position. I'd sneaked another glance at the driver, who was looking at his mobile phone. His short hair and open-necked shirt were unremarkable, and he looked middle-aged and overweight. He could as easily have been a cabbie or a clerk.

Just when I had almost convinced myself that the whole thing was only a false alarm, the feeling began to fade as he turned into the road near the local college and I saw the black Audi coming back towards us with only Magnus in it. He'd dropped Izzy off a little further up the road; I could see her in the middle distance. I'd assumed he was going to drop her off at the government offices, but nothing was going as expected lately. It wasn't the important question in hand, so I didn't give it further thought.

We drivers were converging from opposite directions on the same roundabout. My guy in the Volvo swung around the roundabout, completing a U-turn and closing the hundred metres gap between him and Magnus that had existed beforehand. Magnus seemed to be continuing towards the motorway as expected. I did the same as the Volvo, feeling fairly confident that the guy would have his attention on the car in front, not in his rear-view mirror.

We assembled into a southbound convoy, mingling with the thick traffic. I let the distance between us lengthen since nothing much was going to happen for half an hour or more, but threaded my way forwards through the other traffic whenever we neared a junction, making sure to shorten the gap. My Volvo guy was less edgy and kept a regular distance behind Magnus. After completing the motorway section, we all three continued into the centre of the city and hence to the university, where I saw Magnus turning off into a staff car park. The Volvo continued straight on, with me behind him.

Apart from having confirmed to my own satisfaction that he was definitely a tail, I also had to draw the conclusion that it was Magnus being followed, not Izzy. It was a slight relief to be off the hook knowing that she, and by implication I, was not the one under surveillance. On the other hand, the circumstances now pointed towards a more menacing scenario, possibly that the people who Magnus had referred to as wanting to interfere with his work were keeping an eye on him. I just couldn't believe that Izzy needed to follow him, she had him eating out of her hand.

I carried on behind the Volvo as he headed west across the city. He clearly didn't plan on stopping near the university, and I wondered how he would manage to pick up Magnus on the return journey. Maybe he had a colleague on the ground disguised as a homeless person, or a tracker on the vehicle, or maybe just as likely on Magnus' mobile phone. I was letting my imagination run, still unable to take it quite seriously. I wondered how you would check a phone for that kind of thing. Maybe Izzy would know something about it.

I was more careful now as I thought there was a better chance of being spotted if Volvo man wasn't looking ahead. I lengthened the gap between us to avoid giving myself away and from time to time his car would turn down a side street and disappear from view. Soon our journey led us into the residential area where cheery rows of terraced houses were prettily painted in pastels or more solid shades of pink, terracotta, blue, yellow and cream. The traffic quietened down and there was just the two of us by the time a hairpin bend announced the beginning of our descent into the valley. We followed the steep road downhill towards the river, then I turned another corner and found that I'd lost him. The empty thoroughfare was hemmed in by parked cars, becoming single lane in places, and I crawled along, checking the side alleys and drives. Then suddenly I realised he was parked at the side of the street and I had drawn up exactly abreast of him. He had stopped tight up against the pavement, in a space in front of a van, which had hidden him from view. I knew instantly that he'd marked me, led me on a wild goose chase and that for goodness knows how long, he'd been manoeuvring me into my losing position. He looked straight at me with the tired, almost bored expression of a teacher with a troublesome pupil who had disrupted class and needed ticking off.

I kicked myself for having let him spot me and for a moment I nearly drove on. But I didn't like being beaten, and I thought for all that he'd caught me out, the same was true in reverse. I'd followed him following my brother between two cities, and he was wholly compromised.

I left my car in the middle of the road, jumped out and ran round to the driver's door. He was now attempting to ignore me, messing with his phone. I tried opening his door, but it was locked. So I banged on the window and shouted to him to get out. He went on twiddling with his phone, but I wasn't going away. I was working up to a big confrontation, with no particular plan for what to say except to shout at him and make myself obnoxious and hope that was message enough. Eventually he looked up, sighed visibly and unlocked his door. Then, with a speed of movement which I hadn't thought such a bulky guy would be capable of, he spun round and kicked his own door open from the inside. The door flew out and slammed into my groin. I was unbalanced and fell over backwards in pain and surprise, left sprawling on the pavement. In front of me on the pavement a pair of brown leather brogues materialised, as Volvo man climbed out of his car and stood in front of me.

"I'm very sorry sir. Did you catch yourself on the door?" he asked with an English, Black Country accent. "Do take a moment to recover."

I began to get up, but he used his weight to push me down flat on the ground, stooping down to look at me, and glancing up and down the deserted pavement. Then with the assurance he was not being observed he stood up again and in the same movement gave me a solid well-placed kick in the stomach, below the ribs. I doubled up, winded, scarcely able to breathe as my chest went into spasm.

From pavement level I watched him, mainly his shoes, walk back to the Volvo and climb in. Then it revved and took off with a scraping of metal as he bumped my car out of the way. I was still pulling myself off the ground and trying to suck air into my lungs. After another few minutes, when I'd stopped seeing stars, someone came up to me and asked if I'd move my car out of the way. He hadn't seen my encounter or noticed bits of my headlamp on the road, but once he realised that I was in mild distress, he was a little more sympathetic, within the limits a delivery driver could afford.

My car still worked, even though it was going to need garaging. The drive back to my brother's felt much longer than it had when going out this morning. I knew I would have to broach the subject of the tail with Magnus and Izzy this evening. I wasn't sure how it was going to go down, but badly seemed quite likely, and I wondered whether to lie to them about how and why my plans for today had worked out differently.

Since the weekend, I'd begun to pay my dues towards the household by cooking supper, so I saw a filling dish of winter comfort food as a way to soothe my listeners, together with the right amount of alcohol and careful timing. So to my existing plans for a warming casserole I added an apple frushie dessert, like our mother used to make.

And so it was over the said apple tart, after my brother and Izzy had unwound from the day's work and begun to relax, that I took the plunge.

"Magnus, have you noticed that blue Volvo that's parked outside lately?"

"No, I don't think so. What about it?"

"I think he's been following you."

He sat forward, laughed, half disbelieving and half nervous, and looked towards Izzy for a reaction. Her mind appeared to be somewhere else altogether. Her eyes seemed peculiarly dead and lifeless. When she noticed we were looking at her, she put down her spoon and started to pay attention but said nothing.

"Why would you think that?" Magnus asked, injecting a little scepticism into his tone.

"First off, he waits in the car and sets off just after you and gets back just after you as well. Secondly, I decided to follow him today and he followed you all the way into the university."

Izzy interrupted, "When did you see him first?"

"The Volvo's been around since Monday for a fact, maybe Sunday too. I don't know for sure."

"But it was only me in the car on Monday. Magnus worked at home," she said.

"I only know what I saw. He left straight after you.

Whenever either of you takes the car out, you're being tailed as far as I can see."

"Why didn't you mention it sooner, if you thought it worth checking on him?" Magnus asked.

"I didn't believe what I was seeing. I needed confirmation. He saw you drop off Izzy, then he followed you down to the motorway, watched you park your car at work and then he took me on a tour of the city."

"Do you think he saw you?" asked Izzy.

"Yes, you could say so. He gave me the run-around then blindsided me so I drove right up to him. Then I walked up to him and we had a bit of a tussle before he drove off."

"Is he outside now?" she asked.

"I assume not. He rammed my car with his today."

"Wow, that's amazing, I wondered how you filled your days! Did you get his number plate?" she asked, excitedly, where some sympathy might have gone down better.

"Um no, well I think I can remember it," I said feeling like a complete idiot.

Without further questioning Izzy promptly jumped up and shot out of the front door into the darkened street. I ran out after her.

"I don't think it would be a good idea to go up to him, if he's out here," I called after her, half jogging to keep up with her. "He beat the crap out of me today, no joking. He's a big fellow."

"Don't worry, it's nothing like that," she said. "I'm just going to take a picture of him with his stinking car. We need reciprocity. And your hire car company might be glad of the details to pursue their claim."

Quite apart from the immediate risk of another fight, I was alarmed by what she seemed to be suggesting. As I saw it, if we were the subject of official surveillance, then we'd find

87

that any official complaints were an unequal match. We could be dealing in some way with her employer, I assumed. In what sense did she think we could offer "reciprocity"?

Thankfully, after five minutes' checking cars along the street, she had drawn a blank and so we returned to the house. Magnus was happily cutting another slice of apple frushie, helping himself to seconds.

"Using the same car every day seems a bit careless," he said. I was surprised he wasn't more exercised over it, but he had got over the surprise.

"I don't imagine it's careless at all," said Izzy. "If we noticed then it's because they wanted us to notice. He's not just watching us, he's there to intimidate as well. The proof is that he hit Marcus after he knew he'd been spotted. I bet there'll be someone back again tomorrow."

"It does fit with something else," said Magnus thoughtfully. "I think someone's been looking around in my office at the department. There were a couple of things in the wrong place today, but I thought I'd imagined it."

"Darling, in that case don't you think you'd better check your study upstairs as well?" Izzy asked. "Since we've all been out today."

While Magnus hopped upstairs to his office, Izzy started going through the living room, checking things were in their right place, and looking behind the furniture.

"Are you looking for bugs by any chance?" I asked.

"I'm afraid if we're being watched then it's a distinct possibility," she answered, as she ran her fingers underneath the lip of the kitchen counter. She paused as she felt something and ducked down to look closer.

"Pass me that kitchen knife would you sweetie?" she asked. "I don't want to break my nails on this thing."

With a slight levering, the object of interest came free and she held up something which was quite plainly electronic, small and flat with a flap of rubbery adhesive compound still attached to it.

"In that case, there'll probably be some more around the place," she murmured as she passed it to me for closer inspection.

Magnus reappeared and I passed him the miniature device.

"That's a bug, I suppose," he said, flatly. "Someone's been through my study too. I think some stuff's been moved around but nothing's actually missing. Not to say they haven't left something behind though, like another one of these," he waved the bug in the air. "Or a keystroke logger in my laptop. I'd better look inside it tomorrow in the daylight."

Izzy touched a finger to her lips and leant towards him. "Careful what you say out loud, darling, don't give it all away," she whispered.

Wakeup

That night I dreamt I was high up on a vast sand dune, looking down. In the distance I saw a lone figure, which I assumed was Pete, walking in the valley between the dunes through rows of wartime tank traps and heading down towards an upturned boat by the seashore. I knew there was a giant wave rising on the horizon, approaching fast. He was oblivious to it. I wanted to shout a warning to him, but I couldn't say the words. All the sound was muted, like we were already under water. I couldn't call him. I knew the water would come rushing up between the dunes, sweeping away everyone and everything in its path.

Then I saw that it wasn't Pete, it was Magnus. I was still trying to reach him, to follow him into the path of the flood. I tried but my limbs were too heavy. Then the tsunami arrived, surging towards us, silently but with unimaginable violence. It overtopped even the tallest dunes and I too was dragged away, my arms and legs held down by its weight, pulled downwards under its force and I couldn't breathe. I began to drown.

I dragged myself awake, filled with dread, alone in the dark. It was 5 a.m. and I thought I could hear movement in the house. I crept out of my room and looked around. There was a light on downstairs, and I decided to go and investigate.

I felt the adrenaline began to run and I grabbed a thick leather belt as an impromptu defence while I was on my way, I wound it round my fist to be ready for a fight. Thinking about it, a machete would have been preferable.

After setting off a loud creak from the stairs, I took more care and slowed right down. I crept through the darkened hall up to the living room door and peeped through. It was only Izzy. I sighed with relief and walked in.

"Good morning sweetie, I heard you from a mile off. The stairs are a giveaway aren't they? Close the door properly behind you please," she said. "I'm giving the place another sweep." She walked past me, slowed, leant towards me and planted a gentle kiss on my cheek. As she did so she said under her breath "I found a device in the hall but I've left it there while I think about it. We might think of a use for to leave an open channel."

I didn't want her to walk away. I went to catch her hand but she was busy and unapproachable. I volunteered to help instead and was designated to inspect underneath the covers of all electrical equipment while she did the soft furnishings.

"Have you got privileged knowledge about this kind of thing?" I asked.

"No, not especially. You ought to know what to do anyway, from the movies."

"Except that everything is a lot more difficult in real life," I said, while prising apart a cordless phone to the worrying sound of snapping plastic.

"It doesn't have to be," she said, holding up what looked like another bug which had been stuck under the windowsill behind the curtains. "Besides, how easy it is doesn't matter. Just think whether it gets you a step closer to what you want, if you know. We all have our dreams, don't we?"

I gave her a meaningful look which she laughed off in a

way which suggested that I'd flattered her vanity more than I'd appealed to her sensibilities.

"More nightmares than dreams lately," I muttered.

We worked on quietly for a while but uncovered no more devices. Magnus appeared just after daybreak as the street lights were switching off. He made tea and started taking his laptop apart under a lamp by the window.

Izzy meantime led me to the front door and asked me to follow her outside. We were going to look for our tail again, she informed me. Reluctantly, I followed her down the road until I saw my tail sitting in a different car. He had been downgraded to an old grey Astra.

"That's him," I said. "Just so you know. But stay away from him, he's a real piece of work."

"I can handle it," Izzy replied, stepping forwards, with her cup of tea still in her hand. I trailed a couple of steps behind and obeyed instructions to take some snaps of him and his car with my phone camera. The driver was keeping his head down and out of the shots as best he could.

She meanwhile walked up to his door and with the sweetest of smiles crouched down and gestured for him to wind his window down. I thought I knew this routine and I was ready to leap to her defence but to my surprise he did as he had been invited. Maybe he had reservations about being photographed beating up a pretty woman.

"We were worrying about you sat on your own out here. Would you like a cup of tea?" she asked him, offering her mug. He held a hand up in refusal and shook his head but said nothing. He kept his hand up in front of his face to shield himself from my camera. She shrugged, put the mug down on the pavement and pulled a small diary from her pocket before continuing. "Marcus here says you and he had a bump yesterday, but he forgot to swap insurance details with you.

Would you mind awfully showing us some ID?"

"I'm very sorry madam, but I'm not at liberty to provide you with identification," he addressed her with the affected formality of a policeman.

"Well we've got your registration number anyway. We'll have to think of a name for you. Dudley, if I can call you that, suppose we were to call the police to help sort things out?"

Dudley, like the town, I supposed. She'd placed his accent pretty accurately.

"You're welcome to try, madam," he answered sarcastically.

"So that's agreed then," she said. "Meantime, just to put you at your ease, we'll be leaving in about half an hour. Same route as yesterday." She picked up her tea, stood up and led me back to the house.

"What exactly was the point of that?" I asked her.

"Habituation," she replied with a cryptic smile. "Reciprocity comes later."

She was so directed, I could see from her look of concentration and the way her eyes darted around from left to right that said she was scheming something new. Re-arranging routines and thinking how to rescue Magnus' plans, I supposed. Nothing was going to come between her and the goal. I had a feeling she would fit anything into her grand plan. Was that simply to conquer the world through Magnus? I didn't see my place in that, except for entertainment, but for the first time I wondered whether she had drawn me into her world for more than mere amusement or an infatuation.

♈

Magnus had his laptop in pieces when we got back, but he declared its integrity was unharmed. There were no new additions to the hardware and his disk was fully encrypted, as had been all his important communications. He vowed henceforth to keep it with him at all times to avoid risk of interference.

I couldn't help but point out the irony that he was currently relying on encryption to protect his privacy, while bringing about its practical demise. But he disagreed, saying that he only expected to make it far, far more difficult to set up secure connections over public networks. It wasn't the end of all encryption, he promised. That still kind of made my point, I said. Meantime I wondered what was he intending to do about people breaking into his house and going through his stuff?

"It's paradoxical," he said. "You're bothered about someone breaking into our house, searching it and planting some bugs. But you find the same thing more acceptable when it takes place on a massive scale over the Internet."

"There may be a principle at stake," I answered truthfully, "but you've got to ask what's it worth?"

It turned out that I'd asked the question of the day. Magnus set off as usual but returned home early while I was out on my run. He was loitering in the kitchen when I came back in mid-afternoon.

"Do you fancy a walk? I need a talk," he said, looking around. "The walls have ears."

"Sure, give me five minutes to shower and change."

I couldn't see the Astra as we set off towards the local park. Magnus was composing his thoughts. Beyond the park gates a little frost still remained on the ground, on the shady side of the shrubs. Magnus skidded momentarily on the icy asphalt path and I put a hand on his elbow to steady him. The jolt seemed to break him out of his reverie.

"Basil – that's my head of department – called me in today and started asking about my crypto work," he started.

"Doesn't he know already?"

"Not much, it's my own project. I've done it all in my own time so far."

"You must have said something, or he wouldn't be asking."

"That's a surprising thing. Someone else told him about it and now he's talking about an IP problem."

"What's IP?"

"Intellectual property. It's to establish ownership over an idea."

"OK I knew that really. You mean they think your idea may belong to them instead of you?"

"Basil might want to believe it, but I also think it's a legal ploy. He wants to find out as much as he can and the IP angle is just a pretext for an investigation. We talked about a non-disclosure agreement but I don't want to share anything with him, with or without one."

"Isn't that more or less what you're doing with your new partners?"

"Yes, but those talks are less intrusive than an investigation would be, and there's no argument over who owns the IP. In fact we're just about agreed. I just have to finalise the contract and publication arrangements with whoever puts in the best final offer. The problem is that if I hand the details to Basil now, he could pass it straight on to our government friends and he could start legal action. That could stop me from publishing for a long time. He more or less said we could do it nicely or we could go to law."

"Are you saying that Basil works for the government?"

"Not that it matters, but I'm pretty sure he has ties, yes."

"And you don't trust him, or his pals, to stick to his non-disclosure agreement, is that right?"

"Just so. Cheating, lying and breaking the law are all fine, it's only getting caught that's not allowed. They'll go to almost any lengths to keep it secret. If they can't stop publication they'll do whatever they can to find out everything beforehand."

"You also implied that someone else leaked details to Basil."

"He doesn't know much, but he mentioned a detail which made me think it came from more than an overheard conversation. As if he or someone had seen a synopsis of my work."

"Do you think you've been hacked?"

"That's too unlikely. I'm thinking it may have come from someone within the new partner organisations. There was always a chance of something getting out."

The route we were walking led us to a wide circular path lined with benches, bisected by smaller tracks which formed a Celtic cross. At its centre a grand central fountain still bled a trickle into the pool of icy water. We circumnavigated the path aimlessly, studying the empty plant borders. A little way ahead of us, a man sat down on a bench on his own. He was carrying a rucksack, fairly smartly dressed and warmly wrapped-up. Magnus stared at him and turned to walk in the opposite direction.

"Whatever your department does or doesn't know, threatening you with legal action sounds like a showstopper," I said. "I don't see how you'd get around that. How did you leave it with him?"

"I just left it that it was my own work and I wanted to carry on without interference from him."

"It sounds like you've gone past that point."

"You could be right. I don't think I can progress the work to completion until after I've made the break, so for now I'll just play for time with Basil."

He reminded me that the work was incomplete. "How sure are you you'll get the right outcome in the end?" I asked.

"In the language of the common man, better than evens. I'd give myself short odds. Nine to four on," he answered.

"So it's a gamble," I said.

"The future is always uncertain," he replied.

"Would you stake so much on a horse race?"

"I'd hedge my bet."

"How can you do that?" I asked.

"That's the right question. I'll have a think about it."

As we walked back I saw the Astra was back in its usual space near the house, with Dudley, as we now called him, sitting drinking coffee from a flask. We knocked and waved and he managed a sarcastic smile. Habituation, she'd called it. To what end, I couldn't imagine. Thinking about her raised another question in my mind.

"Has Izzy come under any pressure at work, do you suppose?" I asked Magnus. "It just seems funny that you're fighting this battle of wits but she seems to be sitting undisturbed behind enemy lines, if you see my meaning."

He gave me a very strange look. "Secret Squirrel, remember? She only tells me what I need to know. And no, she hasn't said anything."

Then another part of me died inside as I thought of the really big secret he didn't know, the one about me and Izzy. I knew the pain it would cause him if he ever learned about it. And I also saw the vacuum it would leave, were I to try to give her up, and wondered how long I would withstand the allure of her narcotic powers.

My Father

"Izzy, about you and me," I began abruptly before trailing off, not sure that had been the right introduction. For a moment, the silence sat heavily between us.

"You're worrying about your brother, aren't you?" she said. "I see you're close. You're lucky. That's something I've never had."

"I can hardly begin to explain how I feel about it, or you."

"Have you gone and fallen in love with me?" she asked, cutting rather directly to the heart of the matter.

"Yes, I think so, a bit," I said. Except that the conversation had steered towards her now, instead of Magnus.

"Well, if that's true then it should stand the test of time," she said. She spoke softly and her words were filled with care, lacking in their usual hardness. She checked her mirror and signalled right.

It was evening, and I'd arranged to travel up to see my father, taking the overnight train. After I'd dropped my hire car back with the rental company earlier in the day, I was left without my own transport and Izzy had volunteered to drop me at the station. Up until this point she'd been quiet and untalkative, especially for her. I felt the awkwardness, but I was more uneasy than ever about the dilemma over my brother since he and I had talked that afternoon.

"But what about you?" I asked her. We were pulling up at the station now.

She said nothing for a moment but put a hand to my face and drew me towards her, kissing me tenderly rather than passionately.

"Come back soon. I'll be waiting for you," she said.

Then without a further word, she turned back to the wheel and looked determinedly ahead. I knew it was my cue to get out. It felt unusual for her to show sensitivity like that, maybe even vulnerability, except for a little drama which was her all over. I wondered, had she grown attached to me, or something more? Had I reached a softer, kinder part of her? I spent a long while thinking about it afterwards, but as ever I couldn't work her out. Maybe that was what she wanted.

There were several changes along the route. The carriages were crowded and smelly at the end of a long day, festooned with discarded newspapers and the spilled contents of snacks, and the pungent smell of sweaty people and their sticky kids. You could have told the time by the children in the carriage. They were either snuggled up asleep, looking cute, or behaving like wild animals crawling over the backs of the seats, ignored by their tired mothers and boozy fathers. It was how I remembered public transport, except nowadays there were more people than ever squashed together. I plugged myself in like everyone else, cracked open a can of Tennent's and tried to ignore it all.

I joined the sleeper at eleven for the last leg. I was in a shared berth but found that I was on my own. I was grateful for the solitude, but slept no better for it. The attendant woke me before half past five and I was disgorged from the train onto the platform of the granite-built station feeling slightly raw. It was the dark hour after the nearly full moon had set and before the sun rose. I loitered by the door of the station café and watched the freight traffic going through until it opened. Then I made camp over a fried breakfast, allowing the cholesterol to filter into my veins and deliver its restorative power.

♈

I'd planned to reach my father's house at a more respectable hour but one that was still too early for the local train. As my cab approached our destination I glimpsed the highland hills looming darkly in the distance before we were hemmed in by the massive firs. The driver turned off the main road and drove us over the wide river in whose cold waters I used to swim, then into my home town. Its modest and unspoiled Georgian stone facades were inviting, scarcely changed for two hundred years, its remoteness having cocooned it from the modern world outside.

On the outskirts at the far edge of town, I paid off the cab and walked up to my father's house. I knocked, waited a while, and when no-one answered, went around the side of the house towards the sound of a lawnmower. My father was giving the machine a springtime service. The smell of exhaust fumes from the two-stroke oil came straight from my youth. He looked up, surprised, and immediately ran over to meet me, wiping the oil from his hands with a rag. We embraced as we met.

"It's wonderful to see you. It's been such a long time," he said, giving me a big hug.

I pushed him back as if to look at him, but kept him at arm's length. "You're looking well. Early start for the lawn isn't it?"

"Your brother tells me it's been wet and chilly down south, but we've had it mild and dry for the last week. I couldn't miss the chance to get out here. But never mind that, come in and have a cup of tea." He cut the engine on the idling mower and birds filled the garden with morning song. We walked back to the house.

"How are you getting on without Mum?" I asked, looking round inside. The sense of neglect was palpable: untidy and dusty, a measure of the old man's state.

"I don't feel the same about the place without her around. I'm wondering about selling. Downsizing," he replied.

I felt the twinge of another loss. But the effect of her absence couldn't be ignored. She had been the soul of our home.

Tea was served in the living room, according to custom. "She so wanted to see you before she died," said my father.

"You know I'd just gone out. It was six thousand miles away. I really meant to come, but it all happened so much quicker than we expected."

"And then you couldn't make it to the funeral," he continued.

I hid a scowl by draining my cup. "The milk's on the turn," I remarked, sharply. This was how things always went between us. It confirmed my decision to stay just the one night.

He'd made his point I suppose, so he backed off and there was a moment's lull before we moved on to the more usual topics of news and work. Magnus had told him bare details about the accident and he was anxious to know more. For once he was happy to listen and not to cast judgement and I found myself telling him more about it than I had expected. He picked up on my reluctance to go back to diving.

"You've had a trauma," he agreed, "and maybe that will be hard to resolve. But since diving really seems to be your calling, you should try. Don't give up."

101

"I'm surprised to hear you say that. You and Mum were always against me having a practical vocation."

"Your mother was very strong-willed and ambitious for you children. Funnily enough Isidora rather reminds me of her in that way. I don't know how you progress yourself in your type of work, but we both hoped you'd find a way to make something more of it."

"Not everyone can run their own dive centre from a tropical island paradise, you know."

"Would you if you could?"

"Sure, why not?"

"Tropical island paradise, eh? I'd buy a share in that," he promised. "Your mother wanted you and Magnus and Marina to achieve great things. Before she died she said it had often been more important to her than your being contented. I think she would have told you she regretted that in the end."

Despite myself, a tear escaped and ran down my cheek. I wiped it away quickly. It was too late to be hearing this now.

"Maybe we should have a go at mowing the grass?" I suggested.

The weather held and we spent all morning outside. Then we walked into town for lunch at Davina's Tea Rooms and talked more. We hadn't got on so well for years. My father had taken early retirement during Mum's illness and at 62 he considered himself "still young". He was considering starting to date women again. I was startled by the thought, but couldn't disagree that he needed someone.

We spent the afternoon boxing things up, then in the evening my father cooked us dinner while I leafed through his newspaper. He'd left it open on a page with an article which identified a general complaint which regularly appeared on problem pages, of a type which went: "I found

102

the perfect partner for me, except for one big thing, and now the crunch moment has come". I wondered if my father was further advanced in his dating plans than he'd let on. He didn't usually read this sort of tripe. I wondered what his One Big Thing might be.

He appeared with two plates of food in hand and put them on the coffee table. Certainly, standards had slipped, but at least the food was tasty and it came with a welcome beer.

My father saw the page in front of me. "I hadn't thought of it that way before," he said, "but I suppose if you're in the agony aunt business and seen enough of them, then you would have to get analytical about the whole thing."

"You mean start classifying your correspondents, like a butterfly collector grouping and sorting his specimens," I said. In an abstract way I could have fitted myself into his storyline more than once, and felt mildly offended to be grouped with the type of people who allegedly wrote to the problem pages.

"What's interesting is how they turn it around back onto you," he said. "The problem in every case is you, not your partner, it says."

"You mean 'the complainant', not me," I corrected him.

"Suit yourself," he said. "They say you may be choosing inappropriate partners specifically because of the One Big Thing, and it's because you're afraid of commitment. Slam dunk. How about that?"

I couldn't help but feel my father was trying to deliver me a message, which was bad enough, but to think he had allied himself with someone who had been skewering examples of people's problems, and was now arranging them in their display cabinet as variants of the same species was too much.

"You shouldn't generalise about such matters," I said. "Did you have a particular situation in mind?"

103

"Certainly not," he said. "It's purely a thinking exercise, and a bit of fun too." And so we left it there.

♈

Next day I needed to get away soon after breakfast, but it was a much fonder parting with my father than usual. He drove me to the main station.

"It's good that you're spending some time with your brother," he said.

"How so?"

"You're going through a hard time and he and Isidora can look after you," he explained. I couldn't disabuse him. "What do you make of her?" he asked. "I only know her from the funeral but she attracted a lot of attention."

"She's very nice," I said, which was the most circumspect answer I could come up with. Inside I shrank a little and wondered how to change the subject.

"Charming, at least," he said with a note of reservation. "Do you think they'll settle down?"

"Magnus may be a bit on the quiet side for her," I suggested.

"Or maybe he's the plain backdrop against which she'll be the focus of interest," he replied with a mysterious nod.

"You can't compare them with you and Mum," I said. "You're nothing like. For a start, it's Magnus' star in the ascendant, as far as I'm aware."

He didn't persist with the topic any further, and I mused that nothing highlighted my failure more than comparison with the brilliance of my brother's achievements, and how I had become the rotten core at the heart of his household.

As we were walking onto the train platform, my father said: "There's a chap I used to work with, specialises in

104

trauma. It's a type of exposure therapy where you go back and re-experience it, more of a physical whole-body approach, instead of just talking. I could put you in touch, if you thought it might help."

"Thanks. Exposure therapy, you say. That might be more my thing, I'll have a think about it."

My train arrived, rumbling down the platform, its wheels squealing metallically against the rails before it drew to a halt. We said our farewell, hugged again and I ran to find a door.

Chemistry

It was cold again when I stepped off the mainline train at the end of my journey. A large orange moon faced me, rising over the rooftops, dim behind the twinkling reflections of streetlights on the wet platform. The clouds which had dumped a shower on us were clearing and leaving a cold night sky behind. It would be frosty soon. I was stiff and numb from the journey and decided to walk to my brother's.

I checked but couldn't see any sign of Dudley or his car outside the house. I had supposed he had to have some time off occasionally. I wondered if there was a Dudley II sitting in another car watching me walk up the road.

I was scarcely in through the door before Magnus bounded out into the hall and announced that we were going to the familiar coaching house inn. I dropped my bags and he turned me straight around, gathered Izzy, and we headed out. He was abuzz over something that he didn't want to discuss in the house, but began relaying as we walked up the road.

He had had a second conference with Basil, his department head, while I was in Scotland. He had received what sounded like a great offer. It began with elevation to a research professorship, to pursue his crypto work at the university. Then, in recognition of his outstanding achievement, it had been suggested that an official honour was possible. Not that

106

it was Basil's place to do more than recommend it, but in practical terms the university had a lot of influence and he had mumbled the magical incantation of Officer of the Order of the British Empire.

We were at the pub by the time I'd had the whole story. Magnus fetched the drinks and then, unbelievably, he and Izzy began to pick the whole offer apart.

"It's recognition for you, isn't it?" I asked. "I suppose that means Basil has a pretty good idea now of what you're working on. What about the publishing side?"

"They want intellectual property rights as before, but they've agreed on the principle of publication, so long as it's managed. They're anxious about destabilising the global economy and all that." He didn't sound wholly convinced.

"The thing is it's an offer with a position and money and that's something you can bargain with," Izzy chimed in.

"You make it sound like it's an auction," I said. It was almost the first time they'd discussed the business together in front of me and while Magnus was obsessing that the world should know about it, Izzy's preoccupation with the mercenary aspects was becoming clearer.

"It's more complicated than that," said Magnus. "If I sign away the rights and complete the research under their aegis, they could conveniently start rowing back on parts of the offer. I definitely need a better offer."

"But bear in mind that the other parties can't put in a word towards an OBE, that's not to be sneezed at," she added. "Money instead."

"Are you going to say who these mysterious other parties are?" I asked.

Magnus looked at Izzy and then, speaking somewhat under his breath, at last revealed: "I'm in dialogue with *the* top two academic institutions in the United States."

"I'm not sure what I was expecting you to say, but why on earth the States?" I wondered out loud, thinking he'd be no better off there than here.

"They're wealthier and more independent than anywhere you could find in the UK," Izzy filled in. "And they're simply more ambitious."

"If you say so," I replied. How would I know any better?

"The real point about it is that I could finish the work and publish it, but I still want a job and a successful career at the end of it all," Magnus said. "This seems to be the best way to get all of those things. So I just need to go to see them and finalise the agreement."

Izzy sat back unhappily "Darling, you should have got that business done before you talked to Basil. If you assume he's given the tip-off to the authorities, they'll be getting twitchy about you taking foreign trips. They might do all sorts of beastly things to make it unpleasant or even impossible for you now."

"I can't seriously agree a new contract without meeting them and sharing some information. They'll need to understand some of the detail. It has to be face-to-face. I can't be doing it over any kind of electronic medium," Magnus said.

I had a feeling they'd rehearsed a lot of the argument already. Either one of them on their own might have seen there was a good offer on the table, but the two together were impossible to please. The matter remained unresolved that night but it seemed plain that there was nothing Basil could offer that would satisfy them both. The subject turned instead to my trip and our father's plans to find a girlfriend and sell the family home. Then Izzy prompted Magnus to remember my birthday next week, which coincided with the races, and so we fixed on a grand day out in celebration.

♈

We kept mostly to ourselves for the rest of the weekend, except for when Izzy sought me out in my room to help with an unusual experiment, which seemed to prove something and nothing. She had shown some interest in my laptop having a fingerprint scanner and said she'd like to know how easy it was to hack, if I were interested in helping.

I assumed the real subject of interest was Magnus' laptop. I hadn't noticed whether he unlocked it with a fingerprint, but I was more than happy for the chance to spend a little time with her, if that was the best that was on offer. I'd seen precious little of her lately, except in the company of Magnus, and I wondered if she was avoiding me.

She disappeared and came back after a few minutes with two balls of plastic, soft and warm and pliable. She asked me to press my index finger into them.

"I'll be back in half an hour," she said with a slight air of mystery and expectancy. When she reappeared she asked me to lock my computer screen, then she swiped her own finger over the finger detector. Her finger swipe was rejected, and she didn't look too pleased. Then she tried a second time and it was accepted. She had logged in as me by using the copy of my fingerprint. "Voilà!" she exclaimed and gave herself a small fanfare.

"How did you do that?" I asked.

"You've seen the Bond movies haven't you? It's as simple as he made it look," she replied, starting to peel a thin film of plastic off her finger and waving it at me. "It was in *Diamonds Are Forever*, wasn't it? I did think the technology might be smarter nowadays, but apparently it's still not clever enough."

"Sure, I remember it was how he fooled the smouldering bad girl, didn't he? Was she some kind of role model for yourself, maybe?" I asked.

She simpered softly at me and radiated a sense of longing. I became aware how quiet the house was. She reached out, stroked my jaw until, recognising my growing enthusiasm, she raised a finger to wag at me.

"Marcus Miller, you're showing a bit more cheek than usual, aren't you?" she said, and her parody of a line from the movie perfectly affected the nasal drawl of the villain, with crystal-clear enunciation and cold sarcastic humour.

It was another tease, my desire inflamed and doused in the same moment. I exhaled. "So you can switch it on and turn it off again whenever you want. Did you ever think of becoming an actress? I do believe the world could use a talent like yours," I said ruefully. She giggled.

"So what's the point of your experiment? Are you thinking someone could have hacked Magnus' laptop in the same way?" I asked. "I'm assuming he didn't give them a nice clean fingerprint mould to start from."

"He promised me that he always turns it off properly and you need a passcode as well. So probably not. But it could be a useful trick, don't you think?" She made her way out with a final "'Thank you for taking part in this survey.'"

"Hey, I think I'll have those plastic moulds back now, if you don't mind," I called, chasing after her. She squealed with mock horror and ran down to the kitchen where a surprised Magnus found himself being used as a shield to hide behind. Then after she had extracted maximum drama from the moment, she finally relinquished the moulds.

♈

The hire car attendant in his bright red acrylic jacket looked at me disdainfully as I walked around the replacement vehicle next day, noting the existing dents and scratches on the diagram he had provided. I glanced around at the other vehicles on the forecourt, all of which appeared to be in much better condition.

"All them other ones are booked out to other customers," he said, reading my thoughts.

I'd taken my car back with a banged-up wing and a broken headlight, and I'd expected there would be a penalty. It began with a hefty excess charge and now I got the oldest car available to replace it. I accepted my punishment gracefully and paid the first week's charges.

"I still don't see why you need a car at all," said Magnus, who had driven me there as part of his plan to avoid his boss Basil. "You only used the other one three times in the last week."

He was probably right, but I didn't like to be without my own wheels. The office administrator came out of the kiosk and walked over to us. Her lipstick matched the uniform, but it was too harsh for her ageing complexion and made her look older still. "Can I double-check the registration of the other car please?" She asked. "The one you gave isn't valid."

I was pretty sure I had it right, but I had no evidence to back it up. I showed them the photo of Dudley in his newer vehicle.

"You could try to trace him then, if they're both his cars" she said, while Magnus standing behind her shook his head madly. "Call in at the kiosk before you go. I'll give you some information and the other forms you need. It's worth it for you if you can find him." Then she headed back.

"Sounds like a hit and run then," observed our attendant, sagely.

"You could call it that," I replied, fuming.

"He'll have a lot of explaining to do if you ever catch up with him."

"That's a big if," I replied. I could have added the most infuriating part was that Dudley had followed Magnus' car here today and I assumed he was lurking nearby. We completed our business and Magnus set off back ahead of me. I waited to see if he was followed, which he was, for anyone who cared to look. My frustration began to boil over. I'd had enough of putting up with this game.

I drove my replacement car back and parked it two streets behind Magnus' house, from where I could get to it without being spotted. There was a tyre-change kit in the boot and I removed the crank handle from the jack and carried it back with me. I walked past Magnus' house and found the Astra was not far away. Dudley was doing his best to ignore me as usual, playing with his phone. If he'd looked he'd have seen my face like thunder.

I swung the crank into his windscreen, right at his head. The crank had an awkward off-centre balance and it nearly twisted itself out of my hand on impact, but it made a nice little dent in the screen as it pinged off.

Criminal damage was a whole new excursion for me, and I paused for a moment to inspect my handiwork more closely. The pattern of white cracks I'd made was like a spider's web with radial starring and circumferential contours around a small hole which bent into the centre, and you could have put your finger through. It was going to be very difficult for him to drive. I felt a sense of relief as if the word reciprocity floated past in a bubble, upwards into the air above me.

I learned again that for a big guy, Dudley could move really fast. I was wondering about adding a second dent to the screen, just to make absolutely sure of the job before I legged it, but he was out of his door in a split second and came at me, fists up. I brandished the crank at him and was ready to clunk him with it, if I had to. He saw I meant to do damage if necessary and he stood back a little, although he never took his eyes off me even for a moment.

"I owe you more than that, you bastard," I snarled, and made a feint at him with the crank. My hands were trembling. He took another step back, palms out. I'd done what I meant to, but now I wasn't sure how to end it, so I tried backing further away. He seemed pretty upset but had lost interest in a fight, so I kept going until there was a safe distance between us and I could turn and walk off, keeping one eye over my shoulder. The whole confrontation lasted scarcely thirty seconds.

However justified I felt in getting my own back, I couldn't quite believe what I'd done. This kind of behaviour wasn't what I'd been brought up to. Feeling both glad and guilty, I let out a nervous laugh. The more I thought about it the more thankful I was that I hadn't clocked him with the crank. That was out of bounds. But I'd been prepared to do it, if pushed.

I was fairly sure that Magnus would be outright horrified if I told him about it, and that I had probably messed up Izzy's plan for revenge, whatever that was. But I thought I had better mention it, so I saved it for later, once dinner had settled.

"Sweetie, that was very emotional of you," Izzy commented when I told them. If she was surprised or annoyed then she wasn't giving it away. "I wish I'd been there to see it. How did it make you feel?"

"You could say it was cathartic. I've been bottling up a lot," I replied. Actually I felt great for it. Paying back something in kind had been medicinal. Not that I was a vengeful person. Not normally, anyhow.

But the justification didn't appear to cut ice with her, and she swiftly put me in my place. "I suppose that 'a man's gotta do …' and all of that stuff," she said, dismissively. "But you do need to work on your timing. Please consult us first, next time you're thinking of doing anything radical like that."

"I'll try to."

Magnus had been silent up until now. "Just think first and don't do it again," he said. "That's government property as far as we know, and one of their employees you just attacked. You could get into serious trouble."

"I don't think there were any witnesses," I muttered.

"You could end up in court … all sorts. What would we say to Dad?" he went on. The moral objection went without saying, but the criminal implication was more tangible. Magnus was suggesting the threat of legal retribution would bring shame down on the family. He was prepared to try any angle that might make an impression on his wayward brother.

Izzy thought this was hilarious. "OK, so when the local paper runs with 'Crank man, unemployed, of no fixed abode, believed he was victim of spy conspiracy' we can cut it out and post it to your father."

She screamed with laughter, but it was obviously not funny at all. I don't think I've ever loved and hated someone so much, both at the same time.

The Races

Magnus and Izzy both took the day off work for my birthday. I had five "happy returns" on Facebook and three cards. I wasn't used to having such a fuss made of me.

We enjoyed a lazy breakfast and Izzy went to say her customary and bizarre good morning to Dudley, who was now riding a beige saloon car that looked like it had passed its last MOT. The news of his downgrade was my first birthday present of the day.

Later, when we set off, Magnus took the disk from his laptop with him, locking the lobotomised computer in one of his drawers. We left our cars behind and walked together instead, sneaking out of the back door and going out to the edge of town where the racecourse stretched down the hillside into a wide open valley.

Although it was past midday already the day felt as dull and listless as it had when I woke. Some rain had fallen in the night and the air was still laden with moisture which sat gloomily but unthreateningly above us.

But the pleasure of enjoying my birthday combined with the excited buzz of the throng now arriving at the course left me feeling upbeat. This was how I always remembered the mild and tolerable English winter. People went about their business unconcerned by the overcast sky, the murmur of the crowd muted by the cotton wool effect of the dampness in the turf and in the air.

Visible on the opposite side of the wide open valley was a large hill capped with rough grass and a yellow stone escarpment, which the lowest clouds brushed against. The landscape became progressively less wild further down. Copses of bare trees gave way to green fields separated by scrubby hedges. The fields in turn became neater towards the bottom of the valley where houses began to appear and the hazy grey atmosphere reached its thickest.

Our side of the hill was covered in rich green turf and a myriad of white railings marking the racecourse. The damp had condensed onto the grass and transferred onto my boots, whose toes were dark with the wet and flecked with fresh green mowings.

We arrived alongside a convergent mass of people in country green and khaki colours, swarming into the ground and up onto the enormous grandstands in the near distance like an anthill. Clustered around the finishing line were the rows of illuminated signs flickering and glowing red, displaying the bookies' odds on the first race. In front of them, raised on small platforms, the bookies talked and handed out slips, joking with the punters from whom the damp yeasty smell of beer emanated in profusion.

Magnus had made me do my research the night before and now the preparations began to pay off. He had spotted a runner named Duty Ranger who had disappointed recently, finishing without a place in his last two races despite being favoured. He thought it was a natural "back the beaten favourite" bet at long odds of 25-1 and he shared a couple of other picks for each-way bets to hedge my position.

All three of us made our way down to the bookies' pitches and placed our bets. I put my entire £50 stake on Duty

Ranger to win. Izzy placed her money as advised, except for the addition of a small stake on Guillotine Motion at 30-1, mainly because she liked the name. Magnus spotted overall better odds at the next stall and peeled off to the left.

When we met up afterwards Magnus shook his head in disbelief at my rashness. "You'll learn the hard way, I suppose," he warned. I thought about it for a moment, and decided it was a sign that I'd become fatalistic.

The starting point was some way off and I quickly discarded my binoculars in favour of the big screen which loomed over us. The starter's tape was raised and they got off cleanly, racing in a bunch towards the first jump.

Magnus pointed out a punter nearby who was wearing an earpiece. "Some of these chaps are on the phone to their pals who are laying 'in-running' bets while the race is still going on. I'd give that a go if I was taking it more seriously. But everything can't be work can it?" he said. I had to agree.

As expected, Duty Ranger got off to a slow start but kept with the field. They remained tightly grouped until the penultimate hurdle when they began to stretch out and I could see my horse in second place, next to the rail. I wished I'd gone each way. As the leaders began running up the hill towards us we turned towards the course and looked across the heads of the crowd where I could still see my jockey's green and yellow helmet. Shouts began going up from the crowd which grew into a roar as we urged on the approaching horses and their riders, still neck-and-neck. I felt the tremors rising up through the ground from the pounding hooves and heard their thunder through the noise of the crowd as they hurtled towards the finish, clods of earth flying into the air. From our angle the finish was too close to call and I glanced up at the big screen to discover my horse had been ahead by a nose as he crossed the line.

Our voices joined the whoops of excitement of the other winning punters, while the rest cheerfully applauded the result. I was £1,250 up on the first race, which felt great. Magnus and Izzy were also up by smaller amounts. I thought Magnus was slightly more measured in his celebration after having been outdone by my lucky gambit. Maybe he just wanted me to enjoy my moment, or he was waiting to see how my luck held out. I figured that if I stuck to my per-race limit then I would still be over a grand up at the end of the day, however badly I did on the others. I could certainly live with that kind of fate.

$$\Upsilon$$

I let Magnus lay my bets for me on the second race, and stuck a bit closer to his advice, while I went to get drinks. Izzy came with me to help carry. After we had threaded our way halfway through the crowds she stopped and I saw she was wearing an earnest expression.

"There's something important I wanted to ask you about," she said. "It's better we talk about it here where we can't be overheard."

I was glad of it. We'd had no time to talk together meaningfully for over a week. There were things I'd been saving up.

She put an arm around my waist in an unusual gesture of intimacy and we walked slowly on. "It's Magnus. He needs to skip the country for a couple of days for a head-to-head with these new guys in the States," she said.

I felt deflated. It was all about Magnus lately, and their big project which seemed more and more like a pipe dream the longer it dragged on without a conclusion. She never wanted to talk about me and her at all.

"Thing is he needs to slip off quietly without being spotted and we think there's a good chance it'll draw attention if he hopped on a plane right now. So we wondered if he could borrow your passport. I'm quite certain he could pass himself off as you."

"You cannot be serious," I said, not just for effect. She really had to be joking.

"I am serious, I do mean it," she said. "Don't say yes or no right now. Think about it first. There's no comeback on you even if it went wrong, which it won't in any case. You'd be doing him – both of us – a massive favour. You owe him something, in any case, don't you?"

I was agog. Apart from the fact that the whole idea was sheer lunacy, she was trying to use her infidelity – or mine – as a lever. Obviously the answer was going to be no, the question was how to make her, or both of them, see that this was going too far. They needed to get a grip on reality. I would talk to Magnus first, after the next race, and find out what he really thought, and then give them both my answer. Anything else I might have said to Izzy was now forgotten, cast into the background. We walked apart in silence for the rest of the way to the bar.

But we were still only on our way back to the course with our drinks when she started up again.

"I've hurt your feelings, haven't I?" she said. I grunted an acknowledgement, to avoid giving away too much.

"You want me to talk about us and I'm like non-stop on about Magnus and his problems," she went on. "But I haven't even told you about the other part of the plan yet. You see I have been thinking of you, believe me. I'm going to set up base camp somewhere in the States as a temporary centre of operations and I want you to come with me. You'd like that, wouldn't you? We'd have a few days together all

119

on our ownsomes and then you'd have so much of me that you'd probably get tired of it."

She said it in that playful tone of hers again, which, like the ringing of Pavlov's bell, I had begun to associate with imminent sexual favours. It blew away any more sensible thoughts. Of course I was up for it, now she put it that way. Like a trained pet, I'd sit up and beg, or "die for the queen" if she asked. She'd been so elusive over the last week that I'd begun to think it was over between us, but now it seemed that wasn't the case after all. For all that, I had to acknowledge the proposition was idiotic. The practical risk of failure seemed ridiculously high. But what the hell, I thought. Nothing ventured, nothing gained.

"I still don't think it'll work," I said, but I meant yes and she understood.

"We'll go through the details with you later," she replied.

We walked up to Magnus who handed us our slips in exchange for his drink. "There's only a small field in the next race, so I took the liberty of hedging your bet and added an each way double for you over the next two races," he announced. "Castaway Lad in the first and Petit Parisien in the next. You owe me another £50, please."

The race began moments later. I struggled to spot my first pick on the big screen, Grand Larceny, until Magnus told me it had pulled up after the first fence. So I transferred my allegiance to Castaway Lad and was glad to see him come in third. Izzy was jumping up and down because her horse Maison Maire had won at 7-2 and she charged off to collect her winnings.

"Izzy told me about your travel plans," I said to Magnus.

"Are you OK with it?" he asked, looking out over the racecourse.

"Fuck it, what's the worst thing that can happen? I'm good

with it if you're sure that's what you want to do," I said. "Although it all seems a bit surreal."

"Risk taking may not be rational, except that I need a quick resolution before I blink and cave in to all the pressure. Getting out of the country quickly and quietly has quite a lot of appeal from that point of view."

"Did the idea come from you or her?" I asked.

"That doesn't matter now, we're in it together. Did you talk about your own travel arrangements?"

I had wondered if she had been testing to see if I'd accept the first part of her plan on its own, without the offer to take me along. Now it occurred to me that Magnus might have known more about the way it was put to me than I supposed. But surely that was me being paranoid.

"Yes, that's fine," I said. "Only I'm not sure what you want me to do."

"If you were to lay a false trail, it might make things easier for me. It would just be for a couple of days. Then we can meet up and go back to being ourselves again."

"Speaking of which, what about the beard?" I asked.

"Can you grow one in the next three days?" he said.

"No. Can you trim yours down to a designer stubble?"

"I could go for something a bit less straggly I suppose," he said. "I was sold on the idea that having a beard was less maintenance effort than shaving every day, but that doesn't seem to be the case."

"Were you actually wanting an easy life, before you give up any more of the one you currently have?" I asked.

In the third race Petit Parisien came in third, and I began to wonder whether between us we had gained magical powers of prediction. But when I totalled up my wins over the last two races, I was only £5 better off against a total of £100 stakes, and that was only due to Magnus making the extra bet on my behalf. It seemed like a large stake for a small return, fun maybe but no way to make a living, or not for me anyhow.

"Think of it as a learning experience," Magnus said knowingly. "You have actually made money on it, unlike most people. Losing the lot would have taught you a better lesson, although that would be a shame given it's your birthday." After that I paid more attention to his advice on spreading my bets but the races went against me. There were four more to run and at the end of the third I was up by about £1,300, almost entirely thanks to Duty Ranger's nose. Magnus himself was up by about £200 and Izzy had done slightly better than break even.

I think they must have both been keenly aware that they'd been bested by a rank beginner, because before the last race, Izzy said: "C'mon Magnus, it's our last chance to close the gap with your brother. Let's go for broke, pick us the winner."

Against all his better instincts, Magnus relented and picked out two bets to win from the field of thirteen. They pooled all their winnings from the day and split them over the two horses. Having nothing left to prove, I stuck with Magnus' more cautious hedging strategy. Izzy hurried off excitedly to place all our bets and returned five minutes later with our slips.

The air of competition between us added to the tension of the race and I could hear their voices were charged with extra urgency as our horses set off on the final chase. Izzy nearly flipped when one of their picks was unseated just after the halfway mark, but the other, Randall's Drift, stayed well positioned until the end. He was well-backed and the crowd roared with delight when he took the lead after the last fence and came in the winner, winning a cool thousand pounds for my brother and Izzy. In the excitement, she threw her arms around Magnus and kissed him passionately. I think he was rather taken by surprise, but he soon warmed to it. It did mark a euphoric moment at the end of a fantastic day's racing. While they kissed, she watched me from over his shoulder. It was acutely embarrassing.

However, the awkward moment was soon forgotten in the flush of victory, and our massive luck over the whole day raised my spirits. I felt we were unbeatable and I could tell the feeling was shared. As we walked back to the house I said that dinner out that night would be on me. More than a celebration, it would be a send-off for Magnus who was planning to book a last-minute flight for tomorrow.

♈

As we turned into the front garden we saw the front door of the house was flapping open. Izzy sprinted ahead and dashed inside, with us following. I was last through the door and I stopped to examine the latch, which appeared to be undamaged. There was a cry of dismay from the front room and I ran through to find Magnus and Izzy surveying the wreck of their living room. It had been turned over. Almost nothing was left on the walls or shelves. Food was spilled over the floor and the taps were left running.

We looked upstairs and in the other rooms, where the pattern had been repeated. The others said there didn't seem to be anything missing. Without any evidence I assumed this was payback for my attack on Dudley's car, and for that I felt sorry. I hadn't noticed him when we came past. The others didn't say anything, we just started picking things up.

After half an hour of it, Izzy swore and announced that we needed to get on with booking the flights regardless. The clean-up would have to wait. I logged on to my laptop and began the trawl for last minute tickets while she watched over my shoulder and phoned an order for food to be delivered. The first airport stop was to be in Massachusetts, then on to California and finally to Texas, a state familiar to Izzy, which was our rendezvous before returning to the UK.

After thinking about it, I suggested that my brother and I ought to swap our credit cards – both bearing the name Mr M Miller – as well as passports. It seemed to make for a more seamless identity swap, and besides I trusted Magnus intrinsically. I discovered that I was the last one to have had this thought, but it was good to have come up with an idea independently, for once. I suggested swapping driving licences as well, but Magnus wanted to keep his tucked away as an emergency back-out plan. As a hedging strategy it seemed practical.

He and I had a sit-down together to exchange PIN numbers and our verification passwords and the cards and documents themselves. We kept our voices low, in case we were being listened to. We still had a clear 24 hours before take-off but the sense of imminence was overpowering.

"There's something else," I said to him, cautiously. "I was thinking that today I should've quit placing bets while I was ahead. It didn't work to keep piling them on. You could say the same about where you're heading now. You've got a decent offer on the table, why risk it all?"

"You're speaking with hindsight, and you got lucky at the start," he replied. "That's not a reason to get out of the game when you're still in it."

"It's not just about losing your stake," I said. "There's a sense of menace about this whole adventure. How much further do you suppose these people are prepared to push you?"

"Marcus, it's true that everything is a bit shitty right now and we're all upset about the house being busted up, but actually that helps in a strange way. I'm keen to get away from it for a day or two. The worst case I suppose is that I end up making a painful compromise and coming back here to take a professorship. I could get over it, I suppose, but I still believe I can do better. I'll know by the weekend, Monday latest," he said.

"Promise me then that you'll end it by Monday."

"If not before then," he said. "And then all our lives can go back to normal."

Identities

I just managed to stop myself from shaving the next morning, and spent the rest of the day putting my hand to my chin to feel the unfamiliar stubble. Magnus had played his part by trimming his beard back tightly. He also announced that he was going to walk into town and get a Caesar haircut to match mine that morning.

Over breakfast, Izzy, who'd called in sick to work, announced the pièce de résistance of her plan. Magnus and I were to exchange fingerprints with each other. I completely failed to see the point of it, but her kitchen experiment now began to make sense.

"This is to do with that fake fingerprint you made at the weekend isn't it?" I asked, realising that she'd been cooking this up for days. "But I don't get it. Nobody ever took our fingerprints. What's the point?"

"Keep your voice down please," she warned. "Think about it. Have you never been to the States?"

I shook my head. "My parents take me to Disney World? No chance."

"Well they're going to scan your fingerprints when you arrive and pair them up with your passport," she said.

I remained as nonplussed as ever. Magnus chipped in. "They don't throw them away, you dodo, they're paired with your identity forever. If you registered your fingerprints against my passport then I might never get into the country again, and the same for you."

It was another moment when the intricacy of their plan astonished me. The balance of odds was too delicate. There were too many obstacles. Their confidence in being able to beat the system seemed outrageous.

"Stay chilled Marcus, it's all planned out," Izzy insisted. "Just relax and go with it and you'll soon see that it's way easier than you think."

But she didn't need to worry about me. I was becoming used to acts of wanton recklessness and had resigned myself to it already. I was pretty sure that everything was going to come unstuck somewhere along the way, and in a detached sort of way I was just curious to find out when and how. I guessed that we might all end up being deported, but so what? It was the least of my worries.

Izzy warmed up some more of the soft plastic to make moulds and took impressions of all our fingers and thumbs, marking each of them carefully for left or right hand and which digit it was. I watched the process with some interest and was reassured by the meticulous care she took over it, which should have come as no surprise. Magnus and I were to stick the final transparent layers to our fingers with a kind of theatrical gum normally used for fixing false beards. The finished job was almost invisible. I briefly considered suggesting a false beard as another refinement, but decided there was too much risk that they'd take me seriously, so I kept quiet about it.

She made us practise putting on the fake fingerprints ourselves so that we could fix them at the airport or on the plane at the last minute. It was pretty simple: the trick was to wait until the gum was tacky. We had two sets each, in case of need, and she had a system for marking the final prints discreetly so we didn't muddle them. She even assured us they were edible, in case we needed to dispose of them for any reason. Getting the sticky stuff off needed the most patience, which required makeup remover. But by the time we'd both carried out the procedure a couple of times I almost believed that it would work.

My remaining assignment for the morning was to buy two pay-as-you-go burner phones with cash, one for Izzy and one for me. It was another detail in her plan to drop off and stay off the radar. Magnus was to buy himself his own phone after arriving in the States, and then text us both messages, so that we would have his new number. We would subsequently buy ourselves yet another two phones on our arrival in the States and message him back, to complete the loop and disappear entirely. That promised us a few days of being able to keep in touch without being traced, she said. I had to take her word for it, but I couldn't fault the logic.

So I walked into town again with Magnus late morning. Dudley was near his usual spot and we tipped him a nod. Unlike Izzy, however, I took the precaution of staying on the opposite side of the street. She still persisted in going to talk to him most mornings and I had the impression they sometimes had a bit of a chat. I was beginning to appreciate what Magnus had said: the thought of leaving my real life behind again had grown more appealing, with or without the allure of a fantasy holiday with Izzy.

"Did you ever wonder what it would be like to swap lives for real?" I asked Magnus, by way of making conversation.

"Ignoring the practical impossibility of it, you mean?" he asked. "Why would you want to? I mean, all of this hassle, an uncertain future ... the responsibility of it all."

"You should count your blessings. You have so many

good things: A meteoric career, a beautiful house, an amazing partner." I rather mumbled the last point.

"I should be more grateful, I suppose. You appreciate those things more when you haven't got them," he mooted. His manner could be so direct. I winced.

"And with your psychological issues too, I suppose it all looks a bit glum," he went on. "You didn't meet up with Persi again after you went to the castle together, did you?"

"She's not my psychotherapist," I answered.

"Oh no, I didn't mean that side of things. I meant Izzy thought you had a bit of a thing for her, for Persi I mean. Izzy's very perceptive like that. You should think about it. She might do you a lot of good."

I smiled inwardly. Izzy's story-telling never ended. But the best stories had half a truth in them, didn't they? I made a mental note to see if Persi was around tomorrow, my last day in England.

♈

The last thing Magnus and I did before he left that afternoon was to swap jackets. It completed the exchange of our identities. My nascent beard was still scarcely a match for his reduced one, but the newly aligned haircuts made up even more of the gap and it was hard to think how much more we could have done.

I felt his wallet fat inside the jacket and pulled it out to give to him. It contained a wodge of paper dollars and my credit card. We checked everything else had been properly swapped over and I gave the keys for my hire car to Izzy. They were going to sneak out the back door as we had done on the day of the races and I was to stay near a window, half in sight, enough to create the impression for Dudley that

Magnus was still at home, at least until he had managed to slip away.

We embraced briefly before he left. We had spent so much time preparing for this moment, but it still felt unreal now that it had finally arrived, like the first rehearsal of a play which you've read through but not yet grown into, even though this was the live performance. There was very little to say apart from what the script should have contained. We wished each other good luck and made assurances that we would meet up again in a few days. I had a polite kiss for Izzy and agreed we may not see each other that evening if she was back late. Then he and she set off, fading into the soft drizzle.

♈

I didn't see Izzy on the night when Magnus had flown out, and only briefly again next morning before she went off to work as normal, followed of course by Dudley.

I'd planned to spend all morning in the house with nothing more to do than send a couple of texts using Magnus' regular phone. Happily it had turned out that Persi was free to meet for lunch in town, so there was something to look forward to. Needing to fill some time, I decided to pack my travel bag, even though Izzy and I weren't leaving until tomorrow morning, and I thought I would consolidate my devices and identity papers into my man-bag, once again. It would settle my anxiety, a little.

I turned out the pile of stuff which had accumulated in my bag and began to sort it into a pile to take and one to leave behind. A small envelope fell out of the bag, which I didn't recognise. It was addressed to me, scrawled in Magnus' rough unpractised handwriting:

130

Dear Marcus

I have been feeling guilty about some things we should have talked about lately but never did.

I said I was on the verge of a great discovery. Yes, I've made inroads way beyond my own most optimistic hopes, but the problem is generally agreed to be too hard. So I fear I will be disbelieved and laughed at in the coming week, or find I was wrong all along, and my career will grind to a dead halt, a total failure. But you know there are principles involved, as I said, which affect society. If I wasn't convinced that I was doing the right thing, then I wouldn't have boarded the plane.

So my nerves may get the better of me yet, however much I intend to go through with it, and that would be a terrible let-down. You are taking a deal of trouble on my behalf and I don't want to let you down but if it happens, please forgive me. You think of me as very rational, which I am, but I'm also human.

My interpretation of recent strange events is based on conjecture but has pushed me into our current plan. One moment it seems to be the most logical path forward and the next it's the stupidest. I think you were inclined to think it's madness but I didn't want to agree with you too easily in case I talked myself out of it.

Finally here's some PRIVATE advice. It's awkward to say this and don't take it the wrong way, but Izzy is not the most trustworthy person you will ever travel with, so be warned. It is just the way she is. You are no doubt dazzled by her beauty and dynamism, the same way everyone is at first. But also she is secretive and, if it suits her, she will lie to you about anything. If you find yourself in a situation where it is you or her then look out for yourself (think: prisoner's dilemma). For all that she seems to have found something she likes about me and I am more than content to bind my fortune with hers.

I am really grateful for the help you are giving. Please take care of yourself, and her, until we meet again, soon.

Your brother

Magnus

Bloody hell, I thought and I screwed the letter up, made to throw it away and then thought the better of it. He was keeping all that to himself and now he had led us all on a fool's errand.

After I'd smoothed it out and re-read it, his letter made more sense. In his mind he had chained together all of the most pessimistic assumptions about his trip, and this made the worst possible outcomes seem inevitable. It was the same kind of linear thinking that had probably led to his and Izzy's current desperate plan. He'd been down rabbit holes this way when we were growing up, too. It was what he was like, I should have seen it a mile off. I felt reassured that the worst possible outcomes were probably less likely than he imagined, and was more worried about his febrile state of mind.

But the thing I was wrestling with the most was what he'd said about Izzy. I didn't like it, and I could hardly believe he would say that about her, but having known her for a week I could see that it rang true. For a moment my guilt had the better of me and not knowing if I had the will to go through with it, I resolved that I had to end our secret affair, whatever it took.

Soon after then I received a pre-agreed text message on my burner phone, "BCNU," from a new and unrecognised number, registered in the States, which was Magnus announcing his safe arrival. His cheap burner phone obviously didn't extend to predictive text any more than mine

132

did. I heaved a sigh of relief and started to memorise the number. The passport inspection and the face recognition biometrics had obviously been fooled, and the fake fingerprints must have gone undetected too. It seemed that my own pessimism had been ill-founded, so far.

I took the time to spell out a reply:

Everything will work out. Keep calm and carry on.

I cursed again, folded the letter up and slid it into my shirt pocket.

♈

I was in two minds whether to head into town for lunch dressed as Magnus, or whether to put on my spare jacket and sneak around dressed as me, the guy who was supposed to be in the States by now. In the end I figured that with Dudley gone until Izzy got back, there was little point in worrying about it, so I chose to be me.

It had turned sunny and just warm enough to sit outside the brasserie where Persi had suggested we meet. I was coming to associate her with sunny spring days and the feeling of optimism. We greeted each other and I breathed in as we kissed, getting my fix of her natural scent once again, which remained as delicate and intoxicating as ever. I was happy to see that she was relaxed and smiled a lot, and we had plenty to talk about. Neither of us was in a hurry to go anywhere.

I told her about my trip to see my father, and how I felt more settled about my relationship with him since he'd shown himself a little more positive over my career choice. Carefully, she enquired about my state of mind since the accident, and I had to cast my mind back a week and think about it before I could answer her.

"I'm not sure, but maybe the change of scene has done me

some good. The routine of eating, sleeping and exercising is good for me. It's hard to say," I told her.

"If it's OK to ask, what about the flashbacks? Do you still have them?" she asked.

"Yes, in a sort of way. But they're less 'here and now' than they were and less often. It's more bad feelings and bad dreams. And feeling guilty about Pete, that's a constant. It's just become part of me now I think." My words dried up and I fell into a thoughtful silence. It was true, my state of mind had been getting better all week.

"Those sound like positive signs, or I should say a change in the right direction" she said. "Let's hope things continue in that way for you."

I'd said enough on the topic, especially as it occurred to me that the domestic and professional turmoil within Magnus' household might have something to do with it, and that had been my main preoccupation over the last few days. Fortunately she changed the subject, if only to upbraid me. She was a little jealous not to have been invited to the races as it seemed everyone else she had spoken to had been there this week themselves. I realised that was a goof on my part. I shouldn't have taken her stern words so much to heart the week before. There was something I wanted to say to her on that count, but I didn't feel ready. I ordered another beer instead and a coffee for her, and I asked her about her news.

She was still under-employed, she said, and gave me the rundown on agency work. Her surfeit of free time led up to her plan to visit Westminster Abbey to see Ann of Cleves' tomb, and so to complete her collection of Henry VIII's wives. Would I like to go as well? I said that would be great, after this week. This suited her too as she had a little work, she told me, maybe we could go out one evening instead.

Then the conversation faded abruptly and there was a

moment's embarrassed silence when I realised we had both shared the same thought, which was my complicated love life.

"There was something I meant to say to you," I began, awkwardly. "Following on from the thing I mentioned when we were at the castle last week."

"You don't have to," she interrupted. We both paused, waiting for the other to go first. "I mean you don't need to explain anything," she went on. "I was guilty of judging you when I wasn't entitled. Maybe I jumped to the wrong conclusion in any case." Although she said this, she was clearly a little upset too.

"It's OK. I care about what you think, and besides you weren't wrong," I said. Self-consciously, I slid my hands across the table. A gesture of reassurance.

"Well then I think I can read between the lines and I know enough. You've been a real asshole. And yes, I'm angry with you for it, even if I'm not so surprised. But I am really disappointed in you too."

Her intuition was uncanny, it was as if she could read my mind. On the upside, it was a relief that she didn't feel the need to ask any questions, and doubly so because the two women on the next table had gone quiet, pretending to talk to each other still, but obviously not. Their conversation suddenly had more spaces than words in it.

"What I was going to say was, well, I know I was wrong," I said. "I've tried to make excuses, give reasons. I almost managed to convince myself, but when I talked to you I knew it was just a big lie, and I'm sorry for it."

"So what are you really saying?" she asked. Hell, now the detailed questions were beginning. I hadn't thought this far ahead. I sensed our neighbours unconsciously leaning towards us in their anxiety to get the whole story.

"Um, well I'm going to make it right. Mend my ways. You'll be able to approve of me again."

She seemed partly mollified by that and I sensed there was no point going any further into it or adding more undertakings. I'd just made a big promise, and it was time to shut up before I made any more.

She recovered her usual composure, smiled serenely, and slid her hands forwards across the table until her fingertips just met mine. It was the lightest contact, but it seemed to communicate volumes and I found her touch had a rather pleasing, slightly electrifying effect on me.

"That's good," she said. "You're making progress in all sorts of ways."

There was a slight tension still hanging in the air, however. Her eyes flicked around uneasily. "Is there something you're not saying?" I asked.

"Yes. It's about the new beard," she said. "I'm not sure that's progress."

♈

I was unsure how to follow through my new resolve to end my lightning affair with Izzy. I wasn't looking forward to telling her and a large part of me didn't want it to end in any case. And it felt like bad timing to raise something so radical and potentially sensitive the night before we flew out together, given the nature of the promise she'd made. I decided just to avoid mentioning it, to keep my head down and see how things worked out.

I was doing my work-out using her period French furniture when she got back from work, and she didn't seem concerned, just pulled her stuff together and went down to the gym, taking her Audi, duly followed by Dudley. When she got back she said she hadn't received any messages from Magnus other than the same one I had, but neither had she expected any. That was about it. She seemed to have switched me off in any case, and for once I was grateful for it.

She remained neutral and uncommunicative all the rest of the evening, even over supper, which I put down to her worrying about Magnus. I figured that meant that anything to be said or done between us was postponed at least until another day and I made my excuses and retired early to bed. However, soon after I had gone to my room, she followed me in and climbed in afterwards, on top of me. I started to speak, but she shushed me.

"I don't feel like talking, sweetie. Let's just stick to the shagging part," she said, and got straight on with it.

I would like to say that my heart wasn't in it, or something like that, but my willpower had deserted me, and I craved her just as strongly as ever. So having managed to park my resolve for a more convenient occasion, I joined in energetically and made the most of the occasion. Although that night our lovemaking was slightly functional, mechanical even, she knew me well enough and could bring my desire to an intense and prolonged peak with timing which suited her needs also.

Neither of us had very much to say afterwards, apart from the usual sweet words of assurance, and she walked back to her own room sometime later, having had her use out of me. I lay on my back and promised myself that would be the last time, and wished it could have never ended.

Airports

Izzy, it turned out, had a parting gift for Dudley. On the following morning, before we set off for the airport, she threw some unusual home-made assemblies onto the kitchen table in front of me. Starting with several short lengths of hose pipe, she had pushed half a dozen or more shiny silver nails into each of them so that their sharp ends protruded out of the other side of the hose at various angles. These things stood on their metal legs on the table, and reminded me of caterpillars. Whichever way they landed, some of the sharp ends would always be pointing upwards.

I recognised almost instantly what they were. "Calthrops," I said with an approving grin. Once upon a time these nasty little things were sown on the field of battle to bring down cavalry, and their legacy had continued into the present with the spike strips used at police checkpoints which puncture car tyres. It was an ingenious way of assembling them without needing a welder. Her intended target went almost without saying.

"It's a 'just in case' precaution," she said. "Since we can use your car, he probably shouldn't be following us anyway, so long as he follows form. But it would be nice to think he could have a nasty accident somewhere down the road. Something to remember us by."

"Or at the very least, he'll be on his fourth car. What's the next downgrade? A Reliant Robin?" I said.

"One possible conclusion. I could have thrown acid in his face or something instead." There was a chilly off-handedness in the way she said that which made me wonder how much of a joke it was meant to be. She seemed to have no consideration for the possible consequences of any of it.

"I suppose that'll be the end of the 'habituation' experiment," I said, glad it was all going to be over before things escalated any further.

Late morning, not long before we were about to leave, we agreed a quick plan of action and set off. She scooped up the improvised calthrops and I watched her walk down the road until she got to Dudley's vehicle for the customary skirmish. That was my moment to walk out to the Audi wearing Magnus' jacket, hop into the driver's seat but then get out again and return the house. Dudley would have his eyes on me while she placed the little spikes neatly under his wheel. It clearly worked, as a short while later she came back to the house with the reassurance that it had been all too easy. With that job done, we each walked to my car two streets away, leaving by the back door ten minutes apart, travelling with hand luggage only.

Izzy and I had never been obliged to sit together for so long with so little opportunity for a distraction or physical contact. She was in an excited mood and kept busy on her mobile phone mixing with her friends, who she liked to keep private, and she received two pieces of information from Magnus which he texted to her. The first was that he'd had his meeting on the east coast and the second was that he was about to board his flight to California. Each of the two snippets lifted her further into her state of high spirits. She was so incredibly engaged with the whole adventure and atmosphere of skulduggery. It almost made up for my feeling of scepticism and discomfort. She may have been the architect of the plan, but she was only a passenger during its execution.

We returned the hire car and went through the airport to the departure lounge. I had planned to apply my fake fingerprints as late as possible before boarding and then to avoid touching anything, as much as I could, for the duration of the ten hour flight, so after we'd been through security I locked myself in a cubicle in the loos and got to work. The thin jelly-like pads were in two envelopes, one for left and one for right, and marked with small dots of water soluble ink to indicate which finger they were for. The gum was very sticky and I had to finish one hand before I began the next. It took a good twenty minutes to finish, but in the end it was done and I exited the cubicle using my elbows and the palms of my hands. I didn't think I could have got away with locking myself in the aeroplane loo for that length of time. I felt glad I'd saved that option for emergency repairs only.

♈

Normally I would have read a book, the newspaper and a couple of periodicals on a long flight, or fiddled with my laptop. All these options were closed to me on account of needing to protect my fingertips. I realised that I should have left at least a finger and thumb until the end, but it was too late now and so the journey was unendingly tedious. Listening to music on my player and watching the in-flight movies helped a little but I couldn't settle without having a few drinks, and then a few more until Izzy stopped me. The evening wore on, even if it didn't get any darker, and my anxiety about passport control at the other end overrode the

140

need for sleep, even with the help of the drinks. The cumulative effect made me feel ill. Tired, worried and a little drunk, I went through every detail and then decided that having my own driving licence on me while we went through the passport checks would be a bad idea, and so I foisted it onto Izzy for safekeeping.

We landed at last, and Izzy helped me get my luggage down, again to protect my fingers, and as we disembarked I began to freak out. A cold sweat formed on my forehead. But now there was no choice except mechanically to follow the stream of other passengers out of the plane. To act naturally.

Mentally, I was up past my bedtime, although it was still daylight here. The transfer bus took us to the airport terminal where an icon of a peak-capped uniformed officer and the legend NON-U.S. CITIZENS pointed us down a corridor and into the entrance hall. People fanned out into separate queues underneath signs which read PLEASE WAIT BEHIND YELLOW LINE UNTIL AN OFFICER BECOMES AVAILABLE.

Izzy split off from me, joined another longer queue and remained apart. She avoided looking my way, but I was acutely aware of being studied by her from an oblique angle. I knew she was loving the tension as much as I was hating it. My inevitable exposure and arrest seemed only minutes away, as the queue shuffled forwards.

I studied how things worked at an American passport cubicle. Were all airports the same? Up to a point. The officers were sticklers about the yellow line. I made a mental note to keep a foot clear of it when I reached the front. I wondered if trying to fake a smile and look relaxed was worse than the mask of an impassive stare.

There were cameras pointing at the arrivals. Magnus

141

having got in on my passport had increased my confidence that we were alike enough to each other's pictures, it was more the fingerprint reader that I was concerned about. What if this airport had better machines than the one Magnus had landed at?

Finally it was my turn to step forwards. The officer waved me towards him. I held my passport and declaration papers in a scissor-grip, sideways on. He didn't notice anything unusual in that. I wondered if he could smell the booze on me. Nothing unusual in that either, I supposed.

The man stared directly at me from his cubicle: "What's the purpose of your trip?" he asked.

My mouth had gone dry and the blood drained from my face but with a cracked voice and a weak smile I managed to tell him "Business."

He pointed the camera at me and took my picture. He asked me to press my fingers down flat onto the glowing green scanner screen. The moment of truth. The fingerprint reader beeped or flashed, I don't remember which, and as far as I could tell that seemed to be over with. I wondered if it really only did the tips of my fingers.

The man in the booth looked up and down from my face to the photo and back. I had a feeling something was wrong, and then he waved to another officer from behind the kiosks. The man walked across to us and I figured it must mean only one thing.

"This passenger failed the face recognition biometric," said the man in the booth. I was aghast. However sure I'd been this would happen, it wasn't the same as being here now. I stayed neutral and attentive, trying to give nothing away, offering compliance without resistance.

"Please step this way," said the supervisor, leading me to a partitioned area beyond the kiosks. Another officer was brought over and consulted. They looked to and from me to my brother's photograph and pulled some faces. They asked whether I had any other identification, but they meant only photo ID so there was nothing I could do. They looked inside my bag. One or two more questions about my trip were forthcoming. I'd prepared my cover: I was meeting with some colleagues at the nearby university next week, and had extended my stay over the weekend for pleasure.

After another second the supervisor shrugged and said "This happens sometimes. The picture's obviously you." Then with a smile he said "Thank you for your co-operation, sir. Welcome to the USA."

I was through.

♈

I felt like I was walking on air. I had no baggage to collect and so without a backwards glance I floated past the customs desks. I was into the arrivals lobby before I allowed myself to break into a smile of relief. There was a line of people waiting beyond the barrier. Each of them scanned my face before moving quickly onto the passengers behind as they looked for their family or friends. One or two people held up signs with people's names on them. Their side of the barrier was my target, which I planned to reach before I turned to look for Izzy emerging behind me. I would wave to her from the safety and anonymity of the crowd.

I was about ten feet from the opening, when a man in a navy suit and open-necked grey shirt stepped forward and caught my attention.

"Magnus Miller?" he asked, with a distinct Texan drawl.

"Yes," I answered without blinking or breaking step, looking at him more closely. He was some years older than me, and had close cropped greying hair with receding temples. He had an intelligent face. He turned to walk alongside me and spoke while we walked. I shied slightly to the side while looking across my shoulder at him.

"We've been asked to contact you," he went on. I looked around to see who he meant by "we" and saw a second man, similarly dressed but younger and taller, walking up to me on my other side. The three of us, with me in the middle, walked straight out onto the concourse and towards the exit. I made to slow down and look around for Izzy but with a hand placed gently on the small of my back, the older man impelled me forwards while he went on talking.

"I believe you may be travelling with someone?" he asked.

"Yes, Izzy, my partner. Who asked you to contact me? Could I see some ID?"

"Yessir. We'll bring your lady out to you in just a short moment. Please keep walking."

I examined his photo ID as we continued in the direction of the exit. His name, it said, was Noah Bingam. There was an official-looking Departmental logo with a Texan star on it, and he was designated as an officer of a criminal information centre, or center. I didn't like the look of it at all. What did they want to talk to me about?

He offered reassurances but nothing he said seemed to nail who had asked him to meet me, or why. I was still popping questions at him as we marched out of the arrivals hall and into the pickup area, a concrete cavern echoing with the noise of car doors and engines and the occasional squeal of tyres.

"It'd be quieter if we sat inside the vehicle for a moment and talked" he suggested, gesturing casually towards a large SUV, its passenger door held open by a young guy in a green baseball cap. Despite the underground gloom, he was wearing shades. Otherwise, he was in a paramilitary-style khaki shirt and cargo pants, although I didn't notice any insignia.

His offer finally spooked me enough to offer some more determined resistance.

"There's no need for that. What's this about? I'm going back inside the terminal, you can tell me in there," I said, trying to stay cool about it.

As I began to turn, the two men literally picked me up by my armpits, carried me to the open door and bundled me inside the car. It was done in a second, during which moment I felt a hard lump under Noah's arm, maybe of a gun in its holster. Taken off-balance, I had begun to struggle, but there was a shadowy fourth figure waiting in the back seat who grabbed my arm and held onto me while the younger one, the one in khaki, got in after me. I might have overpowered the smaller younger one fairly easily, but the guy already in the car was another matter. I had another look at him. He was very strong, bald and overweight, wearing jeans and a combat jacket that didn't look like it would button over his gut. The fat on his face reduced his eyes to thin slits and he looked like an evil Buddha.

Noah looked in through the door after me and said: "Don't worry, you're quite safe, Doctor Miller. Please be patient. Your co-operation is appreciated." Then he walked calmly round to the front passenger seat.

The other suited man had taken the driver's seat and we began to drive off from the pickup area and back out into the fading daylight. Despite my struggling, the men on either side of me held my arms and so there wasn't much I could do.

Noah, who was obviously running things, turned round to look at me from the front seat. "Doctor Miller, I do apologise for removing you so rudely, we'll make it up to you. It's really an honour to meet you, sir. My name's Noah." I knew that already, of course. He extended a hand towards me, which I ignored.

"What the bloody hell is going on? Where are we going?" I demanded, with a little less bile than I should have, owing to his courteous and apparently sincere greeting. He withdrew the hand.

"There's a little drive ahead, about an hour," he replied. "We can explain things easier when we get there."

He was dialling on his phone already and cut me off as soon as the other end picked up. He announced that I had been "picked up", and our expected time of arrival, which was nearer to an hour and a half.

"What's happening to Izzy?" I asked as soon as he'd hung up.

"We're contacting her and will bring her to you as soon as possible. Where were y'all staying?"

I knew that in the end she'd be going to the flat we rented in midtown, but I wasn't telling him. I told him instead that we were booked into a downtown hotel, whose name eluded me. He didn't seem too concerned, but said they could locate her easily enough. He didn't try to make any more conversation but ignored my other questions and I withdrew into a truculent sulk. I was wondering whether to tell them they had the wrong guy. It would be a hard sell, given the unlikely scenario, but I soon realised that in any case this was my purpose here: to provide a diversion so Magnus' plan didn't get messed up. Otherwise it would have been Magnus in my shoes, although in the literal sense, our shoes were about the only thing that we hadn't exchanged. And so I decided to wait it out, and find out as much as I could before I was released, whether or not that required me to tell them who I really was.

I was mildly sceptical about whether Noah was quite who he said he was. But he had seemed quite charming and upfront about himself and it wasn't as if I'd been cuffed or blindfolded, so I was inclined to believe some of what he said. Somehow it didn't feel quite like I was being arrested or kidnapped. Even the fact that the fat guy beside me kept letting out small farts added a comical touch. I asked for the window to be opened and he obliged.

I studied our route with care as the car turned onto the interstate highway going south. The land was low-lying and as we sped along, it was only when we went over flyovers crossing other highways that I could see much around us. It seemed at first that we were heading for the downtown area but then we turned onto another highway and drove off in the opposite direction.

The settlements surrounding the concrete highway were plastered in signage and brightly coloured logos, and yet they were all very much alike, creating an anonymous landscape, speaking as one who recognised almost none of them. Tiredness caught up with me and before I knew it I had snapped awake, the darkness outside telling me that I had dozed off for some time.

I noticed oil storage terminals had begun to appear, some lit and others looming like shadows against the darkening sky. Later still, we crossed a bridge which spanned the black waters of a wide bay and finally we switched off the highway onto a local road.

We were now unmistakably in a harbour area. I could smell the sea. We had begun driving past marine merchants, shrimp plants, storage facilities, industrial centres and railways. I saw a brightly lit cruise liner looming over the harbour buildings. We went on a little further before turning towards a wharf where we drew to a halt.

The occupants of the car now began to engage, shifting from their state of bored suspense into movement and activity as they began to get out and pull their bags out of the boot. I followed them out and no-one tried to stop me, but the setting was such that I knew there was absolutely no way these guys were state officials. It was dodgy as hell, and I could hardly believe I'd been duped so easily.

The evening was much milder than I'd been used to lately, if not warm. I stretched and looked around for an opportunity to run away, but I could see we were cut off on three sides by water and on the fourth by a fence whose gate was already being pulled shut. The two guys in combat jackets were both keeping a close eye on me. If the chance came, I'd take it, but I had to choose my moment and this wasn't it.

There was a very fancy yacht nearby, over a hundred footer with three decks. I could make out her name, she was called *Diva De L'Orient*, and sailing under a Cayman Islands flag. She was sleek, streamlined and racy. A macho, man's craft. From a distance, her interior glowed with golden light which looked soft and comfy, warm and welcoming. There were a couple of uniformed crew by the gangway. The whole setup reeked of money, which I sensed was probably not good money, and this provided the remaining confirmation that I wanted. Our group walked over to the welcoming party. Noah, holding a briefcase in his left hand, shook hands with the master in a business-like way, and we were welcomed aboard. As I shuffled onto the boat, surrounded by Noah's enlarged crew, I realised my prospects of escape were now hopeless.

"Where are you taking me?" I asked Noah.

He thought for a moment, then answered: "It all depends on you."

Coercion

The gangway crossed to the fore deck of the ship, and I was led past the cockpit to a door which opened into a small bar. It was part of the main sitting and dining area which was panelled with the most expensive kind of plain elegance.

I was taken immediately down some steps by the young guy, now without the shades, to the lower landing, and into a double bedroom with an en suite, which he informed me was mine. I had gathered by now that his name was Cody. He talked very little. He gave me back my travelling bag, told me to do what I needed and go straight back upstairs. But I just wanted to lie down and go to sleep on the lovely bed. The others could wait. As soon as he left the room I threw myself onto it, shut my eyes and went out like a light.

It felt like only seconds later, although my watch said fifteen minutes, when Cody shook me awake, telling me I was wanted on the main deck. The boat was moving now, and I looked out of my port hole to see the lights of the harbour passing by, although the boat's pitch and roll suggested we were in the sea channel.

"C'mon, get moving, you can see that from upstairs" Cody said and I reluctantly trudged back up to the main deck.

Noah and the other suited fellow were standing outside on the aft part of the main deck, holding drinks and watching the

149

lights go by. The change of air helped to wake me a little and I noticed they had piped country music onto the deck. I hadn't seen this end of the boat previously, so I surveyed as much as I could in the few seconds I had. It had steps down over three levels, leading to the lowest part, the aft deck, a diving board which was nearest water level and had no railings. There was an intermediate level with large sunbeds fixed to it. My guess was the sunbeds concealed a dinghy or jet skis, or both, and could be lifted to allow the smaller craft to be craned out. Not that I was used to this kind of luxury, but naturally I'd read the catalogues.

The highest of the three levels, where we stood, had a table for outdoor eating, but I could see that food was being served indoors and the seats outside were still covered with bags waiting to be stowed. I moved closer to the railing to look over the side and both Noah and the other suit stepped forward gingerly to put themselves between me and it.

♈

"Doctor Miller, let's step inside," said Noah, leading me in and sliding the glass door shut.

There was food on the table, less classy than the boat, with the emphasis on meat and salad. A faint odour of cooked fat and grease hung in the air.

Noah sat down. "This is Connor, by the way, he's my IT guy," he said, indicating his suited companion. Connor looked my age. He had strong shoulders and was obviously very fit. I'd already noticed there was something about the set of his jaw, or his tight-lipped expression, that suggested he was slightly annoyed about something. Maybe it was just too much testosterone, or he badly needed some female company. It seemed to be a permanent condition.

"No offence Connor, but don't mistake me for someone who gives a shit who you are right now," I said. "I'm too tired. You guys do realise that I'm five hours ahead of you? So if you want to tell me why I've been kidnapped, then great. Otherwise I'm going to sleep either here or in my bed."

Noah broke into a broad grin. "Sure, but don't let's say kidnapped, that's such a dirty word. My employer has a proposal for you. He was most insistent that we put it to you before you saw those other people you were planning to see. So we're just gonna sail around for a while, have our talk, eat some dinner, and then we should be done. And with our apologies for detaining you and keeping you up so late."

"You mean we're going straight back?" I asked him, rather relieved that things could work out so easily.

"Sure, why not? Could be we enjoy a pleasant talk, some fine food and we turn right around and drop you where you're staying."

"Or otherwise?" I asked, sensing that his offer was conditional.

"Or, for a longer stay, I know a quiet fishing village down Mexico way. Let's not get ahead of ourselves," he said.

"Who is this employer you mentioned?" I asked.

"He's a businessman. I'm afraid I couldn't persuade him to join us. He's a little protective of his identity, but he would like to offer you ... sponsorship," Noah paused momentarily on the word, and smirked a little as he said it. "He asked me to verify your work and then, based on my judgement, to communicate an offer to you."

I could feel my options for talking my way out of this were narrowing, but hey, I was talking to a bunch of gangsters. I probably knew as much about it as these guys did.

"What do you know already?" I asked.

"Just what you gave out to people when you were asking

151

about work here in the U.S. We were very excited by that," he answered. I wondered who and how many places Magnus and Izzy had been in touch with, apart from the two left on his shortlist.

"It may be quite difficult to explain it in more detail to you, as a layman," I said, playing for time.

"Bless your heart. Lots of folk think us Texicans got shit for brains." He played up his accent for effect. "But if you wanted to we could talk about my work on factoring with elliptic curves. If we had the time that was. It was the subject of my Ph.D. We'll find some common language to talk in, I'm sure."

Bloody hell I was sunk, I realised.

"Well maybe we'll find the time later," I said. "What's the essence of his offer first?" I asked.

"I wouldn't want to disappoint you by offering more than your work's worth, but I can tell you this," he began counting off on his fingers. "Two things. Firstly, in exchange for a regular retainer, we're looking for advance briefings into your work, insights you could say, or masterclasses. But you can go on working for who you like, we'll use what you tell us. We'd like a little head start, but we won't steal your work, and you can still collect your Fields Medal."

"My what?" I asked, stupidly letting my cover down. He paused and gave me a funny look, not sure whether he should go on. Then he laughed nervously.

"Ah, you nearly got me," he said. "Maybe you're better at this than I thought. So let me finish. The second thing is a fixed advance payment, a deposit which depends on my valuation of what your work is worth. As a gesture of good faith."

"My hearing's not great after the flight. You're talking about a bribe I think," I said.

152

"Call it what you like. My employer is a very rich man. It will be a lot of money, and we can help you to keep it private."

"And what do you want with these 'insights' in case I haven't guessed already," I asked. Inwardly I was surprised he'd been prepared to lay so many cards on the table, I thought I would keep pressing for more.

"Admit it. My employer would like to get even richer and in the process some banks and online businesses might lose a lot of money. Nothing more than they can afford to swallow, it'll be more like a middle man's tithe. And you'll not be implicated, we know how to cover our tracks."

I had no doubt that Magnus would have objected to this obviously criminal plan. If he objected to the government intercepting secure communications, then what about Internet bad guys ripping people off?

I could see also that Izzy might have thought it the perfect deal, since there appeared to be lots of money on the table, and some kind of medal too. But my only interest was in delaying the moment of acceptance or refusal, since I couldn't deliver one and the other apparently involved an indefinite stay in Mexico. I was running out of ideas and unfortunately the tables were now turned on me.

"It's your turn now, to tell us what you've been doing," he said. "Any way you like, please fire away."

I'd been watching uncomfortably over the last few minutes as the IT guy, Connor, had produced in addition to his own laptop, a second one which looked like mine. He had been fiddling around with it, thumping the keyboard firmly for a couple of minutes before he showed it to Noah and then he span it around towards me. It was indeed my laptop, I could now see. The request for a password appeared as it should, and above it was my logon name, Marc.

"Before you begin, we're a little bit confused, Doctor Miller," Connor said. "Your name's Magnus as we all know, but this looks like it's your brother Marc's laptop. There don't seem to be any other users of this computer."

It looked bad for a moment, until I realised it was another free gift. I could see a way to blag my way out of this, based on the little Magnus had told me.

"You're kidding me," I said. "I've crossed the Atlantic with the wrong laptop?" I allowed a dramatic pause while everyone had time to absorb the fact. "That's where I've got my results. They're really all the evidence you'd need. Very long integers are not the sort of thing you can memorise."

Noah looked unmoved and said nothing. Connor now turned the other laptop around to face me, the one I didn't recognise. I was confronted with the instruction "Enter the password to unlock this drive".

Noah explained: "Fortunately, in that case, we acquired this clone of your laptop just over a week ago. As you're aware, it's encrypted, but as it's your password, please proceed."

"How did you get hold of that?" I asked, realising the game was truly up.

"I think we've explained enough. Now it's time for you to show us what you've got." Noah replied.

"There's another problem," I said. "Thank you for your interest, but I don't want to deal with you or your employer. I'm not a criminal. We should return to the harbour now."

"That option's not available to you, yet," said Noah. "But we do have an alternative. Well, it's not very nice, I'm almost too embarrassed to say. Better all round if you don't take us down that road. There's no going back once you've started."

I said nothing, just waited for the bad news. I half-guessed where this might be leading. Noah waited for a few heartbeats and then called over Cody and the big guy in the combat jacket, who took up positions behind my chair. There was another moment's silence, during which the big guy let out another discreet fart. Connor's eyelid twitched with irritation at him and Cody sniggered from behind.

"Cody and Troy here would have that password out of you soon enough, if needed," Noah told me. "And the crew will look the other way. But that's not the start of a trusting relationship."

"Go on," I said.

"Doctor Miller, you're at an important crossroads. I can't emphasise that enough. We're partners now, the question is on what terms you'd like it to be. There's a great offer on the table already. Take it. The alternative is imprisonment. I mentioned our little fishing village. It's very peaceful, and it's not all bad, within its limitations. We'll even bring your girlfriend down to join you. But it'll be the end of your freedom and your career."

"And after the goose stops laying golden eggs for you, then what?" I asked.

He didn't answer, but looked at Connor. "Are we outside territorial waters yet?"

"Ten minutes away," Connor replied.

Noah tapped the screen of the cloned laptop, which still awaited a password. "Trust me, Doctor Miller. This is the last time I'll repeat our generous and well-intentioned offer."

"Fuck your mother," I said.

Mirror, Mirror

Noah looked disappointed, a little hurt even, then he shrugged and turned again to Connor. "We'll be heading south then. I'll speak to the captain."

He added nothing more but left immediately, knocking on the door before going into the cockpit. Troy meanwhile put an arm round my neck and held me while Connor directed Cody to strip me to the waist. He also took my shoes, and Pete's watch.

"It'll only get harder for you, so you may as well tell us now and save yourself a lot of pain," Connor said. "Just enter the password,"

I ignored him. Troy moved round in front and slapped me, hard, across the face.

"Come on, enter the password," Connor repeated, cajoling me with an irritated tone as if he'd expected me to capitulate immediately.

Then came another slap. I rolled with it, but my face and ears smarted and I could taste blood in my mouth. My cheek had been cut against my teeth. I said nothing, and tried to think about something else, another place. I looked towards the windows but there was nothing to see through them, no shore lights and no moon to penetrate them. The outside was just a black void on top of which was superimposed a reflection of the boat's brightly lit interior, a ghostly image of the little group of men clustered around my chair. I turned my thoughts in on myself instead and found another dark empty void. No doubt this would end, eventually, but to resist them I needed to think about something else. Anything else.

Connor gave a nod to Troy who punched me several times in the stomach. I saw it coming and braced for it, but he was strong and he wasn't holding back. It was bloody painful. The force of his blows expelled the air from me and I felt sick.

Connor leaned over me and told me again to enter the password. I just tried to focus on my breathing. I was building a story in my head now, of my escape. Troy went on slapping me around the face and head until my ears throbbed, and punched me again in the stomach. Spit and blood began to spread around, covering me and the nearby surfaces.

"Let's go outside, it'll be easier to clean up," Connor said to the others. "Take him down to the sunbeds."

Cody and Troy carried rather than led me out onto the aft deck. The chill of the breeze brought me round a bit.

Connor seemed to know what he was doing, and rapped out instructions. "Lie him down there. Cody take his arms and tie his wrists. Troy, take the legs. Lift him up."

Troy hopped up onto the sunbed and lifted my legs, beginning to tip me upside down. I didn't resist. Connor stuffed some cushions under my back. Then they let me down again, and the pressure of Troy's considerable weight pressed down on my feet, pinning my legs. I felt my wrists being bound above my head with a thin, hard binding. I was uncomfortably arched backwards, with my stomach and groin lifted up, exposed, and my head pinched between my

157

arms, hanging off the end of the sunbed cushion, looking up at the black sky. There was not even a single star. Pure darkness framed the dimly lit figures of my three captors as I looked up at them from upside-down. They moved around me, arranging things in a business-like way. It was a moment's respite from the beating, but the position I was in was stressful and I had a bad feeling about where it might be leading next. My heart was pounding and I realised I was panting shallow breaths.

Connor covered my face with a towel. It was the first time I'd been blindfolded, effectively, and being unable to watch what was happening dramatically magnified the scariness of everything. I immediately tensed up, expecting more blows to the face or stomach at any moment, and listened through my ringing ears for every clue, every sound which rose above the hum of the engines and the wash of the propellers. Someone pinched my nose and when I opened my mouth they pushed a wodge of towel into it.

A few seconds later, I heard water splashing onto the deck and in the same instant its cold wetness soaked through the towel, which now sagged under the weight and hugged my face. I tried to take a breath through my nose but immediately the wet towel tightened against my nostrils, impermeable to air. I was able to take in a few small gulps of air through my mouth but then it filled up with water and I almost took some water down. It made me gag and I began to choke. The explosive force of my coughing filled my whole nasal passage with water, the coughing doubled and my throat contracted involuntarily.

This was the moment when I lost control completely. An animal instinct took over and I tried to kick out but my legs were pinned. I thrashed about, rocking my body and twisting my head as much as I could but the guy on my arms responded by pulling them down hard until they felt like they would dislocate.

The water never stopped flowing onto my face or splashing onto the deck. More of it caught painfully in my throat and I began swallowing it. I didn't know where it was going, just that all my passages had filled up and I was choking to death. There was no air going in. My lungs began to heave, desperate for air. I was growing weaker and struggled less. There was no air, only more and more water pouring over me in an endless stream. I was drowning, fading, dying.

Then I threw up.

The warm acidic mixture of water and my last meal flowed up from my gut with an audible rumble, passed burning through my throat and was ejected into my mouth and stinging nostrils. That was when they took the towel off my face and rolled me over. I heaved again and another pint of watery stomach contents spewed across the deck.

I used all my remaining strength to suck air into my lungs and cough up the remaining dregs of water. Then I lay panting and weak, face down over the end of the sunbed.

Connor leaned across me. "Are you ready to give us that password now?"

I couldn't answer for a few moments, and then I gasped "I don't have it."

"Respect for your pointless gesture," he said. "Go again you guys."

I saw there was a hose pipe in his hand, a slow steady trickle of water pouring out of it. Was that all it needed? The others – their names were a blur – pulled me over onto my back again. It was too soon, I wasn't ready. I hadn't finished clearing the tubes. I wanted to scream but I didn't dare let the air out of me. Darkness came again as the soaking towel slopped down onto my face. I tried to keep my mouth shut but they prised it open and pushed the towel in again.

It was a little different the second time. I didn't get caught out straight away, but held my breath for as long as I could. Even from a bad start I was sure I was good for a minute, probably more. So I managed to stay composed and delay the onset of the choking for a while. But in the end I couldn't defeat the need to breathe and the process of drowning, or not drowning, began all over again. The panic, the futile struggle, the choking and ingesting water, becoming weaker, expecting to die.

It was the same routine third time around, except that time they didn't ask me whether I was ready to give up. They just made sure I was conscious and started all over. I began to think that was probably the end, and they were just going to keep going till I died for real.

I came round at some point, wondering where I was. The fat one, Troy, was patting my face and shouting at me to get my attention. Oh yes, I remembered. The last thing I'd felt before I passed out was a momentary feeling of inner peace. That was gone now. I was soaking and cold, but my trousers were warm so I suppose I must have wet myself.

I realised we were back inside in the warmth of the brightly lit dining area. The laptop was facing me again, requiring the password as patiently and impassively as ever. Behind the laptop screen stood Connor and behind him the glass sliding doors were still open to the dark night. The piped music was an old-time tune that I vaguely recognised. Did Texans do irony? Was there a subliminal message to say that I could give up the fight but still be a man?

"You said you'd had enough," he said. "You have. More than enough. Let's have that password now."

Had I said that? If so, then I hadn't changed my mind.

Going another round wasn't going to help me get out of this situation, so I said: "Give me the other laptop. The one I brought with me."

He raised his eyebrows, but did as I asked and slid my laptop over. They hadn't unbound my wrists and I saw they had used a nylon plastic cable tie. Under the username "Marc" I typed my password one-fingered and the screen was unlocked. I sat back and he pulled the machine back towards himself.

"You see, you've got the wrong man. I'm not Magnus, I'm his brother Marc, like it says."

He concentrated on the screen for a moment, frowning, his hands on the table each side of it. Then he walked around the table and swiped me with the back of his hand out of sheer exasperation. I blocked him but it was enough to send me sprawling and while I was picking myself up from the floor he kicked me in the back and I fell on my face again.

That was the end of it, however, he was just letting out his frustration. It was a very small victory. He went below decks while Troy and Cody sat me up again.

When Connor reappeared it was with Noah, who was holding my various ID papers, passport and wallet.

"Mister Miller, let's drop the doctor prefix for a moment," he began. "From what Connor tells me I'm wondering if maybe you really didn't know about the Fields Medal. I need verification, so please answer some questions for me."

It was late night now, even for them. Noah gave a big yawn, which I saw was catching among the others. Then he asked me for a lot of detail about the people he could see that I'd mailed, to see how fluently I could fill in their back stories. He went back some way. He interspersed his questions with ones about Magnus' and my recent movements, such as where we'd both been and where he was now, which I answered as best I could when it suited me and lied about the rest.

At the end of our interview, Noah concluded: "Your brother would have to be very curious indeed to know so much about your private affairs, and you're a poor liar, Mister Marcus Miller. You know more about your brother's whereabouts than you're saying."

He turned to Connor: "I think he's here to meet his brother. They've exchanged IDs. See what you can find about the real Doctor Magnus Miller travelling as Marc or Marcus, and where the woman is. I'll have the boat turned round and we'll head back to port."

"You," he pointed at me. "Your stock just went down like it was Black Monday. We'll be talking again very soon. Think carefully what you want to tell us. Lock him in one of the crew's berths for now, fellas."

Cody pulled me up, still wobbly on my feet, and pushed me down the narrow steps to the galley. Beyond that was a small cramped cabin with a bunk bed, there for the crew. There was a shower in it, and a loo, and a tiny porthole.

I held up my bound hands for Cody to release them, but he shook his head and walked off, leaving the light on. I heard him lock the door from the outside and go back upstairs, and I was alone again.

The need for sleep weighed on me like lead. There was a buzzing in my head and I couldn't tell how much of it was me or how much was the hum of the engines coming into my cabin through the hull. Yet there was a compartment in my mind where the lights still burned, and in it sat the escape committee. One side argued loudly over the means, the other side pleaded for patience, pointing out the miniscule chances of a successful bid at this time. But one member stood apart, a desperate and determined character who said: "By any means, whatever the chance, take it now." Over the space of a few minutes the other advocates dried up, leaving him the only one talking.

To escape at any cost. The next time a guard opened the door, I would overpower him, run outside, jump overboard and swim off into the darkness. Great plan. That was it, from beginning to end. Survival didn't figure too highly. Noah had mentioned territorial waters earlier, so that had to mean we were fifteen miles off the coast, at least, so it was a fairly hopeless situation at this time of year. Never mind.

I cast my mind back to the conversation I'd had with that colleague of Magnus', Mimi, about martial arts moves. She'd shown me some face and neck strikes. I wasn't too sure if they would take someone down with a single blow. Maybe. Eye-jabs I remembered. They sounded like you'd only need one of them, if placed accurately. Difficult with your hands bound. Or a knee to the groin. I didn't fancy trying that on Troy, there was too much fat cushioning him. I looked at my bare feet and figured that the kicks were out, even though my legs were free. Besides, standing on one leg during a fight seemed to favour one's opponent and space was a bit tight. A machete would have been useful, and it could have cut my hands free as well.

I needed something sharp to cut the plastic tie with. I started looking around the cabin, but it was empty and everything in it was made of wood or plastic, all fixed down, or just plain soft old fabric. There was no kit in the shower room either. I saw myself in the mirror for the first time in 24 hours, and noticed the swelling around my cheeks and eyes from the beating that Troy had given me.

The mirror, yes that was it. Break the glass. I leaned back and lurched forwards to give it an almighty punch with my bound fists, my eyes closed. I probably overdid it, and it hurt plenty, but I heard it shatter and as I opened my eyes I saw pieces of the mirror falling out. There was some blood on the glass, which was mine, where I'd cut my hand. There was a splinter of glass sticking out of my knuckle which I pulled out with my teeth. One or two fair sized shards had landed with a clatter in the metal sink. Someone above decks had to have heard it. I pinched the biggest piece between my knees and began madly rubbing the plastic tie against its sharp edge. It was working beautifully. While I freed my hands I realised this would make a makeshift weapon, good for stabbing at least.

I heard footsteps above the ceiling, crossing the floor above and heading towards the galley stairs. I counted the steps on the way down while I frantically cut a strip of sheet off the bunkbed and spun it round the thick end of the glass for a handle. I was scarcely ready when the door was unlocked and it opened inwards towards me. It was Troy. I leapt forwards and swung my stabbing tool at his face. He tried to block me but I felt that I'd connected with his forehead or cheek with a slicing action across his left eye. He cried out and his hand went to his face. Copious blood immediately flowed between his fingers. I'm not normally squeamish, but neither did I ever try to take out someone's eye using a deadly weapon. I flinched, looked to see what I'd done, and for a moment I lost momentum.

Injured though he was, Troy also used the moment's hesitation to recover somewhat. He was still standing and he blocked the door with his considerable bulk, and called for Cody. I needed to get past quickly. I threw my whole weight at him, bodily, and the two of us went sprawling into the narrow corridor between the cabin and the galley. He took hold of my leg to stop me scrambling over him and I stabbed my glass knife into his arm. He let go of me with another shout, but the glass dagger had stuck too firmly in him and wouldn't come out very easily. I had to go without it.

I ran across the galley in time to meet Cody skidding down the steps. I had a slight advantage of weight and strength over him and he was off balance. I punched him in the nose, as hard as I could. He cantilevered backwards and collapsed onto the floor where he stayed prostrate, groaning. I wish I'd had time to hit him a second time, but I just jumped over him instead, onto the bottom step. Nine steps later I emerged into the dining area, which was empty. The music coming through the speakers was *On the Road Again*. Was that Willie Nelson? Country was suddenly growing on me.

I could hear either Cody or Troy was coming back up the stairs behind me and at the same time Connor's face appeared through the door from the cockpit. I yanked open the sliding door at the back and made for the stern, snatching up a couple of odd bundles left lying on the outside seats as I ran, or more accurately fell headlong down the steps to the aft deck.

One of the things I'd grabbed was a lifejacket. The last thing I did as my feet left the deck was to discard it. Buoyancy and visibility were two things that were not going to increase my survival chances right now.

Sea and Sun

I dived deeply, entered the water cleanly and used my momentum to carry me as far down and away from the boat as I could get. The water was pretty cool and I had to hold down an urge to gasp. It was hard to gauge my depth in the darkness, but I swam for as long as my breath would last and didn't break the surface. Eventually my lungs began to convulse with the instinctive need to breathe and these became so intense that I gave in and allowed my natural buoyancy to lift me back up to the top. I breathed out a little as I rose, the action seeming to calm the spasms as I anticipated the lungful of air which I needed so much.

As my nose and mouth cleared the water I drew in breath as steadily and as quietly as I could. I was again able to choose when to come up, when to breathe and where to go. That little bit of freedom felt so sweet.

Willing myself to stay calm I took a few moments – a few more breaths while the fresh oxygen flowed through my arteries – before I looked around for the first time. The boat was pretty much behind me, like a little island of light in the middle of the dark ocean. It had been sailing when I jumped off the back and I'd swum reasonably straight, so we'd put all of 150 metres between us. As I rose and sank with the waves, the boat was alternately obscured or in full view, although the sea was reasonably calm. They'd turned halfway around and were on their way back towards me. I could see my former captors on the deck looking overboard and calling out to each other. One of them had a flashlight and was scanning the surface, but was not yet looking far enough out. I was convinced that they would catch sight of me at any moment, so I turned away again and carried on swimming my stealthiest breast stroke through the swell, at right angles to the course which I judged the boat would take.

My eyes began to adjust to the darkness and I saw there were enough breaks in the clouds to make out some stars. There was also a silver glimmer on one horizon which could have been the moon rising. Low down on the opposite horizon, the night-time clouds dimly reflected the orange glow of a city's streetlights. It was enough to give me an approximate orientation. I couldn't guess the distance to shore, but I could tell that the coast was many, many miles away. I didn't foresee my swimming that far. *Just don't get caught again. Better to die alone here in the middle of the ocean than under the hands of those crooks.*

I kept swimming, promising myself to do another five minutes, gaining about a quarter mile on my current position before changing stroke or looking round again.

I'd counted only half my strokes when I heard a shout go up, which carried over the water as if they were almost on top of me. Moments later, the boat's engines revved. My heart sank. I was certain that if I turned round now, there would be a torchlight in my face and it would be game over. I dived again and swam several metres to my right before surfacing to take a quick look. The boat had finished turning around but it was still more than twice the distance from me than before, and they had cut the engines already. They were scrambling to retrieve something – maybe it was the

167

lifejacket which I had ditched at the last moment, in favour of being able to swim underwater.

But there was something else too. I could see they were launching a dinghy from the boat. I turned around and got on with swimming away from them, but it wasn't long before I heard the dinghy's outboard motor join the sound of the boat's engines. I determined not to stop again to look, but changed to a crawl stroke to increase my speed.

I went on for another ten minutes. The sound of the boat engines and the dinghy's outboard grew and faded again. They were quartering the area to find me. Many lights scanned the water, the two search craft buzzed around and the men on board shouted out to each other. Their search grew slowly nearer. At one point the larger boat passed within a hundred metres of me and I ducked down underwater for a minute.

When I rose, the clouds had parted just above the horizon, revealing the three-quarter moon. It cast an intense steely white light across the ocean, which responded by breaking into a million shining stars. I realised my danger of being silhouetted, and ducked down again long enough for the boat to move some way further off. After that the search moved on and their engines only grew more distant. A bit later and I realised they had either drifted too far away to be heard, or they had given up and gone home. Increasingly I realised I was on my own in the cold water.

The sense of relief was tempered by the gloomy prospects for a lonely death here at sea, if not with company under extended torture. I tried to tell myself it was OK. I'd experienced inner peace when I passed out earlier, which was not such a bad thought. But in truth, welling up inside me was the certainty that I could not give up hope. To stay alive, I had to keep on hoping and breathing.

♈

I began to form a new plan. However unlikely it seemed, I'd made it this far, against the odds. Firstly, I remembered the bundle of waterproof fabric that I'd grabbed on the boat and was currently tucked into my waistband. I held it up above the water to have a proper look while the moon was still out. It was a cagoule, as I had hoped. I put my head and arms through it, zipped up the front, pulled up the hood and tightened everything that I could. Soaking as it was, I thought it might reduce the chilling rate and buy me more time. I kept my trousers on too, for the same reason. In my line of work I probably should have known more about how long it would take for hypothermia to set in, but normally I would be suited up for these conditions. I was used to being cold, but I didn't normally plan to die of it. After my ordeal on the boat, I was shocked, weakened and cold to begin with. My best estimate was I had a few hours – more than two, maybe eight, probably not twelve.

Judging by the position and phase of the moon it was going to be daylight in four or five, possibly six hours. The clouds were continuing to clear, so I could get a proper look at the stars. The North Star was easy to find. The dim glow of the town was pretty much below it, very roughly in the direction that the boat had gone. With no great expectation of reaching land I headed north as well, mixing my strokes and pacing myself. If the currents were against me then I could have been swimming in order to stay in the same place, for all I knew.

Swimming had always been the thing I loved, before diving became my passion and then my work. It occupied a part of my mind, but freed another part to wander. And so even in these, probably my last hours, I was back in my element. Having escaped another greater danger, and in the familiar monotony of the long distance swim, I'd forgotten to be afraid. The sea had become my refuge again.

My thoughts soon turned to Pete and his watery death, however. I'd not swum or dived since then, and first time back in the water I was facing a similar ending. It felt like quite a coincidence, although I no longer possessed his diver's watch, which I'd considered to be my bad luck charm – it was on the boat now, if they hadn't thrown it overboard. So much for superstition. Or was having left it behind a good omen?

Amy had no idea what she was setting up when she gave me that damned watch. Would she miss me, one day? I hoped she would guess I'd met with a misadventure, somehow. I accepted her reasons for not wanting a relationship, but she'd given me something better. Of any living human, surely she could have resented my part in Pete's death, but she didn't. She'd forgiven me automatically, without hesitation. I was still toying with the Madonna-like vision I'd had of her and now I could see she could fulfil the role of intercessor too. Maybe I wouldn't share that thought with her, though, even if I had the chance. She might take it wrongly.

My freewheeling mind now recalled a condition called the Madonna-whore complex. Was that me? Except I had a feeling that would have meant being unable to get it up for Amy, which hadn't been a problem at all, rather the reverse. I wondered how things would have worked out with Persi if events had gone differently. She was the next nearest woman to a saint that I could think of.

On the flip side, what about Izzy? I'd charted a path to hell before we ever met, but she had been the perfect vehicle to help me navigate it, with her auto-pilot already set squarely in the direction of trouble. She was irresistible and without conscience. I'd used her every bit as much as she had me, but had I debased her? No, dammit, it went much deeper than desire, in both directions, I was almost certain. Much more, and at all sorts of levels.

Testing yourself for complexes was like reading a medical dictionary: you shouldn't. But I was glad to have resolved that in my own mind before I died.

I wondered whether my dying here on this night would even up something between Pete and me. Cancelling the life I'd gained unfairly. A week earlier that was how I might have felt, but there, at that moment, I couldn't describe it that way. It just wasn't realistic. Besides, I still had business in the land of the living: Magnus wasn't in the clear yet.

Magnus, yes, the reason to stay alive. To use the life I'd gained to save another. I liked the ring of that. Could I somehow also pay a debt for my infidelity to my brother by saving him from a fate like this, or worse? It might atone for something.

Yes, I remembered why I loved to free my mind on a long distance swim. Things could be settled. These were my peaceful thoughts as I reviewed the last few weeks and months of turmoil and reconciled myself to my likely fate. My mind kept on wandering and I ploughed on through the water with a vague notion of reaching Magnus again.

Time passed, a great deal of it. The black sky shifted almost imperceptibly to Prussian blue and then deepest indigo. The water seemed colder than ever.

About the time the moon reached its zenith, the eastern horizon began gently to fill with light, less bright than the moonlit part at first, until a smoky pink appeared, low down. Then as the moon seemed to fade, the pink turned into a faint apricot and eventually it was hemmed in by a yellow hue which spread upwards.

Finally, the sun at last peeped over the glowing orange horizon. It found one of the few remaining clouds, which it lined with silver-gilt and through which it radiated its shafts of light, crepuscular rays which reached across the sky. It was a picture postcard scene.

The glow of the town had long since faded and disappeared. My guide now was the Sun, behind me and to my right which I took to be due east. It was also my clock. Between the moon and the sun I felt I'd been going for upwards of seven hours, at the upper end of my survivability estimate. As if to confirm it, I'd been shivering quite badly for the last hour or two, but I figured that was OK so long as I could still swim.

Occasionally I used a wave to get higher in the water and try to see if there was any sign of life or land, but that was optimistic in this part of the world, where I'd seen the coast was low-lying and swampy.

My best bet I thought would be if a sailing vessel passed my way, now that there was light. I'd seen two or three ships heading one way or the other, but none of them near enough to wave at, me being such a tiny speck in the great expanse of sea. I was even wearing blue. The only other things I'd seen since daylight were seabirds and at one point a school of dolphins which overtook me. *Hey guys! Aren't you meant to rescue people or something? Nobody ever told you that?* Or maybe they were sharks – that would have been more like my luck.

I saw a light plane, flying across my path, not so far ahead. I waved, unconvinced that it would see me but unwilling to give up without trying. I wondered if it were tracing a path along the coast then maybe I might be drawing closer. In

172

which case, I wondered, had we been closer to the shore than I realised, or had I been caught on an inshore current? Either way, I couldn't manage the maths. My concentration was fading fast. I was quite unsure about how long I'd really been in the water or if I had my bearings right.

I redoubled my efforts to swim on. Although I had hoped my exertions would generate some warmth, the shivering had grown far worse in the last few minutes. The tremors became so violent that I would have to pause swimming until they subsided again. Shivering apart, I would occasionally wake up to the realisation that I'd slowed down or almost stopped in the water and was slipping into daydreams. It was so hard to get going again – and then I began to lose power in my limbs as well. In truth, I should have known that my number was up, but actually I felt at the time I was doing unbelievably well.

Dimly at first, but steadily growing louder, I heard a distant roar, and I slowly realised that it had to be the sound of surf. I must be near to a shoreline.

I was lying on my back and I tried to kick out once again. The shivering had passed but my arms and legs were so stiff and weak that I couldn't summon the strength, even with the sound of my salvation so near. Swimming like this had been the simplest way to keep my airways clear up until this point, but now the water's surface grew steeper and more choppy. As the low-lying shore came into view I concentrated on keeping my head above the water instead, facing away from the oncoming waves. Swimming wasn't an option any longer, I had to rely on the forward momentum of the breaking waves.

Then a large wave broke right over me, crushing and submerging me in the same moment, filling my mouth and nose with salty water. The reflex was so familiar now: I tried to cough it up but gulped down more instead. Finally I broke the surface, retching and coughing as I gasped for air. Even the effort of breathing was exhausting.

Seconds later another wave overtook me, but this time I lay limp and dazed while it held me, rolling me under and through the water. So close but so far: I gave myself up to the sea. Then there was only darkness.

Later – maybe much later – I became aware of a gull's cry and somewhere else in the distance, the sound of the shore again. I cracked open my salt-crusted eyes to the shock of seeing a man's face very close to mine. I was lying in darkness under a makeshift shelter which seemed to be made of wood, and he had crawled half into the space, through a canvas flap. The light which entered the crack beside him was dazzling white and made me flinch. He was lying on his front, on the ground, right next to me. His face broke into a warm smile.

"Hello mister," he said. "You cause me no end a'trouble, but it look like you OK now."

Therapy

And so I found I was still alive, kind of. The violent shivering was back with a vengeance and I hurt like hell, all over. In fact, if this was me recovering, then it felt worse than dying of hypothermia had felt.

"W-w-where am I?" I asked as best as I could manage between the shivers.

"In my boat, near where you wash up," said the man. "And when you talking properly I wanna know where the fuck yo' from, 'cause you sound like you come from the other side of the fuckin' ocean. Time enough for that. We gotta get you on yo' feet first."

I looked away from him and blinked away the imprint of the light outside. My eyes began to accustom themselves to the gloom again and I realised I was looking up at the hull of an upturned boat, which may have been a small skiff, little more than twice my length. It reeked of paraffin from a small heater down by my feet. He had created a really good close fug in the tiny space. I was lying on a thin blanket, folded in half and packed on either side of me were a few rags which were keeping me propped on my side and stopped the draughts, but otherwise I was naked.

The man gave me a hot drink, reminiscent of black coffee, very sweet, which I almost immediately threw up. I managed to miss the blanket, mostly.

"If you gonna be sick again, try and use a fuckin' bag," he said, pulling a carrier bag towards me. "I don't think this one got no holes. My name's Jordan, in case you was wondering."

"M-M-Marc," I stuttered in reply, holding out my hand. Without hesitation he took it and gave me a thumb-shake.

"Good to meet you, Marc," he said. "You was so near dead when I pull you out the surf. You was cold as a John Doe. I brought you here and been trying to warm you up since."

"V-very g-g-grateful."

"Shit, you polite, I like that!" he said through a broad smile. "Not like me, worse'n Aunt Fee. I gotta warn you I got a short attention span too, so I gonna leave you here while I go do what I got to and I come back later. Don't try to do nothing in the meantime."

He had a profoundly deep voice, which lent gravity to his words, and despite every other sign of goodwill, I noticed that his searching, deep-set eyes never left me, and I sensed that his trust had yet to be earned.

With that he dropped the canvas flap and left me in the dark.

I went on lying there, shivering and hurting for a while. On a second attempt some of the hot drink went down and stayed there. It was in an enamelled tin cup like the ones we used to take camping and the heat from it made it difficult to hold. As for the rest of my body, I was reminded of how my hands used to ache after playing too long in the snow as a kid, except that now it was all over me.

I snoozed for a while and by the time I woke it was getting pretty snug inside, uncomfortably so. I really wanted to find out where I was, so I wriggled across and popped my head through the flap. I was in the middle of a thicket, so there was very little to be seen except for the scrubby bushes around the boat and the sand on which we rested. My trousers were hung up to dry on the bush opposite. The sea was out of sight even though I could hear it in the distance. The sun was high and beginning to beat down on the boat, which might have been hotter by now except for the shade from the thicket and an insulating thatch of scrub and grass laid on top of it.

What were the odds on me ending up here, like this? Wherever "here" was, I knew it had to be the Gulf of Mexico coast. Jordan seemed to be OK but I couldn't understand how I'd ended up under his boat instead of in a hospital. There was something odd about it. I wondered if Izzy was doing her nut looking for me; I'd have liked to believe it. But it was all a bit much for me at that moment, so with as many questions as answers about where I was and how I came to be there, I crawled back inside, extinguished the flame from the heater's wick, finished the cold coffee and went back to sleep.

♈

Next time I woke, it was roasting hot and I was sweating.

I lifted the canvas enough to allow in some ventilation and let some light in too. It was then I noticed there was a large and battered paperback beside my head. On closer inspection I discovered it was a Bible, its corners left dark and dog-eared from many hours of study. The pain of re-warming and the shivering had passed by now and I was left feeling really thirsty. All good signs. I crawled out from under the boat to see what I could find, starting with my trousers. But when I tried to get to my feet I discovered I was still very weak, and

I staggered the few steps towards my trousers. Almost immediately, I heard voices on the far side of the bush. Naked as I was, my instinct was to duck down onto my knees and then peer under its branches. Within thirty metres of me, there were a couple of men, hikers with baseball caps, rucksacks and long carry-bags that I took to contain fishing rods, walking along a path in the direction of the ocean. I could see now that the coast was only a couple of hundred metres to the east. The sight of them was reassuring as I knew I was in reach of civilisation, when I chose my moment to return there. But I was wary of presenting myself to the next random passer-by. There was no telling where that might lead.

I finished retrieving my trousers, which had dried as stiff as cardboard, and bent and shook them until they were soft and supple enough to put back on. Then I had a bit more of a look around, despite there being not much to see. The compound, that is the sandy area bounded by the bushes where I stood, was one-third filled by the boat, which was a one-man skiff, flat-bottomed with a narrow stern. It was very effectively camouflaged and looked seaworthy besides, although I couldn't see any oars or a mast. On the open patch in front of it there was a dug-out hole containing charcoal from an extinguished campfire and beside that a rusty one-gallon can which smelt oily but contained tepid fresh water, which I took a sip from. In the bush I could see what looked like drying fish. I was ravenous, so I took one down and ate it on the spot, and then another. If he had any other food stored, I couldn't see it.

It was a long time before Jordan returned and when he did, he seemed to spring up out of nowhere. I'd been peering in the other direction, looking for more signs of life, and I nearly jumped out of my skin.

He had a small bundle of clothes under his arm, which he now unrolled. In the middle of the bundle were two bread baps in a plastic bag which he set to one side before passing me the clothes – a white t-shirt and some trainers. The trainers were too tight, so he took them back and opened up the toes with a knife so I could wear them like sandals, with my toes poking out of the ends. While he was doing that I had a proper look at him. His clothes were dirty and worn and he was in dire need of a shave and a haircut, but underneath it he had a strong, knotty build, and his maturity and self-assuredness shone through. He was a little younger than me, I judged, and yet in some ways he seemed a little older.

"You feeling better now, want something to eat?" he asked.

"Thanks, yes. I'm sorry I helped myself to some of your fish," I answered. I hadn't had time to think about it yet, but his accent suggested what I could have assumed, that I was still in the state of Texas, or nearby.

"Lot more where they come from, have another. I got these too," he said, and threw me one of the bread buns. "They look like fish bait, you might wanna pick them green bits off. You see them dudes go by?" he asked.

"Yes, the two hikers walking over to the coast."

"Their boat a half a mile that way," he pointed inland. "Bread come from there." From which I gleaned I was eating stolen goods. I assumed the same went for the clothes as well, and then I began to wonder whether even the boat was his.

"Maybe I'd better not talk to them when they come back then," I said.

"No shit. I ain't in the habit of stealing. I trying to keep a low profile, y'know," he said.

179

"A low profile. That suits me too. Where are we?" I asked.

"Barrier dunes, about the quietest spot I can find," he said.

"What barrier dunes?" I asked.

"Hell, you're asking a lotta questions, mystery man. Now you talkin', I got some of my own. Like how come you was washed up on the shore like that, middle a' nowhere? You fall off a fuckin' boat?"

"Yes, that's right, but not one I want to get back to. It belonged to some bad guys. They kidnapped me, so I jumped off and swam ashore."

I didn't expect him to believe it for a moment, but he accepted it without a flicker of surprise, and just came back at me with a quote.

"'The sea give up the dead which was in it, and death and Hades give up the dead which was in them; and they was judged according to they deeds.' Book of Revelation," he said.

"That's pretty impressive," I said. "Have you got the entire Bible memorised, or is that a favourite bit?"

"I reminded myself, while you was sleeping, motherfucker," he said, shining with his good-humoured grin. I began to see he was a little shy, even if he swore a lot. "So then we both fuckin' fugitives. Except you probably wanna go to the law," he said.

"Not really. I'm happy to keep out of their way too," I replied. He took his eye off me then, and I realised I'd given the right answer from his point of view.

"What you do to them motherfuckers that they wanna kidnap you, anyways?" he asked me.

"It's my brother they want, really. A case of mistaken identity," I said.

He was not so easily fobbed off. "Why you afraid of the law, then?" he asked.

180

"I need to get to him before anyone else does. The police are probably going to make that harder. Too many questions they'll want answering." That seemed to satisfy him enough for now, so I followed up with a question of my own. "Do you mind my asking, why are you hiding out?"

At this point however, his ears pricked up as he heard something carried on the wind and he shushed me. We kept low and peered out through the bushes as the two hikers came past, going back in the direction of their boat. We kept quiet after they'd passed downwind and what with the food and the warmth, I felt my eyelids begin to droop again. I signalled to Jordan that I needed more sleep. The sun was only halfway down the sky, but my body clock was really messed up. I crawled back under the boat and as I drifted off it occurred to me I had lost track of what day it was.

♈

I must have slept for several hours because it was early evening by the time I woke up. I was on my own and decided to venture out carefully, to see the lie of the land. The way into and out of Jordan's compound entailed weaving round a low-lying bush. As soon as I'd gone outside I turned round to check my path back and saw it was very well concealed. I didn't suppose anyone would want to leave the narrow track for it in any case. Most of the strength had come back into my legs, so I walked down to the sea, where the beach stretched as far as the eye could see in both directions, without a soul in sight.

There was still plenty of heat kicking off from the sand but the onshore wind was cooling and helped the incoming tide to bring foaming waves right up to the strandline. I pulled off my clothes, dropping them further up the beach and then

181

stepped over the line of brown seaweed and walked into the water for a swim. It was a test, and I was glad to discover that it felt right to be in the water again. I swam out for around a hundred metres before I began to tire and then turned back in. During that short time the longshore current had taken me quite some way down the coast. As I walked back up to find my clothes, I saw Jordan combing the beach, working his way down the water's edge towards me.

As I drew nearer him, I saw he was picking through the seaweed.

"Shit, you recovering fast," Jordan said. "Ain't you had enough water for a fuckin' lifetime?"

"I'm trying to get back into it," I called, over the noise of the surf, feeling a bit shaky and wondering if I'd overdone things. "What are you looking for?"

"Shrimps, for supper. They living in the seaweed," he replied. "You gonna pull some clothes on and help?" He passed me a spare plastic bag for collecting in, while looking the other way to avoid staring at me naked.

I continued up the beach to find my clothes, dressed and re-joined him. Then we worked the shoreline for the next hour while the sun dropped and the tide began to recede. As we walked back, we compared our pickings and found we had a decent-sized haul.

We reached the compound and Jordan started making up a fire. He didn't have one during the day, he said, as the smoke would make him too easy to spot. He lit the fire with a cigarette lighter, explaining that the purpose of the pit was both for shelter and to reduce the visibility of the flames. The shrimps went into a tin of briny water to be boiled together with some of the dried fish, and I discovered he had buried a biscuit tin which contained a few precious ingredients – sugar, instant coffee, cayenne and one or two other spices.

"I'm normally a diver you know, except I've been off my form lately, not felt like going in the water at all," I told him, out of nowhere. "But I'm going to give it another go, starting with some home-baked exposure therapy."

He went on tending the growing fire. "The Lord musta brought you back to the land for a reason," he said, "not just so you could get back to work. Did you say you need to find yo' brother, rescue his ass?"

"Yes, you're right, he's probably in the same sort of danger I was. The same goes for his girlfriend. I'd better get back tomorrow, if you can point me in the right direction," I said.

He didn't answer directly, just gazed into the fire as the dusk began to settle round us. The light of the flames flickered and sparkled in his dark eyes which seemed to be looking far away, but I could tell he was still listening, maybe for something I hadn't said.

"It's not just because he's my brother," I went on, filling the silence. "There's a debt I have to repay him, or an act of atonement I have to carry out, or something like that. I've done wrong by him. I've been cheating on him with his girlfriend. In theory I gave her up, except I'm weak-willed that way, and besides she'll be hard to replace. So I still need to show myself I can do it."

"I think you closer to the truth now," he said. "I seen guilt in yo' eyes and you restless like a man that's not at peace with himself."

He thought for another moment and then added: "Weakness for pussy ain't no weakness at all, but stealing yo' brother's girl, that's disrespectful. My brother done that to me, I shoot the motherfucker, except he dead already, bless his soul."

We talked until the food was ready, and surprisingly it was

183

both tasty and filling, despite the very basic cooking arrangements. For the sake of variety, I'd suggested we tried eating some of the seaweed, which seemed worth giving a go, but it tasted quite bitter. Afterwards, we sat back with some of the sweet black coffee, Jordan having reclaimed his tin cup served me my drink in the sawn-off bottom half of a plastic bottle.

"I been on my own on this island a while, thinkin'," Jordan said after we'd both ruminated for a while. "I remember something, from long time ago. They says ain't no way we can atone for things we done. That what Christ done for us. We just got to accept God's forgiveness, repent and walk humbly with Him. That the path to righteousness."

It brought me up short to recognise there was a cultural chasm between us. He didn't question the existence of a higher power, and I didn't want to start arguing with him over whether it was true or not. That would have been disrespectful.

"Did you say this is an island?" I asked.

"Shit yeah. You need a boat for getting on or off," he said.

I thought I would wait until tomorrow to talk about my departure plans, and lapsed into a thoughtful silence. I would have dozed off except for the noise of my stomach rumbling.

"Yo find a latrine round the other side of that bush down there," Jordan advised, helpfully. "Just throw a bit of sand on top yo' shit to keep it covered."

Grateful for some advice I had a genuine and urgent use for, I picked my way around the bush in the last light of the day, found the pit and turned around. From my squatting position I surveyed the ground nearby, more shadows than light. There was something protruding from a pile of heaped up sand in front of me which looked not right and as soon as I could I crawled forward to investigate, peering into the gloom, partly feeling my way ahead. Then to my horror and disgust I discovered I had laid my hand on a bare human foot and was looking at its underside. Alongside it was the matching foot, pointing skywards. Both legs had been levered up out of a shallow grave.

I let out an involuntary cry of surprise, and jumped back, but having regained my composure, felt compelled to investigate further. I crawled further along towards the other end of the grave, where I found a bare torso, scarcely covered by the sand. Whether it was male or female, young, old, black or white was hard to say. To the right of it was the shadow of another mound, which I took to be another grave. I didn't look to see if there were any more, I'd seen enough to realise I could be in danger. I stood up and looked around, wondering how best to escape from this place, starting now.

Then I heard rather than saw Jordan appear from round the corner, pushing past the scrub, and I stood ready to defend myself.

"I shoulda said about them two dudes. Give you a fuckin' s'prise, right?" he said. "They come poking around in the evening a couple a' days ago, so I shot them."

"These clothes I'm wearing, did they come from them?" I asked.

"Sure, he ain't got no use for them," Jordan said, which was undeniable.

"What about all that stuff you were telling me about the path of righteousness, does that include killing people?" I asked.

"They come too early for me. I ain't done repenting yet," he answered. "Time for me to move on though. I best come with you tomorrow."

For the first time I saw that his existence on Earth was even more fragile and uncertain than mine. He had rescued me, nursed me to health, fed and clothed me. He'd even shared his philosophy and theology, however unreceptive I was. Meeting him this way, as if through the eyes of a child, I'd mistaken his self-reliance and assurance as meaning he was confident of his future, whereas he was in fact just what he'd said: a fugitive, running for his life. Except he'd made something more of it as he went, and achieved a state of grace. Recalling the hero in my recent book, I began to see him as something like a modern-day Robinson Crusoe. And if that were him, then what did that make me into?

"What day is it today?" I asked him.

"Shit, how'd I fuckin' know? Maybe Saturday," he said.

Rebirth

I knew before the sun came up next morning that I was running a fever. Jordan had given up his space under the boat for me and was snoring outside under a tarpaulin. I prepared to make a dash for the latrine, when it was needed, but the moment never arrived. I just went on burning up and sweating like I had flu.

When Jordan woke up an hour or so later he took a look at me and announced I'd done too much too soon. I wanted to blame the shrimps or the seaweed, except he looked fine on them. We agreed to wait at least until the afternoon to depart, and I spent the rest of the morning dozing on and off.

Wanting to show willing, I got up and started moving around at about midday, even though the heat was oppressive and I still felt pretty raw.

Jordan walked me down to the inland bay behind the dunes, where he had hidden the small outboard motor that belonged to the boat, and from where we planned to launch it. He had a map with a route marked on it to a town on the other side of the bay, which was at least a twelve mile trip, although he didn't know exactly where we were he knew near enough. He had it all figured out nicely.

As we walked back to the hideout, Jordan showed me how he had managed to maintain his supply of fresh water, even

187

though he said it hadn't rained since over a week ago. He had dug a dozen pits, all within a hundred metres, and from them built solar stills – miniature greenhouses to catch condensed water – using plastic bags and bottles gathered up from the beach. He'd gone round collecting water twice a day since discovering me, and begun to build some more stills. I'd heard of these things, but I was surprised to see how productive they were. It would have been difficult to do without his knife, he said, which he treasured as a survival tool above even the cigarette lighter, partly because the knife was a survival tool in the city as well as the country.

"You ever handle a gun?" he asked me.

Only a shotgun, I said, which he answered by pulling out a small black handgun with a silver strip down the side and passing it to me, sideways on.

"That's your gun, is it?" I asked.

"This one for you," he said, and pushed it into my hands.

I held it up for a closer look. It was not much heavier than an air pistol and more compact. Jordan briefly showed me how to click the safety off with my thumb, pull back the slider and then it was ready to shoot.

"Go on, take a shot, hold it in both hands," he said, pointing to one of the plastic collecting containers a bit more than ten metres away on the adjacent sandy hillock.

I aimed and pulled the trigger. The gun kicked back with a decent loud bang and the bottle went flying off over the top and down behind the dune.

"The fuck? See if you can do that again," Jordan said. "Wait here."

He disappeared over the dune and ran up the side of the next one, driving the neck of the bottle into the sand, now at least twenty metres distant. He ran back to me and told me to try that. My first shot went wide – we saw the sand thrown

188

up a few inches to the left of it – but the second shot knocked the bottle into the air once more.

"Shit, you an expert already, and you still got five left," Jordan said.

He showed me how the rest of the mechanics worked. It seemed simple enough. The ammo inside met with his approval, comprising hollow-pointed bullets with notches in them, which he explained would expand on impact to inflict maximum damage on their unhappy victim. The coldly calculated appraisal of the bullet's wounding potential seemed rather brutal, but then I supposed that shooting people was hardly done for their own good. Maybe it was better to hold no illusions about it.

Then he pulled out his own gun from the back of his pants for comparison. It was about five centimetres longer than mine, and a fair bit heavier, which he said was partly due to it having fifteen 9mm rounds in it, instead of my measly eight, now down to five, of .380 ammo. The logo on his gun meant nothing to me, but he assured me it was a much more expensive brand and came with more features as well as holding more rounds than the one that he'd just given me. His was more professional he said, in the way of a man for whom a gun was a tool of his trade.

Mine being simpler to use would be better for a raw beginner, he continued, although it hadn't done much good for the dead dude that he'd taken it off: that motherfucker couldn't hit a mark no more than he, Jordan, could hit a high-C. But they were both good guns, he said.

I couldn't foresee myself using the thing, so I thanked him for the demonstration and tried to give it back, except he wasn't having it. He said to see if we could get back to the city without being shot at and then to think about it. I didn't have the strength to fight over it. I just made damn sure the safety was on before I stuck it down the back of my trousers. I had one bum-hole, and I wanted neither one more nor less.

We ate as much of the remaining food as we could before we lugged the boat down to the shore. It was quite some way, but easy enough between the two of us, going downhill more than up. It must have been harder for him to drag it up there.

The two of us fitted into the boat quite comfortably, with no loose luggage except for Jordan's Bible. Once we were afloat, he asked me to start the outboard, which was unexpectedly deferential of him. More surprisingly still, it started almost immediately.

"How long was it sat there?" I asked him.

"Two, three days," he said. "This ain't the same boat I come on. It belong to them dead gangster motherfuckers."

"Is the map theirs too?" I asked.

"Yo, I figure the X marks where the boat come from, and we not leavin' on a fuckin' bus neither," he said, opening his hand to show me a keyring. It bore the easily recognisable plus-shaped Chevrolet logo.

The boat's small engine buzzed cheerfully as we set off across the inland bay. The boat rose and fell gently over the small waves and the sun beat down on us, countered by the cooling effect of the breeze and occasional splashes of water. It was impossible not to enjoy it, or to feel a new sense of optimism as we left the dunes behind. The feeling came from deep down and I realised something had changed in me. Exactly what it was, and when, was harder to say. So much had happened lately: although there had been plenty of people and things that I wanted to forget, there were some that I wanted to remember. Who could undergo such intensity of experience and emerge as the same person? There and then I knew that I'd turned a corner and I was ready to take my life back.

190

I began to get our bearings as we travelled along, matching the shore to our map. There were also quite a lot of small boats out on the water, whose position and direction gave more clues as to where the settlement was. Towards the end of our boat ride, as we picked out the marina, we could see it was the base for a small fleet of commercial fishing boats as well. And so our arrival was unremarkable at the dozy end of a warm afternoon, just one more boat among many, so long as no-one looked closely enough to notice how dirty and unkempt we both were. We tied up against a quiet jetty a short distance from a park filled with motor homes and caravans, and set about looking for the Chevrolet.

The waterfront was small enough for us to do a snaking circuit of it within the space of an hour, but as it happened it was only ten minutes before Jordan spotted an SUV whose size, black paint, wheel trims and dark tinted windows marked it out as a strong candidate for investigation, and moments later we were sat inside it. Jordan checked himself in the mirror and swore at the motherfucking wild man facing him. Then he found a packet of cigarettes in the glove compartment and lit up. I had one as well: my first smoke for a couple of years. I knew that it was a mistake, and I'd be pining for another one for weeks to come. For a few minutes we just chilled and appreciated the comfort, until Jordan found the music system.

He agreed we drive back to the city to drop me off, on condition we found some scissors, a comb and a razor along the way, and that I helped to make him look presentable. The local drugstore and hardware shops were closed, but it was a hundred mile drive, so eventually we found the necessary tools at a gas station and I was relieved to discover that he intended to pay, using some dollars which he had hidden about him. He'd found some shades and a hoodie in the car as well, so by the time he'd shaved both his face and the rest of his head, with my assistance, he was almost another man.

Before we embarked on the final leg of our journey to the city, we sat for a few moments longer on the tailgate, watching an endless freight train grind its way past us, crossing the fresh green of the coastal plain, heading north under a big sky. My thoughts had turned increasingly to the end of our journey together and, while I had my own plans, Jordan's remained as mysterious as the reasons for his being on the run in the first place. Our brief friendship was drawing to its conclusion.

"How about you, Jordan? What are your plans after you've dropped me off?" I asked him.

"I ain't got no home no more, and only so long before the police check the car, so I gotta park it up and disappear again."

"Do you have any idea where you'll go?" I asked.

"Disappearin's hard, man, and lonely. I was glad when your ass washed up on the beach. But last time I told someone where I was going, result was I had a fuckin' hit squad on my ass. So I best not say, no disrespect to yourself."

"I wish there was something I could do to thank you for saving my life," I said.

"Save your brother life instead," he replied. "And walk your ass away from that girl of his, even though she a Bad Mama Jama, going by what you says."

We continued on our way into the city. I could remember the midtown address that I'd booked. We did a drive-by and saw the lights were on in what I recognised as the apartment we'd rented. Jordan drove on another fifty metres before parking, and declined the offer to come in with me. I went to get out, then an idea struck me.

"Wait for me here, give me five minutes," I told him. "I'll

192

go and get you some cash to keep you going." I was glad he didn't object to the offer, and I walked off down the leafy suburban street into the dusk.

As I reached the flat and turned off the sidewalk, two smartly-dressed men jumped out of a black sedan parked in front and ran up to me.

"Mister Miller, can we have a word?" asked the nearest one, reaching inside his jacket. It was a routine I thought I recognised, and I didn't wait to find out what he was about to pull out. For an answer, I just kicked him in the nuts and ran for it.

♈

The chase didn't last long. I'd started off in the wrong direction if I'd been heading back towards Jordan, even if that might have seemed like a good idea, which it didn't. It turned out there was nowhere to run to. The small suburban blocks were fenced off with assiduous care, and the street grid system really meant that no amount of imagination on my part could make up for the lack of a car.

I felt the gun Jordan gave me digging into my back and thought maybe it was time to turn and fight. It was an all-or-nothing decision. The guy who I hadn't kicked was doing a good job of keeping up with me on foot, and the distance shrank every time I took a look around or turned a corner. He wasn't waving a gun around or anything like that, so I chose not to escalate the situation any further.

I gave it one more block to see who would tire first, but a moment later his partner overtook me in their unmarked car and pulled up a few metres ahead, lights flashing. I was tempted to believe the flashing lights meant these were the real police department. Two against one and surrounded, I knew it was either time for my last stand, and go down shooting, or to give myself up.

I took the thinking man's gambit and put my hands up. "Who are you? Let me see your badges," I called out.

But we'd gone beyond politeness, given the manner of our introduction, so it wasn't a complete surprise to find I was sprawled across the bonnet a moment later, being cuffed and advised I was under arrest for assaulting a federal agent. So that was good and bad news: at least I hadn't tried to shoot him. They found my gun and took it away, and shoved me into the back of their car, which smelt sour, sweaty and lived-in. We set off while they talked into the radio.

The one on the passenger side, the one I'd kicked, was the older one of the two, and he twisted round to look at me.

"Mister Miller – you are Mister Miller, aren't you?" he asked. I nodded, wondering which one he thought I was, but keen to find out as much as I could either way. "You're a British Citizen, visiting the United States on a tourist visa?" I nodded again, waiting for the next question, but it didn't come. He just turned to face the front.

The cogs in my brain whirred. I was as sure as I could be that these guys were real cops, except they'd said federal so that meant FBI as far as I knew. They'd been waiting for me, or more likely for Magnus. Why? A few possibilities raised themselves, but the one that made my blood freeze was that maybe something had happened to Izzy.

I leaned forwards. "Do you know anything about my partner, Isidora Moran? Is she all right?"

"S'far's we know," he replied, looking round again.

"Then I need to talk to someone about my brother. He may be in danger," I said. "And before I forget, can I offer a personal apology for kicking you – I didn't realise you were cops. I thought you were some other guys."

194

"We'll take a full statement from you when we get to the office," he said, rather dispassionately I thought, as if being kicked in the nuts was all in the line of duty. I had to admire his professionalism and be grateful they hadn't beaten me up, which in retrospect was what I might have expected. But that was all the conversation I could get out of him.

It was hard to overcome the frustration of having been so close to Izzy, literally within ten metres, and then having been snatched away, imprisoned again. Reason told me the quickest way out of there was to be patient and allow events to run their course, despite the nagging temptation to try to talk my way out. So I practised deep breathing and kept my mouth shut.

It was a fair drive to the large faceless federal building, and fully night by the time we passed through the security gates into the brightly lit courtyard. Lights shone through all the lower floor windows, but above them far fewer of the grid-like windows in the upper stories were alight, and the top of the building faded into the darkness. The large repetitive facade seemed suggestive of bureaucratic administrative procedures and the grinding slow wheels of justice. Adjusting my expectations for a Sunday night, any hope I had of a quick turnaround died there and then.

If things had got off to a bad start that evening, then they began to go even more pear-shaped when I was asked to confirm my personal details. They were expecting Magnus, I looked like him, I'd answered to his name – so they thought – and I'd referred to Izzy as my partner. When I told them I was his brother Marc, and no I didn't have any identification papers, they looked at me with weary eyes.

"It's a crime to make a false statement," warned the older agent. "Don't make things worse for yourself, Mister Miller. You're on a gun possession charge and assault misdemeanour against an officer. These are all federal crimes. You'd be advised to start co-operating."

"I'm telling you the honest to God truth," I said. "If you don't believe me, get Izzy to come and identify me. You seem to know where to find her."

The agent looked perplexed, but filled in the form according to the details I gave him and I had my fingerprints taken. That had to help.

"Do I get to make a phone call?" I asked. The answer to that was yes, and they pointed me to a phone opposite the desk.

There was only one number I knew, and it was the burner phone which Magnus had used to send me a text, which I'd memorised. My call went straight to voicemail, so I left him a message, with as dire a warning as I could give about stranger danger, in the thirty seconds I had before the beep went.

Then the agents who'd arrested me took me for another drive to a courthouse, where I was left to stew in a holding cell until the morning, and without so much as an aspirin. So much for getting my life back.

Release

My fever from the previous day did not return and I wolfed down breakfast next morning. It was pretty busy in the cells. I'd been put in with a cell-mate who was barely an adult and he kept to himself. He was taken away quite early and didn't come back, leaving me on my own. I supposed that people had been stacked up over the weekend and were now being processed. Surely I was a special case, I thought. Would that mean I would be processed sooner rather than later? I asked the guard, but he denied knowledge.

By my estimate another hour ticked by. As far as I could remember, Magnus had been expected to arrive at lunchtime. It had to be getting close. I really needed to speak to someone about it and I called the guard, who said it wouldn't be long now. I tried explaining the urgency to him, then my temper frayed, but he was impervious to that kind of behaviour and he walked off.

Another age passed before an officer came to escort me to an interview room. The corridor passed between an open plan office on the left and a row of doors into internal rooms on our right. Finally the officer turned, opened a door and guided me into interview room five.

The woman sitting at the desk facing me was reading through some papers when I walked in. She pushed her hair back behind her ear with a gesture that I recognised immediately, and then she looked up.

"Bloody hell, Persi, what are you doing here?" I asked.

"They asked me to come in and identify you," she said. "My God Marc, you look awful. And those clothes, and the shoes. What happened to you?"

"I'm so glad to see you, but I don't understand what you're doing here, in America. I mean, why are you here in Texas?" Questions were filling my head, then I got a grip and pushed them all to one side. "I suppose it can wait. If you can confirm who I am, that's good news, I need to get out of here as quickly as possible. The thing is that Magnus and Izzy are in imminent danger. Do you suppose you can help?"

"Yes I can try," she said. "But slow down a moment, I'm still catching up. How come you showed up at Magnus' flat yesterday, saying you were him? You were meant to be in California, flying here today, weren't you?"

Cogs whirred. I paused to put things in order for a moment before I let the words tumble out. "I never said I was him last night. That was a misunderstanding. Those guys who brought me here only heard what they expected to hear. And about the flight, since you know about it – you must've been talking to Izzy – she may have told you it was me on board, but that's not true. It's Magnus on the plane. I've been here all along ... well, we might get to that."

I stopped myself from going into details which might have been superfluous, and fast-forwarded to what I thought she needed to know: "The point is there are some bad guys looking for Magnus who found me instead, but they're onto him now. He needs to be warned, and we need to get to him before they do. They're very serious trouble and as far as I know they're going to kidnap him if they find him. They were after Izzy too."

She froze and stared at me, her mouth opened and closed as if she had meant to say something and had changed her mind. Then finally she said: "I'll be back in five minutes."

She stood up and left, leaving me in the room with my escort, while I sat back, relieved to have unburdened myself to someone I could trust. I sat there puzzling over the coincidence of her having been around at the right time and place, here especially. I thought she said she was from San Francisco. What were the chances of that, I wondered. How did anyone know even to get in touch with her? Of all the lucky flukes that ever chanced my way, this capped them all. Seriously, what were the odds?

With hindsight, I can forgive myself for having been so slow on the uptake, but the realisation did catch up with me in the end. My excuse was that a lot of things had happened which didn't fit in the normal world, not mine anyway. I wasn't used to questioning everything. Until very recently reality had consisted of the normal. Things had generally been as they appeared on the surface, instead of everything being a lie. But it seemed that I'd walked into a world of unreality on the day I walked through Magnus' front door. Or maybe sooner. Had I already left it behind when I used my relationship with Milena as an escape from realities that I didn't want to face?

When Persi reappeared, I said to her: "You're some kind of spy, aren't you? Magnus is just an assignment for you. That's all. You lied to us all. You're acquiring him, like an asset. Or worse, maybe he's a hazard that you just need to remove."

She sat down again and sighed. "I wish it was as simple as that, trust me."

"Trust is what walked out of the door with you and didn't come back in," I said.

"Some facts then," she said. "We know why your brother's here, even if we couldn't figure out where he was. The whole thing's such a mess. That's probably another charge on your sheet, by the way. You switched passports? Really? I saw you in England on the day when you were supposed to be here, didn't I? What kind of stupid game have you been playing?"

I didn't try to answer her many questions, but began to realise why she was so annoyed. If she had thought a moment ago that I was flying in from California, then she must have seen my itinerary and somehow not noticed that I had been in two places at the same time. She and I had actually been drinking coffee together in England when my travel plan said I'd be interviewing in Massachusetts. That would be a big "oops" against her record, if anyone else noticed it, I imagined.

"We also know your brother's in jeopardy, which is why we were trying to bring him into protective custody last night. We were staking out Izzy for when your brother showed up. Anyway, we're in touch with the airport now and sending some guys up there to see if we can intercept him."

"That's something, thanks," I said.

"Touting himself and his research interests on the open market the way he did was not a smart move. There are many people who would rather see him dead than let him share the stuff he's worked out, unless he wants to give it to their side," she said. "That goes for both governments and commerce. And he seems to have attracted the attention of some very shady business people."

"That's the impression I got," I said, seeing that as she knew so much there was even less value in telling her my story. "Would your lot act any differently?" Then it became her turn not to answer my question.

200

"Tell me something," she said, slightly riled. "This whole farcical game you've been playing. It has to have been Izzy's idea, yes?"

"Not entirely, Magnus has his own good reasons. He'd have found it harder to do without her help. He was being put under various sorts of pressure at home. I don't know they would have wanted him dead, but they were making his life unpleasant."

Persi tapped her finger on the table while she scanned the documents in front of her and mulled something over, but I was the first to fill the silence.

"You knew more about the significance of his work than you let on. And you played a part in getting him to come here, didn't you?" I asked her. "You mentioned you had a contact to me and Izzy said so too."

"Sure we did," she said. "He was ready to jump ship, so we offered him somewhere safe to go. Actually, the best place he could go for his subject, anywhere in the world."

Somewhere safe. Safe for whom, I wondered. Then I asked again: "Were you anything to do with applying pressure on him in England?" She just blanked me in response, as if she had no idea what I was talking about, but I thought it had been worth a try.

"I was saying about Izzy," she continued. "You should understand that she's a fantasist and a parasite. I'll tell you about her maybe one day, unless you want to hear it now?"

"There won't be another day, will there?" I said. She didn't like that.

"There's a test, a checklist they use on people," she went on. "A psychopath checklist. They're not all killers, you know, they live among us. Sometimes you find where they've been from the trail of ruined lives they leave behind, instead of bodies. Well, Izzy ticks a lot of boxes on their test.

It's why she didn't complete her probation with your government surveillance people. You see, people like her have no empathy, it's all about themselves. There is only number one."

"You're not such great friends after all, are you?" I said, my heart hardening towards her, Persi.

I could see what she meant about Izzy, of course, but it was too much at once, I couldn't grasp the magnitude of it. Besides, I wasn't taking her, Persi's, word for anything. For a start, ticking boxes might work for the civil service, but it wasn't enough to condemn somebody in my books. Lining up all the negatives was to overlook the positives.

"Izzy's exceptional in a lot of ways. And I also fell for her charm and beauty, at first," she replied. "But don't be thinking she's the femme fatale from a spy film. Her grandiose plans aren't for the real world."

Something about what she had just said jarred, but Persi went on: "Stay with me on this, we've strayed from the point. You need to tell me how you came to be in the condition you are, and what you know about these bad guys."

I remembered now. Izzy and I had shared a joke about the Bond movie a week ago, when she came into my bedroom to do the fingerprints thing. It seemed like more than a coincidence that Persi just recalled almost the same thing. Was my room bugged? Had Persi been listening? I started to join more dots. Her other intuitions about my private circumstances … maybe there was less guesswork there than I'd imagined.

"The bugs in Magnus and Izzy's house. You put them there, didn't you? The first day we met," I said. "In the hall, behind the curtains and under the kitchen counter, where you sat and peeled the pomegranate."

"I can't talk about operational stuff, sorry. There's no

point asking me questions about that kind of thing," she said.

"And you bugged my bedroom too. You've heard it all."

She didn't even blush. "Focus. Tell me about the bad guys," she insisted.

I was disinclined to tell her anything more than she needed to help Magnus. I felt she'd betrayed us and made me feel like a complete idiot into the bargain. I gave her names and descriptions of Noah, Connor, Cody and Troy, and the allusion Noah had made to their employer, and the vague mention of Mexico, but I skipped over the whole boat trip thing. I thought it might seem too fantastical.

I had to make up a few alternative facts to fill in, so I said I'd been imprisoned in a farm shed which I'd escaped from, and stolen the gun at the same time. I'm not that good a liar but it seemed to pass as good enough. She raised an eyebrow but didn't test me too hard on the detail.

We continued through my return to the city, my arrest and detention, right up to when I was dropped in the cell the night before. It was only when she asked me whose phone number I'd called from here last night that I remembered my omission.

"It's Magnus' cellular, I should have said," I admitted. "But it was turned off. It went straight to voicemail, and then he was on the plane. I don't think it will be much use. I plain forgot to mention it."

"Give it to me now please." Her tone was flat and unemotional as it had been increasingly since her outburst.

"I'll trade you Magnus' number in exchange for Izzy's," I said. "I can tell you've been in touch."

"You still want to talk to her?" Persi asked.

"There's no-one else left," I said. "Someone said to me once, you have to take help from wherever you can find it."

"OK, here it is," she said, taking it from her dossier and

203

copying it onto a piece of paper which she passed to me. Then I gave her Magnus' number from memory and she went outside again to find whether it could be traced. She was gone for some time before she came back in again.

"Marc, we're done here, but here's the deal as far as you're concerned. I won't run through all the charges that could be brought against you, we don't have all that long," she said.

"For whatever reason, we're going to do you a big favour, better than you deserve probably, and have you released, so long as you promise to come to the courtroom tomorrow to meet with an attorney. They will arrange temporary travel papers for you. You won't let me down, I hope." She took my piece of paper from me and wrote down the details – a time, a name, the address – underneath Izzy's number. "You'll be required to leave the country within a reasonable period, which won't be very long, but in exchange we'll not pursue the numerous charges against you."

She asked the escorting officer to stand outside the room for a moment before she pulled her wallet out.

"This is a hundred dollars from me. You don't need to pay it back," she said, pushing the money into my hand. "It should pay for a cab, and you can buy some proper shoes. Now I'm going to have you escorted to the desk to be discharged."

Her small act of kindness showed a crack in her professional armour. It was true she had lied to me and spied on us all. But she and I had been friends. I felt there had been something genuine about that, partly at least, and for a short while I'd felt it could have become more than that. We got on well together so naturally, she might have been good for me in another life. Even Magnus had seen that, for goodness' sake. I felt a stab of regret about parting on harsh terms, no doubt for the last time, and I held onto her hand.

"I'm sorry it's ended like this," I said. "I may be a bit upset now, but I don't want to be mean. You've also been very kind to me and I won't forget it. In truth, I'm going to miss you."

Then she surprised me by putting her arms around me in a hug. "Don't say it's ended," she said. "You don't know that. I'm gonna miss you too."

I was stuck for how to answer, our imminent parting being a judicial matter and a courthouse interview room was not the easiest place for romance to blossom. But she saved me the worry. She stood back, gave me a sad smile and then smoothed herself down and led me briskly back out into the office, while I hurried to keep up. A little way down the corridor I heard her sniff and wondered if that was the result of her suppressing a tear. I have to admit that I had a lump in my throat.

♈

I was free again. Freedom's underrated by people who have it all the time. I was not just out of jail, but lightened of my responsibility, now that Persi's people were looking out for Magnus and Izzy.

Still, I was as keen as ever to confirm that they were both all right. A cab had been summoned for me, and I asked the driver to head for the airport via a cellular phone shop, where I bought a basic phone. I called Izzy, then Magnus, but neither of them answered, so I left messages. A short while later my phone rang. It was Izzy, at last.

"Who am I speaking to please?" I heard her say. In the background, echoey sounds like an airport terminal.

"It's me, Marcus."

"Where the hell are you?"

"Outside the airport, coming to find you. Long story. Have you met up with Magnus yet?"

"Well tell me about it later. It's a bit strange, Magnus texted to say he was boarding at the other end but there's no sign of him here. He should have come out by now. Ages ago, actually," she said. "There was even an announcement for him. Come and find me here. I'm in the arrivals lobby on level 1."

It only took five minutes for us to be reunited, but instead of a greeting she drew back from me. "Sweetie, for God's sake, how on Earth did you get in here looking like that?" she asked.

"Like I said, it's a long story. Have you been contacted by the feds or any other government-type people?" I asked.

"Don't get me started. Yes, is the short answer. They came to the flat. And one of them walked up to me here, half an hour ago. I told him to sod off."

"Can I see what Magnus said?" I asked. She passed her phone over, a top-end smartphone, not a cheap model like mine. I checked we'd both been calling the same number so there was no doubt. His last message only said *Boarding JSYK*, and I could see they'd been chattering quite a lot over the last few days.

I knew there and then that the nightmare was not over yet and we were heading for more trouble. For all that, we decided to wait another few minutes, just in case Magnus appeared or called either of us. Besides, I had to fill her in over the events since I'd been in this very same spot three days ago, and the type of people we were up against. She was the first person I'd told about my interrogation and torture on board the boat, or about my escape in any detail.

She didn't waste much time offering sympathy, but then it wasn't the moment. Neither was it the right place or she the right person. In fact, I was grateful now for the emotional distance I'd begun to try and put between us.

"You think they might have kidnapped Magnus, the same as they did you?" she asked, probably knowing the answer, but like me struggling to accept the truth.

"It was always meant to be him. So unless the feds got to him first, that would probably still be their plan," I said. "You were also a target. As a bargaining chip, I think. I take it they didn't find you."

"They can't have him, he's mine," she said. "How dare they! We'll have to get him back."

It struck me that she had a strange way of putting it, sounding almost petulant, but at least there was no disagreement over the next step.

"I'd better say too, the person who came to see me in my cell and had me released was Persi," I said, and then I told her what I could about Persi's reappearance and my assumptions over the bugs in the house, while skipping over Persi's insights into Izzy's psychology – it wasn't the time for that conversation.

"Persi's a spy, huh?" Izzy said, coolly. "I guess she's off the Christmas card list then."

"I gave her Magnus' phone number, in case they could get to him in time. I didn't go into details about the boat," I said.

"What if he's on the boat, or being taken there now? Can you remember where it was?" she asked.

"Only vaguely, and remember, they're armed. We'd need help and I don't have the number of a tactical squad I could call up, do you?"

"Not here, no," she said, which seemed to leave open a suggestion that there might be one, somewhere. Persi said she'd not completed her probation with the security services, and I'd seen Magnus dropping her off at the college campus.

These two things made sense now, and I saw straight through her lie.

But while I was thinking about that, the name of the boat had nearly come back to me. For a moment it was on the tip of my tongue … "Cayman Islands flag, *Diva De L'Orient*, that's the name of the boat," I remembered suddenly. "Pass me your phone, please."

"Is there some way of finding it?" she asked.

"Yes, there's a thing called the marine Automatic Identification System, AIS for short, it's a tracker for boats and ships. Any boat that size is bound to have it. It shows where the vessel is, or was, on a map. They'll have had it switched on at some point in the last few days, for sure."

It took me less than five minutes to locate the boat using Izzy's phone and a website, and the location of the docks where it had arrived two nights ago, following my escape. There was nothing to suggest it had left since, and I passed her back the phone with the location information on it, around ninety minutes' drive away. That could easily have been the same place where I'd boarded it.

"This is easier than tracking a bleeding elephant through fresh snow," she said. "We need to go and have a look for ourselves. Let's get my car."

Naturally she had hired a car, but to my surprise it was an economy Nissan, in silver. She saw the way I looked at it. "It'll do seventy-five," she offered in explanation, before I had time to ask.

We never dropped below the limit as we headed south east towards the docks, but she took it steadily nonetheless. As we made our way, I recognised each section as the same route that Connor had driven us and I grew increasingly confident that it was the same script run again.

I sent Magnus another text, just in case, and periodically

used Izzy's smartphone to check for any update on the position of the boat. We were not far past the downtown area when it popped up on the map again.

"So the good news is they just reappeared on the map," I said to Izzy. "The bad news is that they're making six knots out of the harbour into the Gulf. Our ship just sailed."

Contingency

After the boat left harbour we carried on towards its disembarkation point for another quarter hour in the vain hope that it might return, or that we'd come up with a better idea. But as the truth sank in we both realised there was little to be gained in completing the journey.

"What happens next?" Izzy asked me. "I mean, run through their evil plan again for me."

"Well, if Magnus takes their offer," I began, interrupted only by a sceptical puff of breath blown by Izzy, "and if they weren't lying about the deal, then they'll turn around and bring him home. He knows where the apartment is, and so might they by now."

"That's not going to happen. He's far too principled," she said. "How did the alternative work through?"

"Don't underestimate how sneaky Magnus can be, if needs be," I said. "Call it canniness if you prefer. He'll know as well as I did that their promise to take him home may not be true. But either way, if he holds out for too long then he gets a beating and the waterboard treatment and they set sail for Mexico. Then it's imprisonment and forced labour in a fishing village somewhere remote for a long time."

"Well, we've got to track them down the coast then," she said. "We can't rely on anyone else to do it, or not quickly enough anyway, especially if they cross the border. We can go faster than them. If we can catch up, then we can see where they take him and sort out some kind of rescue."

"That's OK so long as they leave the AIS tracker switched on," I said. "Big assumption. And remember that I don't have a passport."

"I'm not sure they bother to check you on the way out of the States," she said. "As far as I remember, leaving was a lot easier than coming back in. I'm sure we can blag or bribe our way through if we have to."

"You're sure?" I asked

"Twenty dollars buys a lot of goodwill," she said. "I'd be more worried about running into one of those vigilante squads on this side. What do they call themselves? Border Patrol or something. They'll mess with you just 'cos they're bored or think they've got something to prove."

"What videos have you been watching?" I asked. She didn't have a very good opinion of officials, any more than Magnus. I just couldn't work up the same amount of attitude.

She paused and thought for a while before continuing: "You'd better have something to show them to prove citizenship. I've still got your driving licence that you gave me, and I made some photocopies of your passport which you could use at a push."

"Just give me a minute, let me do some calculations," I said. I didn't ask why she had copied my passport, but it came as no surprise. Nothing she said or did was going to surprise me now and it sounded like she had half a plan, ignoring the problem of what we might do when or if we caught up with Noah's crew.

I checked the map and estimated the boat could get as far south as the first major port in the space of twenty-four hours. We could drive it in not much more than half that. The only thing was the slight problem of crossing the border without a passport. Even if it could be done when we were headed south, I was damn sure that for the return journey I'd be swimming the Rio Grande like any regular illegal immigrant wanting to get into the States.

"Here's an outline then," I said. "We follow them down the coast tonight, and only go into Mexico when we can see they've crossed the line out at sea. That would be in the small hours tonight, or later if they turn the tracker off and on again. That leaves us a few hours to get some equipment together, before we set off."

"Equipment. You mean like, guns?" she asked, obviously relishing the thought.

"We'd best find a shop and ask," I said, hoping the gun laws which I'd supposedly broken this morning would be flexible enough for us to get our hands on one or two. "And I could do with getting some clothes and a bite to eat."

"And a shower," she added, while she peeled off the freeway to turn the car around.

♈

Gun shopping was a major disappointment. As foreign tourists, there was no way the stores were going to sell us a gun, not even a small one. We downgraded our plan to knives and batons, which looked like a better prospect, and found that there were rules for them as well. What had happened to the Wild West when you wanted a piece of it? Then I mentioned the planned border crossing and found it may not be so simple. There was a decent chance of being thrown into jail for carrying weapons into Mexico.

To cap it off, now for the first time it crossed my mind that taking the hire car across the border in a few hours' time

212

might not be so simple either. I began to feel pessimistic about the whole lashed-together plan.

Izzy was all for just breezing across and ignoring the rules. Nine times out of ten it would all be fine, she assured me. I thought my brain would burst trying to count up all the ways she thought we could wing it, trusting alternately to luck and back-handers. I checked the progress of the *Diva*, hoping they would solve the problem by turning round, but they were still heading determinedly south. Worse than that, it looked like they were aiming for one of the Mexico-bound shipping lanes. There was still time for Magnus to be talking about a deal, maybe, but it seemed that their destination had been set, which didn't look too good for him.

"What if we just walked across the border with credit cards and cash, and buy or hire what we need on the other side?" I asked Izzy.

"Plan B," she said, thinking it over. "Sweetie, it's a pretty good idea, you're on a roll today. And we can walk across separately just in case they catch you and turn you around or shoot you for not having a passport."

I didn't like the thought of her travelling on her own, but those were desperate times. At least it meant that the shopping business could be cut short after we'd picked up some new clothes and changed some dollars for pesos. Izzy bought me and herself some dress-down faded jeans, t-shirts, sneakers and baseball caps so that we could blend in, and two lightweight jackets. I'm not sure where she thought we would blend in, apart from the border crossing, maybe. Two Brits wandering around a non-tourist part of Mexico? She chose neutral earth colours, tastefully well-matched, which was no surprise, and yet our two outfits were differentiated so we didn't look like we were in uniform. I supposed that as well as looking good in a restrained kind of way, she was also thinking about hiding in the bushes somewhere. Somehow we also ended up with knapsacks, water bottles and binoculars, which added to the whole paramilitary feeling. I had to admit I liked the feeling of adventure. That was always my thing, even if breaking the law came less easily to me than it did to her.

Then I drove us to a currency exchange and from there back to her apartment while she arranged a hire car on the phone, on the far side of the border for the next morning. I discovered without much surprise that she had working Spanish, from her travelling experience, and she managed to persuade the hire car office to open half an hour early, especially for us. The timing could still work, just about.

As soon as we got back at the flat, I pulled off my filthy clothes at the threshold and walked naked to the bin, and dropped them all into it. Izzy busied herself preparing some food and pretended not to notice me.

I headed straight for the bathroom and had my first decent wash in days. The shower was warm and relaxing and with several generous gloops of perfumed shower gel I washed away all the grime and brine that I'd collected since taking off in London. The shower room was like a sauna by the time I stepped out, and I wiped a streak through the steamed-up mirror, through which I saw a tired, gaunt and grizzled face staring back at me. It was time for the beard to go, so I set to work on it, with a pair of nail scissors and a lady's razor. As I sloughed off the fuzzy layer, my cleaner, better self re-emerged. I felt the keen sense of being ready for the mission ahead and the same feeling of returning optimism that I'd had when on the boat with Jordan. Although it seemed I was fated to stumble over every hurdle, nonetheless I'd picked myself back up every time and kept going. That's what mattered, wasn't it?

Izzy breezed into the bathroom, clad only in her underwear.

"I need the nail scissors," she said, before realising they were in use. She stopped to admire me in my naked state and she wiggled her body to draw my attention. "Ooh sweetie, you're having a deep cleanse, aren't you? Got all your pores open. The clean-cut hero prepares himself for battle. Male rituals really do something for me. If only we had a few more minutes we could give ourselves a proper send-off. But if I start to go out of control, you're allowed to tell me no, for once."

She really was incorrigible, which of course was part of her attraction. Despite my lofty intentions, the lower part of my anatomy responded swiftly to her suggestion, and I turned away from her slightly to disguise the tumescence. It wasn't lost on her, though. She cackled with delight and walked back out of the room.

Half an hour later we were both dressed, looking like regular tourists, and finishing the lamb pitta salad which she'd thrown together. It was the best thing and the healthiest that I'd eaten for a long while.

I checked the online map again and saw the ship was still heading south, about a third of the way down the coast. I turned it round to show Izzy, who shrugged her shoulders and started clearing the table. If anything, its route seemed to indicate that Magnus was sticking to his principles at the cost of expediency. It was no surprise to her but it seemed I'd misjudged him over that, or overestimated his craftiness, and now I shivered at the thought of what he might be going through. It renewed my determination to make our sketchy plan work.

Izzy came back from the kitchen. "The bags are all packed, are you ready to go?" she asked.

"*¡Ándale!*" I said, getting into the mood but wishing my Spanish stretched a bit further.

She replied "*¡Órale!*" which sounded even more convincing, even if I didn't know what it meant.

♈

"Theoretical question, I know, but did Magnus say how he got on with his meetings?" I asked, once we'd settled down.

The streetlights had just come on as we walked out of the flat. Then we'd driven out of town and joined the same highway that Jordan and I had come up only yesterday. It had grown straighter as we left the town behind, and eerily quiet in places.

"He said the California bunch were most interested," she said. "Strangely enough, it was Persi handed me the name of the guy to get in touch with there. We should have guessed there was more to her than met the eye."

"That was good then," I said without conviction.

"Well no, it was a bit of a disappointment really," she went on. "Magnus could have sounded more enthused about it. And it sounded like he had an even more mixed reception in Massachusetts."

"He was worried about that," I said. "He thought they'd be too sceptical. Although it's funny, he was quite convinced he was onto something. I can't see why it would be so hard to convince those others."

"Maybe they're all more sensitive to the politics than we realised, the cowards," she said. "There are kinds of knowledge that some people don't want. They don't want their comfy lives upset."

Mention of Persi had set me thinking about her again. I wished she'd given me her number. It might have made a

216

difference for Magnus now. In any case, it would just have been nice to hear her metered, reassuring voice. I wondered what she was doing now. I guessed she had probably spent the day trying to track Magnus down, the same as us. Except that she got to go home at the end of her day's work, wherever she called home.

"Where – how – do you suppose that Noah's crew got wind of what Magnus was doing?" I asked Izzy.

"We didn't contact that many people," she said. "Four actually, here in the States, all of them academics. But I doubt it could have been the two he went to see. They'd have known where he was, and when. The others wouldn't have known anything."

I continued the line of thought: "They did know what he'd said to at least one of those four, so maybe they've already got an insider working for them. That would fit. But they knew about the flight booking as well, so two sources."

We weren't going to solve it like this. I checked the position of the *Diva* again. Izzy, who had been hanging back letting other cars go by, now saw one go past that was right on the speed limit. She sped up and latched onto it, following its two red tail lights like devil's eyes into the pitch darkness.

"I think someone bugged your laptop," she said after a while. "It was you who booked the flights. We know they penetrated the house on at least two occasions. More, if you include Persi's social visits, and you know for a fact that's what she was up to."

Whenever Persi's name came up, I could feel the tension rise through the darkness. When she said Persi was off the Christmas card list, she wasn't joking. I flushed, knowing my laptop security wasn't the best to begin with, but also I instinctively wanted to defend Persi. As far as she was concerned, personal feelings were still involved.

"Well it couldn't be Persi, could it?" I said, knowing my logic was subjective and emotionally biased. "I mean, she's a *bona fide* official of the secret service. Noah's crew were keen to get out of US territorial waters. The flag means the boat's under British jurisdiction once it's in international waters. I'd plump for it being whoever Dudley was working for. They weren't on the same side."

"What I mean is someone – I don't care who – got onto your sodding laptop," she said. "Maybe everyone with an interest paid us a house visit while we were out. They were probably tripping over each other."

"It's still a bit weird, if the States were trying to poach a British academic from under our noses," I said. "Given that they're meant to be on the same side."

"Hah! You think so?" Izzy said. "Like they're going to miss a chance to get one over us? Who do you think owns the Internet? How can you be so naïve?"

"I suppose you're right," I said. "I just keep getting caught out every time I make an assumption or assign a motive to someone. I'm becoming allergic to thinking I can guess the answers to things."

"Well if you don't think you have the answer, what's the question?" Izzy asked.

"It's this," I said. "How did Persi and her crew come to bump into Magnus in the first place? What were they doing?"

"You don't mean enjoying free cocktails at our house-warming party, do you? Neither of us could work out who she came with, or how she got invited," Izzy said.

"It's still too hard for me. Maybe we just stick to the rescue bit," I said.

"Best thing you've said the whole journey," she answered.

♈

We switched positions after a while, so it was me in the driving seat when we reached the Texan border town in the small hours. The place was completely dead of course, apart from a strip club, and even that looked like it was shutting up for the night. Going by the looks of the town, and the language of the signboards, I wondered if we'd somehow crossed the border without noticing.

We were an hour or more ahead of the *Diva* and I suggested we got some sleep. So we drove around until we found a less sleazy part of town and parked on the side of the street, in a line of cars. It did for a quick nap, more for my benefit than hers. She seemed to get by without much sleep, which was maybe lucky for her.

She woke me at about four in the morning, her face eerily lit by the brilliant light from her phone. "Marcus," she said. "Look, see, they crossed the line."

I sat up and screwed my eyes up to look at the dazzling rectangle of light as she turned it towards me, bright white against the dark. As my pupils contracted, the light resolved into a map which confirmed what she said. The boat was well off the coast, and had now gone south of the US-Mexico border. Its route still seemed to be bound roughly for the first major port, which didn't tie in with the small fishing village that Noah had mentioned.

"Great, thanks. Wake me up again in a couple of hours," I said, and slumped down and tried optimistically to go back to sleep again. But whether or not I succeeded was hard to say. The anticipation of the border crossing pervaded my thoughts and dreams alike.

Highway

Leaving the US involved simply passing through a turnstile for the cost of just a dollar.

It was still dark when we walked across the no man's land of the footbridge, carrying only our backpacks. I looked down on the Rio Grande and wondered what happened if I couldn't get through the other side. Whose jail would I wind up in, or did they just leave me out here like that Iranian guy stuck in Paris airport? Still, I'd done it now, made the commitment and crossed the bridge literally as well as figuratively from the point of view of our plan.

Most people crossing at this time were in their cars, and only a few early birds had walked across the bridge at the same time as us. Izzy seemed to have forgotten about separating from me and I didn't remind her. The staff at the Mexican customs post weren't interested in our bags, but we joined a short queue for foreigners wanting to travel any further than the frontier zone, which extended for the first twenty or thirty kilometres inside the country. The customs building had had some recent refurbishment and I wondered how many other things might have changed since Izzy had come this way a few years earlier. The border had been a political hot potato for a decade or more, after all.

There was only a couple in front of us, and it was obvious

there was some form filling, ID checking and rubber-stamping going on. I nearly turned around on the spot, thinking there had to be a way to avoid this, but Izzy held onto me. Then it was our turn and we walked forwards together.

The Mexican official was very nice and polite and spoke English too, but Izzy handled the questions for both of us in Spanish, in order to maximise rapport before the crunch moment came. Izzy's command of the language was far better than mine, and I could only follow the thread. We filled in the forms. At the point where passports were needed, Izzy produced hers as expected, and I slid across my photocopy together with my driving licence photo ID. The word "no" translates clearly enough, and the woman politely slid them straight back to me. The details of her explanation were wasted on me but the general meaning was clear enough: nothing less than a passport would do.

Izzy now began talking quickly and flashed plenty of smiles and a fifty dollar note while I cringed. She'd said twenty, wasn't fifty almost too much? Evidently whatever the story, she was lying shamelessly but she never turned a hair. She was as relaxed and upfront about it as if she was buying a candy bar and having a chat with the cashier. The woman looked at us like we were two pieces of shit, not unreasonably, and I wished that a hole would open up and swallow me. When I came to think of it, I reasoned that a Mexican jail might be a near equivalent, so maybe my wish wasn't so far off the mark.

The woman stared at the offending bribe for a moment, while I inwardly pleaded for her either to hide it or to give it back. The "little bite" just sat there, in the open. Then she asked for more money in pesos, which made me think she was even more shameless than Izzy, except that it turned out she was actually asking for the piffling amount we had to pay for our official permits. Amazingly, she'd relented and decided to let us go through, I realised. I couldn't conceal my gratitude and she offered a sympathetic, slightly patronising smile. I was, after all, still a piece of shit.

That was my second illegal border crossing of the week, and I hoped it would be the last.

♈

As we exited the customs building and began walking towards town in the growing light of dawn, we quickly found ourselves outnumbered by taxi drivers eager to give us a ride, even if it was only as far as the car hire shop.

It really was scarcely worth the short ride, except as Izzy said to pick up some local knowledge from the driver, and that seemed a good enough reason. We walked past a few before we chose our cabbie at the cheaper end of the walkway. Carlos seemed like a decent enough fellow and he drove us around a little and pointed out some key points of interest.

What couldn't be ignored was the overpowering military presence in the town. There were a lot of soldiers driving around in the back of army trucks, carrying big guns and wearing ski masks.

The streets were still in early morning shade, but the rooftops caught the sun, and looking up I spotted a couple of gunmen with scarves covering their faces looking down at us. Whose side were they on? The taxi driver informed us casually that there had been a large-scale gunfight between the rival drug gangs, or factions within one of them, which had run across town the night before last. The security forces were still on a high alert. Obviously I'd known there was violence in Mexico, but it was a surprise to be dropped in the middle of it.

"I wasn't expecting this," I said to Izzy.

"It was all just beginning to liven up when I came through a few years ago. I thought it might be something like this, maybe not so much," she said.

"What kind of people are Noah's crew, that they come here to hide out?" I asked.

"People who are friendly with one of the cartels, or the paramilitaries, or the government, wherever you draw the distinction," she said, her cynicism shining through.

"I suppose the boat is a decent way of skirting round all of this," I said.

"A lot of cocaine from Venezuela and Brazil lands on the East coast, and not a lot of American tourists," she said. "They need local contacts for protection, especially as they've got to draw some attention coming down here in that boat. Whoever you are, it looks weird, even if they're going to go all the way to the Yucatán Peninsula."

It sounded convincing enough for me, and despite the warning Persi had given me, Izzy seemed to know a bit about how things went around here.

We got to the hire car shop and Izzy ran ahead while I paid off Carlos. There was a silver Volkswagen sedan with tinted windows on the tarmac at the front, which looked suspiciously like it might be ours. But even by the time I saw Carlos off, I could see Izzy was waving her arms around in the office in a way which didn't seem quite right. I walked in, and she turned round to me.

"The manager's nervous about renting us the car because we're going south," she told me.

The fellow looked at me and seemed to relax a little. Maybe her having walked in as a woman on her own had made things worse, it was a patriarchal society, after all. The manager shook hands with me and I addressed him politely with the name on his badge before standing back. Things calmed down, and Izzy wound up the business. Forms and money were exchanged, and we went outside with the keys for the sedan.

Izzy took the driver's side and wasted no time setting off. She was still rather uptight.

"You managed to smooth his nerves, then," I said.

"Not much," she said. "He saw I was a white non-Hispanic woman and the price suddenly went up. He said he'd assumed from my name that I was a local and it was dangerous here to look foreign."

"Did you talk the price down again, then?" I asked.

"I just put down a huge deposit – we'd better try to get the car back in one piece. The bit from him about the journey south was mainly an excuse, I think, although what he said was interesting."

"Interesting, as in the Chinese curse?" I asked.

"Apparently the road we're taking has become known as the Highway of Death owing to the number of hijackings, murders and robberies on it," she said. "Not to mention the thousands of people who've just gone missing completely."

"That counts as interesting," I agreed. "Is there anything we can do about that, like go another way?"

"There was some good news too. There's a daily caravan that leaves here at nine," she said.

I looked at the time. "That's a bit tight isn't it?"

"We ought to be able to make it, just about. Worth a try to have a police and military escort until the point where we turn off," she said. "If the violence is worst here in the north, then that covers the part that counts the most."

"I've got the map book here if you know where it sets off

from," I said, leafing through the pages to find where we were.

"Yes, I'll mark it on the map while you're having your retail experience," she said. She was heading into the narrow streets of the shopping centre, where Carlos had pointed out there was an ironmongers, at our request. A few streets later we pulled up outside it, blocking the traffic for five seconds while I hopped out to a chorus of car horns from behind, before Izzy continued driving around the block until I re-emerged.

It was that wonderful old-fashioned type of ironmongers that you rarely see nowadays, with the front of the shop festooned with samples of their wares, from galvanised buckets to kitchen pots and pans, brooms and garden implements. Inside there was the faint but pleasant smell of sawdust and oil. Despite the pressures of the moment, the Boy Scout in me saw half a dozen implements useful for an outdoor expedition, and I had to hold back from making an impulsive purchase.

My task now was to find the garden tools section, or an assistant, whichever came first. Happily, I spotted an attractive lady who looked like she could help.

"¿Tengas machetes?" I asked her, after the customary friendly greetings.

"Tipo Rambo, no," she said, not the Rambo type. We both laughed. I was sure it was meant as a compliment. I think she understood immediately where my mind had wandered, so I didn't feel the need to pay her any more compliments than the appreciation she'd already noticed.

"¿Tienes alguno como cuchillos?" I asked, the sort like knives? The answer was yes. She had some with polished blades about forty centimetres long, sharp enough to be going along with. I bought two at the asking price and had her wrap them. At almost any other time I would have haggled over the money and asked her out to see a movie with the change.

I got my focus back and walked out onto the street to wait for Izzy to drive around again. It was a long wait. I texted her after ten minutes and received an answer back telling me to walk round to the corner. From there I could see our car on the wrong side of a police checkpoint and thought better of crossing it carrying the blades, and so I waited another five minutes until she was allowed through. She skidded to a halt beside me and I leapt in.

"There's the meeting point," she said rather tersely, jabbing a finger at the map. "I hope they're not leaving on time." I checked my watch and saw we were already late. The car's tyres squealed on the corner.

♈

Getting out of town to the meeting point wasn't any quicker just because we were in a hurry. We followed signs to the highway, but we joined it without ever seeing the caravan.

"So we missed it," Izzy declared. "Which just means we go a bit faster until we catch up."

She floored the pedal and we watched the speedo climb. The traffic was two-way but it was really quiet, more so after we left the outskirts of town. There were enough slow vehicles to add more delay, and enough roadside shrines to past road fatalities to make one think, but we were in no mood for caution or politeness. Then as the sporadic small settlements faded out entirely, the traffic all but ceased and we experienced the open road and cut a direct line south, hemmed in by the scrubby oak-green road verges and beyond them the flat sandy brown arable fields lying bare, which stretched out endlessly on either side of us.

The hold-up happened not much further on. A white SUV pickup was pulled up some way ahead, with its hazard lights on. Three young men spilled out of it and strung themselves across the road as soon as we hove into sight. There could be no doubt over their intentions. We could see that the handguns they carried were already out, dangling lazily by their sides, scarcely hidden. One of them began flagging us down with his free hand, while the few hundred metres between us shrank rapidly.

Izzy's foot never faltered from the pedal. "Slide down as much as you can," she said at about two hundred metres distance.

It may have seemed like longer, but we covered the gap in six, maybe seven seconds. About the time that we'd halved the distance between us, and it must have been clear that we weren't stopping, one of the guys raised his gun and started firing, far too early to be on target. I was looking over the top of the dashboard and saw the gun kicking. His two partners were slower and had only just begun to raise their guns when they saw the wisdom of jumping clear instead. So the one who seemed to be their leader stood alone but kept shooting until the last moment before he went to jump out of our way. Except that now he discovered he'd backed up to where the SUV was blocking him, on the roadside. As he leapt backwards towards the verge, he collided with their car and was halted in his tracks in the road. He twisted his head to see which direction we were going in, and I saw his panic-filled eyes open wide when he saw there was no space left. I do believe that Izzy had allowed our car to drift slightly towards him. Then there was a hell of a bang and he was suddenly whisked out of sight, sheared between the two cars and propelled to the ground in an instant.

Our car bounced off him, or their car, or both, and swerved

across into the opposing lane. For some moments it was as if we were floating on a layer of molten rubber, fishtailing our way across the road, before Izzy gently steadied our course and steered us back towards our own lane again.

I sat up. I didn't need to be stood outside to see that the car was messed up badly. The windshield was starred on my side from a bullet, and from what I could see the bonnet and wing were bent up. My passenger window had gone completely, and the door panel seemed an inch or two closer to me than it had been before.

I looked back and saw we'd nudged the SUV right off the road. There was a small heap on the road beside it, which I assumed was the remains of our shooter. The other two guys were banging off some rounds in our direction, but we were a good way off by now and picking up speed again.

"There's the deposit gone then," Izzy said, as a matter of fact. I assumed this was meant to pass for irony, otherwise her remark would have been too horrible.

"That's the thing with trying new places. You never know who you're going to bump into," I quipped, trying to respond in kind. In truth I was shocked to the core by what just happened.

Despite her flippancy, there wasn't much conversation in the car after that. The gravity of it didn't escape me, even if it was necessary to put on a brave face. I doubted the lawfulness of our action. Those lads may have been enemies to our lives, if we'd known their actual intent. Yes, we acted somehow in self-defence, but I couldn't reconcile myself to the shedding of human blood, not even for our deliverance.

On the other hand, as the immediate shock began to wear off, I began to see the possible advantages of Izzy's unusual temperament, for our particular circumstances. The killer instinct had its place here, and the evidence showed that nothing was going to get in her way before we had completed of our rescue mission. I heaved a sigh and decided just to get on with the job in hand.

"Don't worry, it'll get better sweetie," Izzy assured me. "We're just down on our luck at the start. The law of averages says things will go better for it."

"Isn't that what they call the gambler's fallacy?" I asked. She ignored me. I should've known better than to challenge her opinion, especially when we really needed a dose of good luck. Being right only made it worse.

Not long afterwards we drove up to an official checkpoint, which was an inland customs post as far as I could see. Fortunately for both sides, it was well marked and the dozen or so well-armed police and young military guys looked convincingly enough like the real thing, as did the sandbags piled around the kiosk. Izzy pulled off the road and pushed me out to do the talking. Despite any reasons to the contrary, she assured me that as a man I would be "less threatening", and this made more sense to me having had the experience in the hire car office.

I proffered our papers to the officials, but the damage to the car was far more interesting to them. It was my first glance at it from the outside and, as expected, my side was badly wrecked. I noticed there were some dried-on bits of meat stuck to the inside of the wheel arch, beginning to go brown in the heat.

The policeman asked me what had happened, and a couple of other guards now wandered over as well. I blustered my way through with a mixture of Spanish and English: we'd swerved to avoid a dog, hit it, hit a road sign, kept going. Lots of hand gestures and sound effects when my Spanish ran out. What else could we have done?

The group walked around the car and one of them put his

finger to what was quite obviously a bullet hole in the boot, to complement the one in the windscreen.

"El perro tenía un dueño," I think is what he said, looking at me quizzically. The dog had an owner, yes of course. I smiled and nodded, waiting for the final confirmation that our plan had just come to an end.

"Era un canalla," said another policeman and they all had a laugh on me, who had no idea what they just said. He or it was something – a *canalla*. I saved it up to ask Izzy later. Then it was suggested I had better take over the driving from the señora, which led to more jokes and I realised I had actually become the object of some sympathy. We were blokes together, I realised, the mood became unexpectedly friendly and I relaxed a bit. Things went perfectly smoothly after that. They checked the boot and our knapsacks for drugs, bundles of money, firearms or whatever it was they were interested in, and asked me a few questions about where the "dog" had been when we hit it, where we were going now and so on. I had my answers ready and thankfully they weren't too thorough with the search.

Izzy and I swapped seats when I got back in the car, and I asked her "What does canalla mean?"

"It's pejorative. It means a low-life or a dog," she said. I got the joke at last, and smiled, and a memory floated up from what seemed a lifetime ago, of a light-hearted moment shared with Pete and Enrique, of a joke almost lost in translation, and now the tables had been turned.

"There's something else," I said, "before I forget. I have to take back what I said to you before about the gambler's fallacy. It seems you were right about the law of averages. They do apply to you the way you meant, even it works for no-one else the same way."

She liked that.

Off the Map

As I drove us south at antisocial speeds and the road grew rougher, the noise of the car made it less easy to talk. Izzy catnapped. I noticed there were still regular army patrols passing us going in the opposite direction, with bigger guns and more armour than the police. I took it to mean we were not yet out of the most high risk area.

I wondered whether they'd find the body of our gunman up the road, or if his remains had been tidied up. Would they even stop to look at it? Would he just be plus-one in the statistics. If they felt as I did, then they might leave him for the crows, but all the same it was another incentive to keep my foot down hard and put distance between us. So I hammered the engine until, at last, we finally caught up with the convoy and tagged onto its tail.

It was a relief then to feel we had some protection and to slow down a little. The cumulative tiredness of the last few days was a tax on my concentration. To be able just to follow the car in front for an hour or so helped to ease the effort of covering the endless plains.

The convoy stopped at a gas station just before the road where we planned to go our separate way. We took the chance to top up the car for the last time under the watchful eyes of our armed patrol. The banged-up car attracted some

231

attention again, but there were more eyes trained on Izzy, who had gone to ask the officer about the road ahead. She came back with his suggestion that we allowed a slight detour in order to stay with the convoy a little longer.

So we stuck with the convoy for another half hour and then with slight reluctance we separated and took the branch of the road which cut towards the coast. We were off the plains now and it became hillier. The arable farms began to give way to ranches. The road was poor, and the phone connection worked only intermittently. At our last checkpoint we had seen we had just about closed the gap between us and the *Diva*, with a chance of overtaking her in the next hour.

We made better progress after reconnecting with our original planned route and passed through another settlement which was a fair-sized truck stop. The road was lined with shops, garages and cafes set back far enough for the massive lorries to park and turn around. I began to slow down, aiming for a roadside grill when Izzy got signal and checked the map on her phone again.

"The map's stopped showing the *Diva*," she said.

I glided the car to a halt and to see for myself. She wasn't lying. The boat had disappeared since the last checkpoint, quite some way back. "I'm not sure what to do next," I said. "Except wait."

We bought some food and drink and rested while we thought it over. The people here seemed very pleasant and friendly, so unlike the bad boys we'd encountered on the road. It was hard to get my head round how different these two aspects of the place could be, but I found I was beginning to feel almost at home among the locals.

After we'd given it another quarter of an hour, there was still no sign of the *Diva*. It seemed they'd gone dark, either because someone had at last remembered to turn off the AIS, or because they were pulling out of the shipping lane and had less use for it.

"There's no reason why they couldn't be docking somewhere around here," Izzy said, as we looked at the map. "It's quiet, not many people, but there are a few villages on this part of the coast."

The main north-south road which we were following was well inland, but I'd noticed there were very few roads connecting the coastal villages directly. "Agreed," I said. "But we'd need to drive down each and every coast road to get eyes on, which could take a long time. If the *Diva* was still sailing south then we would lose ground."

"We could make it up again if we had to," she said.

"OK so if we start a local search then we need to prioritise locations around the better moorings," I said, "and make sure we go through places where we'll pick up a signal."

I marked the time and last location of the *Diva* on the map and drew concentric circles around it with possible arrival times further down the coast. It provided a series of time zones down the coast which we could use to plan our itinerary as we worked our way through the likeliest moorings.

"At least then we'll have an idea what the places look like," Izzy replied. "There can't be a better option. We'll have run out of money before we get to Belize, though. We might have to sell your body."

We decided to set the northerly extent of our search by backing up a little way along the main road, to the previous place where a metalled road had branched off towards the coast. The other road led to a small resort, the largest settlement for some way north or south. It was built around a decent-sized inland waterway and seemed to include a small marina. On this silty coastline the *Diva's* harbouring

233

options had to be quite limited – I guessed the boat would have a draught of two metres or more – and that improved our chances of finding them in a place like the resort.

♈

A wind-blasted banner, whose cheerful Bienvenidos message was faded, blown to tatters and hanging in rags, marked our arrival on the coastal plain just outside the resort.

The road to the coast had been better than expected, although as we had climbed up and over the low-lying hills, the pale dust of the arid landscape had encroached along the roadside, blurring its edges. Nonetheless, what traffic there was, had actually been going somewhere: home for the siesta quite likely, and so we'd made good time, leaving a dusty cloud in our wake. Briefly, as we dropped down onto the coastal plain, we had been able to see ahead to the coastal haze, and then we had joined the flat again, overlooked by a big sky, as hot and dusty as the road we ploughed along.

Now the map told me that we were about to converge with the river which led down to the resort. I was keen to get a look at it as soon as possible, to gauge how far up it was navigable and also check the opposite bank, which appeared from the map to be uninhabited, as was most of the area around us. There were no bridges marked so I suggested that we go down a farm track, to see whether it led down to the river. The countryside was pretty well deserted with little farming going on, and the first track we tried was rough and falling back to scrub. It eventually opened onto a mudflat which I didn't fancy trying to cross in an ordinary road vehicle, and we were too far shy of the river to see, even while standing on the car roof.

We returned to the main road and moved a little further

down. The first signs of settlement appeared: small, flat-roofed block-built houses, some of them smaller than a trailer home. The edges of the properties were delineated as much by the contrast between sandy scrub and smooth lawns and deciduous fruit trees, as they were by their flimsy barbed wire fences, which were roughly made with crooked posts cut from local scrub or driftwood. But of greater interest was between the simple pastel-shaded buildings where an increasing number of sandy tracks pointed in the direction of the river. Before long we saw one which looked slightly more worn and led to several other residences. We decided to go down it. Then within half a mile we were looking out over the river from the bank for the first time, parked beside a dusty uninhabited shed and a rotten landing pier. The river was easily two or three hundred metres wide here, and we could see more than a mile upstream and down.

With the binoculars, I could see there were dozens of small piers like ours, in both directions, leading out from the shallow muddy banks on our side of the river and into the deeper water. The only boats I could make out were small bay boats and runabouts, fishing and recreational boats for shallow waters. The opposite bank was deserted.

I marked our spot and the time on the map, and we went back to the main road to advance another two miles along the bank. The fences here were a little smarter and palm trees began to proliferate. The river grew closer to the road, and we invaded the car park of a scruffy hotel for the five minutes it took to sweep the banks. The owner came out to try to sell us a room and I detained him as best I could, trying to steer his eyes away from our car and from Izzy while she finished scanning the riverbanks. When I saw she'd finished, I extricated myself and we made our escape before I asked her what she'd seen.

235

"It's no different here, just small pleasure boats and not many of those. There's a posh house on the opposite bank, but no boat parked outside. That's it, almost everything's on this bank," she said.

"We should go on further this time," I suggested. "I'd like to see the lower reaches down to the estuary as soon as we can, then we have an option to look around some more, or to drive down to the next village before dark. Then maybe we could press on down the coast overnight."

"Driving at night in Mexico is meant to be more dangerous than in the day," Izzy said. "So it could get interesting."

We were walking back when our eyes fell on a grey car, just like the Astra that Dudley had driven and whose screen I'd smashed. Obviously it wasn't the same one, and there was no Dudley sat inside, but we'd both become tuned to looking out for it and here was its doppelganger. It was an unpleasant reminder that we, currently doing the following, had been the ones being followed not long before.

"I don't think we'd be here now, if it wasn't for Dudley," Izzy said.

"You still think he's linked to these guys?" I asked.

"I mean that was the thing that got Magnus off his backside and made him go do the interviews," she said. "That and the house being turned over, which was quite likely Dudley's people too."

"I'm sorry things worked out this way," I said.

"No, it was the right thing to do. It'll still be worth it if we can rescue him. I'm sure we can pull it off yet," she said.

"What was the right thing?" I asked.

"To twist his arm and get him to come over here," she said.

"Hang on, you're not suggesting that you had something to do with Dudley's appearance, are you?" I asked, suddenly alarmed.

"Oh my God, sweetie, what do you think of me? Of course not," she said. "That's a horrible thing to say, you should be ashamed of yourself for even thinking it. Say you're sorry."

"Yes, of course. That was unjustified," I said.

"You're Goddam right it was!"

She got over it quickly enough, and we drove on to our next stop, which was at a river bend, in an empty building lot. Here the curve of the river was in the wrong direction for us, bending back behind us, with the effect that it badly restricted how far we could see on our own side. It was not far downstream from a station run by the coastguard or the military and they had a much bigger, longer pier with a coastal patrol vessel tied up to it, its purpose made clear by a large machine gun or cannon on the rear deck. End-on, the coastguard boat looked about the same size as the *Diva*, although its battered hull showed it had many more miles on the clock. But it did confirm that we had found a viable harbour, navigable for larger boats to at least five miles above the river mouth.

Below our current spot, looking downstream, we could see only two or three piers. The buildings they served were much smarter than any others we'd seen, and I reasoned we had just reached the prime waterfront location. The map indicated that the river meandered more and more from here on, and I marked out two more vantage points which would offer the best fields of view between here and the coast: firstly, a point two miles further on, where the river bend was in our favour, and then a little further round, where there was an inlet just above the main resort, there was a point which would give us a clear view down to the river mouth, and to any marina such as might still be a part of the resort.

♈

"Take a look at that one, to the left of the terracotta building," Izzy said, pointing as far upstream as could be seen.

I swung round and noted the small white blob where she was pointing, which was a mile or more away. It was no bigger than a pinhead to the naked eye, closer to where we had been looking out from fifteen minutes earlier than it was to here at our penultimate lookout spot. I refocused my binoculars. It was the only boat of its size in view and the nearest distinctive building to it, visible from here, was a large terracotta building which may have been a large casa or a small hotel.

"It's about the right size, so certainly worth a closer look," I said. "We should go back now in case it moves."

The boat seemed to be standing slightly off the bank, but its movement if any was hard to judge as we were looking at it stern-on. We studied it for another few minutes and decided that it was either moored, or making only very slow headway. We ran back to the car and jumped in, Izzy driving, me on the lookout. We drove to the terracotta building which was our landmark. It appeared to be another hotel, and we left the car on the road while we walked up to the riverbank, going round the back of the hotel to avoid drawing attention.

I could see the boat through the trees before we reached the riverbank. I recognised the *Diva* in an instant. Instinctively, my hair stood on end and my pulse quickened. We ducked down and edged as close as we could get, and I checked the name on her bow in any case.

"It's her," I said, as if Izzy couldn't read for herself. By some amazing good fortune we had stumbled on her almost straight away.

The *Diva* was moored some fifty metres off the bank, and about a hundred downstream, close to the next pier along the river, beside a large private house which, like many here, was being extended. The house was unusual only in the solidity of the boundary wall running around it, to within a foot or two of the riverbank, which seemed to be the only place it could be viewed from. A silver pickup was parked beside it, and a small digger stood silent on an area of recently levelled ground. Although from where we stood the pier was partly obscured by a stack of pallets and building materials, it seemed there was no dinghy tied up and no activity outside the house or on the boat deck either. Everywhere was calm and peaceful, with humans and wildlife alike having gone quiet in the middle of the day, and the only sounds were of the river current and the gentle throb of the *Diva's* engines.

"We've got to go round, to find out if they're in the house," she said.

"If you can look through the windows of the house, I can swim out to the boat and see what there is," I said to her.

"You think that's wise in broad daylight? Someone's bound to spot you," she said.

"I should be able swim out underwater," I said. "Just to do a reconnaissance. You need to be as careful looking at the house. If you have to run, take the car and we'll meet up later, at the last lookout spot."

"I thought you had a problem with going in the water?" she asked.

"Exposure therapy seems to be working quite well for me," I replied. "In any case, needs must."

Then unexpectedly my phone started to ring, loudly. I madly scrabbled to get it out and answer it before we disturbed all our neighbours from their siesta.

239

Intervention

"Who's that?" I asked.

"Marc, it's me, Persi. You didn't show up at the courthouse this morning, you rat."

Switching context was a struggle. Was today really only the day after yesterday, when we'd sat together in the interview room? So much had happened during the interval, the fact of it was hard to grasp.

"I'm really sorry, but I've been a bit caught up in something. It's not a very good moment for us to talk," I said. I turned away from Izzy and began walking back towards the road, putting distance between us to avoid being overheard. I didn't dare look over my shoulder.

"When will we ever find a good moment?" Persi said. "There's always something else getting in the way."

"Fair point, but I'm not joking," I said. "It's important, sorry. I really do have to go."

"Supposing I said I might be able to help you with that boat you're so interested in?" she asked.

"You say what?" I asked, wondering how Persi would know anything about the *Diva*. Come to that, I didn't even own this phone the last time she and I had spoken, so how did she get my number? The back of my neck began to prickle uncomfortably and suddenly my paranoia seemed wholly justified. She seemed to have guessed – or to know – far too much. I was still connecting the pieces. She'd had Izzy's phone number, I'd rung Izzy. That must have been how she located me.

"Hold that thought for just a moment, there was something personal I have to say," she told me. "Important for you to know before you go get yourself killed or disappear into some jungle forever."

I was still walking past our wreck of a car and down the road when I heard the door open and I looked round. Izzy had followed me out of the hotel grounds and was getting into it.

"Despite it all, despite everything I know, I have feelings for you," Persi continued. "But try to see where I've been coming from. It's not straightforward."

"Complicated," I said.

"Yes, complicated," she said.

I was beginning to wonder if the depths of her feelings might have run ahead of where mine had been. She seemed prepared for some reason to overlook a lot on my account.

"So you could afford to trust me, a little," she said, after a pause.

I knew this was not the time and place for the conversation, or maybe it was the time and place which had made her say something. I wondered what it was that she knew about present circumstances.

"We should talk about this some more, soon," I said. "By the way, is this a private number?"

"No, that's on government record now. You needed to know, anyway," she said. She didn't sound comfortable saying it, and I realised other people might be listening, or would be one day in the future. In my mind, the imagined listeners-in were either screaming at her through some glass,

241

telling her to bloody get on with her job, or goading me to say something romantic. But I didn't want to say something corny or superficial, just because that was in the script, and on reflection the screaming through glass scenario seemed far more likely.

"It's awkward timing, I know," she said. "But so long as that's understood, then here's the next thing: I'm looking at you on a monitor, real-time. You're in the road just in front of your car, and you just stopped dead in your tracks and looked round. Izzy just got out of the car and she's walking in your direction, carrying something shiny."

I saw Izzy was walking briskly towards me, carrying the two machetes and looking pretty pissed off.

"What have you got to gossip about that's so important? Who the hell is that?" she called out.

"It's Persi, she seems to know more about this show than we thought," I said, holding up a hand to beg for more time. "Persi, tell me what you know. We're about to have a closer look at the boat."

"I'm looking down on you from about half a mile above," she said. I instinctively looked up, but I couldn't see anything against the sun. "We've been jamming the network connections on *Diva De L'Orient* for some time and I'm told we disabled their navigation system when they entered the river, not so long ago. They got there about the same time as you. How did you know where they were going?"

"Tell her to go fuck herself," Izzy raised her voice towards the phone, loud enough for Persi to hear in any case. Then she prodded me rather hard with the business end of a machete until I took it away from her. I noticed she had put camouflage paint on her face, Native American Indian style, with a broad horizontal stripe drawn neatly across her eyes. It accentuated them dramatically and highlighted her fine

242

cheekbones, with the result that she looked devastatingly chic with it on. It even had some camouflage value.

"Just a lucky guess on our part. Have I got time to ask how you know all this?" I asked Persi.

"No. Just let me know if you see anyone you recognise," she said. "I'm on this number. By the way, your cellulars are the only ones in town which will work right now. You're connected through us. I can't tell you anything more, and I know you gotta go anyway. You can try and calm your psycho companion down now."

Persi hung up, and I turned to Izzy and pointed skywards to explain our situation: "We're being watched from up there, and they've worked out we're following the *Diva*. They're jamming her systems so she probably isn't going anywhere for a while."

"Can we get back to Plan A now please?" Izzy said in a rather sarcastic tone. "Give me your phone to hang onto. Get back to your starting blocks and in the water. I'm going in that way." She pointed towards the house entrance which was closed up. "Actually, on second thoughts, give me a leg up over the wall before you go," she said. "I'll see what I can and then try to work my way over to the jetty and watch out for you."

♈

The river water was warm and pleasant and with the little added weight of my machete, having let out some air, I sank gently down to the riverbed to gain cover. I swam straight out to where the current would carry me downstream. Propelled mostly by the flow I swam lazily along with it, keeping an eye towards the surface ten or twelve feet above, until I saw the dark hull of the *Diva* loom ahead. Although I scarcely had time to think about it, my recently acquired aquaphobia had quite subsided. Calmly and with plenty of breath to spare, I ascended, coming up under the prow where I'd aimed, and I caught hold of the anchor cable to guide me up.

Minutes earlier, when I hid my clothes under a bush in the hotel garden, I'd been unable to see any movement. But as I broke the surface I could hear activity down by the stern. The Texan drawl which sounded like Noah talking carried across the water, and I swam across the bow to look down the side of the boat. They were boarding the dinghy on the side nearest the shore. Cody was on board already, still wearing his sunglasses and combat fatigues and evidently on transportation duties. I saw Connor hand him down several bags before hopping down himself, keeping Magnus' laptop bag clasped to him all the time. It confirmed for me what we had already assumed, namely that they had captured my brother. For someone who I had only ever seen wearing a suit, it was strange to see Connor wearing a gaudily coloured shirt, Bermuda shorts and sandals, but his powerful bearing and irritable tone of voice were unmistakeable. Noah was the last to jump down, looking cool and elegant in a pale linen suit. Cody started the outboard and cast off from the *Diva*. I could see no sign of Troy or Magnus.

I looked across to the jetty in time to see Izzy ducking down behind the pallets, apparently undetected so far, but her hiding place looked precarious from my angle. She was hidden from the stern of the boat and the approach course of the dinghy, but to avoid the landing party she would have to move round, into a position which was clearly visible from the boat. If she was detected, she'd be up against three armed men. I couldn't leave her like that.

They were already moving off as I dipped down again. I

began to swim back towards the jetty, scarcely a pool's length away, and I saw the dinghy's shadow pass in front of me before I arrived. I popped up as silently as I could underneath the jetty while the landing party was still jumping onto it, and worked my way up to the shore end, ready to jump out and do whatever was needed, if the situation demanded it.

Through the slats above I could see the three figures and hear them talking. They were in no great hurry. Noah was handing out instructions to Cody, who was lighting himself a cigarette. The cloud of aromatic smoke permeated down to water level where I appreciated the distinctive oriental scent of an American blend, probably Marlboro. I hadn't noticed before that he smoked.

"We don't need you inside right away," Noah said to Cody. "Finish your cigarette before you bring the bags in. It may take a while for Connor to get us back online."

"Not so long, the equipment here's fine," Connor assured him. "Pass me a beer, will ya Cody?"

The jetty shook slightly as the two of them walked towards the house, and I could feel the vibration pass down the posts. Then the clatter of their footsteps became muted as they stepped onto the grass and made their way up the garden. I could just see Izzy sliding behind the pallets for cover and I looked back towards the *Diva*. There was no-one on deck, although it was impossible to see whether there was anyone looking out through the tinted windows. She was as exposed as she could be now, pinned behind her scanty hiding place, surrounded on three sides and always vulnerable to one. Her best bet might be to run for it, keeping on the opposite side of Cody who was nearest and the one most likely to see her.

But she didn't move. Cody stood looking vacantly out over the water, his cigarette burning down, while I looked up at him from underneath the slats, gauging my chances of getting up out of the water before he had a chance to jump clear and shoot me. The odds didn't look good, he was a little too far out of reach. I decided to wait till he was about to discard his stub. In that moment of distraction, his hand busy with an automated movement and his eyes elsewhere, I might gain a fractional second longer to hop out and take a swing at him.

The moment never came. There was a rush of footsteps on the jetty and Connor turned around to face Izzy charging down towards him. He hesitated for a moment and then pushed back his light combat jacket, where his gun sat in its belt.

With a ladylike sound like a *hip!* from her sharp intake of breath, Izzy swung her machete at him with full force, her whole body raised onto her tiptoes for a moment as she extended and rotated her arms balletically. Her blow connected almost silently with his neck and he immediately fell backwards onto the deck, dropping the gun, clawing at his throat, gasping.

He wasn't getting up. His legs squirmed and his feet flailed, weakly pushing him a little further along the gangway. His completed cigarette rolled along the plank, leaving behind a wispy smoke trail before it dropped between the slats and landed with the faintest fizz in the water beside me.

Izzy, meantime, dropped to all fours and crawled forwards towards him until she was face to face with her desperate, dying victim. To my horror, I saw her aping his expression of pain and horror, her face like a mirror of his, mimicking the contortions of his mouth as he gurgled his last breaths through the mucus and blood which I could see he was spitting out. Spots of it rained down through the slats and

246

into the water in front of me. With no regard for getting back behind cover, she invigilated the whole process, placing a hand on his shoulder to keep him on his back, studying him closely as if she was admiring the grisly aesthetic of the scene.

And so she savoured every moment, storing the memory, until his death rattle faded away. When he was quite dead, she calmly sat up, pushed a lock of hair back under her cap and looked around.

Any doubts I previously had over Persi's warning about Izzy were now despatched, and yet knowing her as I did, I found it strangely easy to incorporate this most repellent aspect of her personality with the rest. It changed but didn't transform my understanding of her. However uneasy it made me feel, she remained as fascinating to me as ever, even if now I felt the distance between us had grown again.

I chose the moment to announce my presence, making a deliberate splash, as if I had just surfaced, and taking a deep breath for effect.

"Hey Izzy, I'm down here," I whispered. "Are you OK?"

"I just killed one of the bastards, as you can see."

I pulled myself up onto the jetty. "That was Cody. We need to get under cover," I said. "And we need to get this body hidden." I started pulling off some of Cody's combat gear: his jacket, cap and sunglasses.

"Explain yourself, is this something kinky you're doing?" Izzy quietly demanded, sounding amused. She wore a twisted smile which together with her camouflage paint made her look quite manic.

"Give me a hand with this, quickly. I need his trousers," I whispered.

"What're you doing here, anyway? Surely you can't have been aboard the *Diva* already?" she asked, removing his

247

boots while I undid his belt and pulled his trousers down.

"I thought you were in trouble so I came over here. Not that you needed any help, it seems."

"Thank you sweetie, it's the thought that counts," she said, generously. "I only hit him once, you know. I got the blade the wrong way round, otherwise I think his head might have come off. It was quite interesting, though. I must look it up later to find out what it was I hit. "

I had removed enough of Cody's clothes to get dressed in, and so we rolled his semi-naked body over and lowered it into the water with a small splash, and then as it floated, we steered it under the jetty, where the gentle pressure of the current trapped it against the uprights. I noticed he had eight-pointed stars tattooed on the front of his shoulders. I wondered whether it was callous of me to care so little about his violent death. But this day had been like no other, and I was becoming inured to it.

Cody's pistol lay on the jetty and Izzy looked at it with greedy eyes. "Best if I take the gun," I said. "I'm going to ferry us both over to the *Diva* in the dinghy and we can both go on board. I haven't seen Troy yet, he may be there or there may be a replacement. If anyone comes out, they should be looking at you, wondering who you are. Hopefully my disguise as Cody will be good enough to get me on board."

I picked the gun up and had a look at it. It looked new and expensive, black and blocky, with hard-edged corners. The German name embossed on the handle seemed to have a ring of Nazi connections, which seemed quite appropriate for a shady gangster's henchman to be carrying around in Central America. It was about the same size and weight as the one which Jordan had owned, but it didn't obviously have a safety catch, which made me wonder if I was missing something. I checked and saw that there was a bullet in the chamber already and I holstered the gun with superstitious care.

I was acutely aware that we'd been on the jetty in clear view of anyone who cared to look for the last five or ten minutes, and I thought we'd used up our ration of luck on that count. So I guided Izzy into the dinghy, where she wedged herself between two bags at the sharp end, and I cast off, started the outboard and set out across the short stretch of water towards the stern of the *Diva*.

Reciprocity

The little boat ate up the fifty metres of water within a few seconds, and as we drew up beside the *Diva*, an overweight figure wearing an olive green t-shirt emerged onto her deck, with a large white bandage over his eye, held on with a diagonal band.

In Troy's hand, he held a chunky-looking sub-machine gun, almost brick-like, and he reached across his paunch with his other hand to slip on a shoulder strap, revealing a second white bandage wrapped around his forearm.

He trod heavily down the steps to the diving deck at the very end, the place where I'd dived off from so recently, and casually pointed the gun at us as I cut the engine and glided the boat up to the corner where he stood.

"Who ya got there, Cody?" he asked. I shrugged to avoid saying anything, kept my head down and threw him a rope to tie us up with, which he caught nimbly and threw a couple of loops one-handed around a cleat, which suggested that his injured arm was working well enough, and that he knew his ropework.

He took a quick look at Izzy, dressed in beige and green and wearing her war paint, and made his own mind up.

"Some kinda squaw sneakin' up on us, huh? Well step aboard darlin', nice and easy." He stood back to make room for her and she hopped up lightly while I held the dinghy against the boat.

"Get down on your knees, hands behind your head," Troy ordered her and as she did, he gave me a much harder stare with his one cruel eye. I carried on climbing up, but as I stepped across, Troy raised his gun towards me, pulled back the lever to load the first round, and put his free hand to the trigger.

"Miller, is it you?" he asked, his aim never wavering from my chest, his one eye fixed on mine. His confusion was written all over his face, unable to believe who he was looking at. My two eyes reflected back his look of hate, doubly so. "Or you got another brother? Get on the floor, face down bud. You too, darlin', flat on the deck," he said, recovering from his surprise.

Izzy shuffled forwards on her knees slightly and then suddenly, unexpectedly, sprang up from beneath him. She batted his gun to one side and swung her fist into his ribs. She made no impression on him at all, and he simply brought down the weapon on the back of her head, upon which she fell down again as if poleaxed.

But she had bought me the moment I needed. The muzzle was pointed elsewhere and I took my cue, throwing myself towards him, using my whole weight as I had done once before, grabbing his gun and pushing it into his face. He stepped backwards, but his rear leg found only thin air and he went over the side, floundering, and I followed him straight into the water with a very large splash.

As I left the boat I managed to thrust off the side enough, so that while he landed more or less the right way up, I dived and managed to turn him over, bearing the two of us down head first deeper into the water. He instinctively tried to swim to the surface, but I was taking him down, holding him by the shoulder strap across his neck. He was a poor swimmer, and I could tell straight away that I had the advantage.

As he tried to wriggle free, I caught hold of his shirt from behind and began to get him into a lock, turning him over again as best I could and trying to propel us both further downwards all the time. He delivered one or two extremely painful jabs into my ribs using his elbows but I held on with grim determination and while he used his effort against me we continued our descent. But his breath hardly lasted and as it began to run out his panic rose and he began to struggle more for the surface than to hit out at me.

Too late. Once we had hit the water, there was never a moment when I wasn't winning the fight, and now his struggling grew weaker. I folded him closer into my embrace and took us both down to the riverbed. By the time we had reached the bottom, he had gone quite limp, and I looped his gun securely around his neck to weigh him down. Given the amount of gas in his guts, I wasn't sure how long he'd stay down there.

As I ascended I decided that reciprocity, revenge in kind, didn't feel so sweet. I thought he'd earned his ending, but now that I'd repaid him I found there was no reward in it for me. It was just necessary business, and a rather nasty business at that.

♈

The crew of the *Diva* had shown themselves adept at remaining scarce during the time I'd spent on board, but now at last I got to meet one of them. I vaguely recognised him from the harbour when I was first kidnapped. He was watching me swimming back to the boat, standing on the aft deck where I'd left Izzy, who was now gone. He dropped a ladder over the stern as I got closer and called me over in his direction. He must have mistaken me for Cody.

"I've taken the lady up to the main cabin, sir. Is everything all right? I can't find Mr Troy."

As I climbed the ladder, I pulled Cody's gun out of its holster and pointed it at the hapless crewman. Goodness knows if it would have worked full of water, but it had the desired effect. His jaw dropped with incomprehension and he raised his arms in surrender.

"Take me up to the cabin. Who else is on board?" I said.

"Just me and the captain, sir. And the lady. There's no need for that, sir," he said, walking compliantly up the steps past the sunbeds, towards the cabin. My wet clothes sagged and slopped and dribbled onto the deck as we walked up. I didn't care to dwell on the last time I'd seen those sunbeds.

"What, no other guests?" I asked.

"I'm sorry sir, I don't know. Some of them went ashore."

We entered the dining area through the sliding glass doors and found the captain ministering to Izzy with a drink and helping her to sit up. He looked up at me, then down at the gun and up at me again. He certainly recognised me, or thought he did, and waited for me to speak.

"Back up," I ordered them. "Both of you go and sit on those bar stools. Keep your hands on your knees where I can see them." The bar was empty and there was a nice clear space between me and the high stools. Neither of them appeared to be armed and it was as good a place as any for me to keep an eye on them as well as Izzy.

"Have you got any aspirin?" Izzy asked me. "'Cos I've got one hell of a headache."

"You did a great job," I said, and raised my hand in front of her. "How many fingers am I holding up?"

"Oh do fuck off. Six," she said, standing up, if still slightly uncertain on her feet. She snapped her fingers: "Machete, please."

"Hold my gun and point it at these guys while I nip down and get them," I said. "They're still in the dinghy. Try not to shoot these fellows, please, unless you have to." I ran back down the steps and retrieved our blades, looking across to the riverbank as I did. Noah and Connor must have been in the house for twenty minutes at least by now, or what felt like it. Had they been outside at all? I would much rather have known where they were.

Izzy was in control of things when I got back, and I ran down the small steps to the crew's quarters to look around. The doors were all open and the berths themselves were empty. The one where I'd been confined a few days ago still had its broken mirror.

I ran back up, swapped a machete for the gun with Izzy, and then nipped down to the luxury berths. Unlike the crew's quarters, they were all locked. I suppose their doors could have been kicked in, but I preferred to call the captain down to open them, which was probably as quick, after I'd made him shut up. He was pleading to be forgiven. It was all a misunderstanding, he didn't know what was going on he said. He piped down when I poked him with the gun and got on with opening the largest berth. It proved to be empty but had an elegant writing desk in the corner, scattered with papers. Noah's briefcase was parked underneath.

The briefcase was also locked, but gave in quickly to some solid machete blows, whereupon the contents spilled onto the floor. My wallet and Magnus' and our two passports were there, and I quickly thrust them into my damp pockets. Then, after a moment's hesitation, I picked up Pete's orange-faced diver's watch. Although it felt like a significant moment was passing, I was too short of time to reflect on it, and now I also spotted the scrunched up letter which Magnus had written to me. Noah, or somebody, had added a note next to the paragraph about Izzy: *I've got to meet this lady!* Qué sorpresa, I thought. What was so compelling about her? He might soon learn to be careful what he wished for.

I tucked the letter away and we moved onto the room I'd been given on arrival. The captain unlocked it and I pushed my way in. A body lay in a foetal position on the bed and I ran over to examine it. It was my brother, Magnus. He was fast asleep.

♈

"Magnus, darling!" cried Izzy. She ran over to the bed as he began to stir. I looked around and saw that she'd followed us down.

"Where's the shipmate?" I asked her.

"He'll be no trouble, don't worry," she said, which was worrying, coming from her. "Magnus, love, everything's OK we've found you. I'm here to rescue you and I brought Marcus along too."

Magnus was blinking himself awake and looking at us with a mixture of incredulity and delight. The swelling and bruises on his face were obvious and he winced slightly as Izzy pulled him to his feet and gave him a big kiss. For a moment they were alone together again, in their little love bubble. I gave them another moment and then went and hugged them both, and just for a moment all our troubles were forgotten.

"Thank you, both of you," Magnus said when we let him go, his speech a little slurred by a thick lip. He looked at me: "They told me they took you first but that you were dead, lost

255

at sea. I don't understand, were they lying or did you somehow beat the odds?"

"The latter of those two. I'll tell you about it later," I said. "We need to get out of this place first."

"Do you fancy a holiday in the Yucatán?" asked Izzy, "since we seem to be the current owners of a very nice boat."

It sounded like a jolly good idea for a variety of reasons. Plan C. But first I had to settle the doubt over Noah and Connor's whereabouts.

"Can I have my phone please? I need to make a call," I asked her. She knew what that meant and she gave me a dark look as she passed it over. "We've a guardian angel watching over us," I said to Magnus, by way of an explanation. "I'll see what she can do for us."

"By the way, have you got my laptop back?" Magnus asked. "I held them up for as long as I could, but things got rough and they had the passcode and a tutorial out of me in the end."

♈

"Hi Marc, you'll have to speak up," Persi said when I called her. "I'm on the move. What's happening?"

"We found Magnus, he's OK," I said. "We're on board the *Diva* with him."

"What about Noah and the others?" she asked.

"Noah and Connor went into the house on the riverbank and I haven't seen them come out," I said. "The other two are dead. There are two crew here with us, but they seem mostly harmless." I'd walked upstairs, half expecting to find another body but instead found the shipmate bound with cable ties to the pole of a bar stool. I doubt he had any idea how lucky he was that day.

"Did Magnus give up his work to them?" Persi asked.

"Yes, and I think they took his laptop onshore with them, I think they had a network connection there," I said.

"Shit. Is there anyone else in the house?"

"Not that I know of."

"Could you try to be more definite than that?" she asked. I shouted the question down to Izzy who replied she was sure the house was empty when she looked in through the windows, before Noah and Connor arrived. I relayed the information.

"As of this moment," Persi said, "you're in a very dangerous place. However far you can get yourselves downriver away from the house in the next three minutes, do it now. Three minutes, not four. Go now," she said, and promptly hung up.

For once, I was right on script. "Izzy, Magnus, get up here NOW," I shouted. Running over to the shipmate, I cut his ties free. Izzy and Magnus were up the stairs already, followed by the captain. I noticed Izzy was holding a rectangular black padded bag.

"We found this in Connor's cabin," Izzy said hurriedly. "Magnus thinks it's a clone of his laptop."

"Great, but for Chrissake get down to the dinghy and climb in, all of you. We need to scat, not a second to lose. Go quickly," I said, ushering everyone aft with my machete in one hand and gun in the other, like an Action Man. The group picked up speed and we climbed, jumped or fell into the dinghy, which was overfilled. Izzy started throwing Noah and Connor's luggage overboard, the shipmate cast off and I started the outboard.

I turned the dinghy in a sharp U-turn and headed downstream at full throttle. Looking back towards the house, I saw Noah emerging, at last. I was relieved to see him, having a fairly good idea of what was going to happen next. He started by walking across the lawn towards the jetty, seemingly curious about where the dinghy was going. Then he saw us and must have guessed some of what just happened, because he began to run, skidding to a halt when he reached the bank. He had his gun drawn and raised, but we were a hundred metres down the river already and gaining, and he didn't waste any shots. I wondered if he'd recognised me.

He looked back to the house and called to someone, which must have been Connor, and turned again to watch us, right until the moment when the explosion occurred. It came from the house, behind the trees, so the first thing I saw was a bright flash like a flicker of lightning reflected off the white hull of the *Diva*, followed a split-second later by the thump of the explosion as a ball of red fire and black smoke billowed up above the trees.

Maybe the boundary wall around the house funnelled the force of the explosion towards the river, but I saw Noah's pale suited figure launched cleanly into the air, where it passed through a graceful arc from the bank into the river, where it disappeared from sight. In the same moment, the *Diva's* windows blew out and I saw her rock in the water as scores of birds flew out of the trees up and down the river. Then fragments of the demolished house began raining down into the water and all around. A cloud of dust billowed out across the lawn. The smoke from the explosion continued to rise, mushrooming up into the sky, like a giant black map pin, marking the point of the explosion clearly for all the neighbourhood to see.

I supposed this was the biggest thing to happen in the quiet fishing village for quite some time, and no doubt it was going to draw a crowd. Any likelihood of taking back the *Diva* seemed to have been ruled out. She looked messed up, even from this distance and no doubt the locals would be swarming over her soon enough. Without a better idea I continued to steer a course downstream, wondering what Plan D would look like.

Point of No Return

My phone rang again.

"Me again. Are you OK?" Persi asked.

"Fine," I said, "although you just spoiled our plan for a luxury floating holiday."

"We couldn't allow any chance of your brother's research being passed on. Not like that or to them, at least," Persi said. "We've probably stopped them, but we still need to check." And I remembered what Magnus had told me: *They'll go to almost any lengths to keep it secret.*

"Have you any useful suggestions as to how we get out of here?" I asked her.

"Yes, that's why I was ringing you really, not just for the chat," she said, a little sarcastically. "There's an inlet on the north bank about three miles downstream of you. Go up there, to where there's a road bridge. Some cars should be there soon to pick you up, if you don't mind hanging round waiting for a while."

"Did you see what happened to Noah?" I asked. "He was blown into the river."

"That's good to know. I can see there are two patrol boats on the way down there from the naval base, not to mention a small flotilla of locals. They'll find any floating bodies, although we may not be on talking terms with the Mexicans for a day or two. We'll need to soothe some hurt feelings first, but that stuff's above my pay grade."

We rang off and I checked the time on Pete's watch. It would only ever be his watch. That and the warmth, the river, the boat and the gentle hum of the motor conspired to remind me of his last day, when he held us up, but gave me that grin, like the one my brother flashed me just a moment ago. The grin which always made me forgive him, Pete. Now I pictured it again I knew that Pete would, with the same easy care, forgive me for having traded lives with him on that day. So many people had been trying to tell me that, but I hadn't been ready to listen. He always believed in life as an adventure, and he never held a grudge, did he? And in that moment, I began to forgive myself.

I looked at Magnus and Izzy cuddling up, enveloped in their love bubble at the bow of our little dinghy, and I knew that I no longer needed her in the same way. The pain of grief would subside and I could stop the addiction.

I was tired but I felt like we were going home, in some way, and I steered the dinghy towards the shady side of the river and continued cruising at a gentle pace, feeling really quite mellow.

As we rounded the final bend in the river I realised that the inlet Persi had directed me to was the one where Izzy and I had planned to make our last reconnaissance stop. From its entrance, it had a good view across the village and down to the river mouth. Much more than a fishing village, I could see it was indeed a small resort, no doubt quite lively at the weekends. There were quite a few boats heading upstream – sightseers who had heard about the explosion, I supposed – but we were far enough from the scene that most people must have been unaware of it.

The small tributary was a quiet haven in the low-lying

estuary, its calm waters lined with moored-up boats on both sides, but few habitations and more pelicans to see than people. It seemed like a good place for us to stop where we could remain out of sight for a short while. We tied up to a bush on the bank and stepped back onto dry land.

Knowing we had a ticket out of here, the captain and shipmate seemed happy to stay with our group. I was amazed by their audacity, but it was their necks they risked, so we left them with the boat while Izzy had a scout around. I strolled a little way up a farm track with an arm on Magnus, who was a little unsteady on his legs. It was our first chance to talk.

"You know what they did to me?" he asked.

"They thought I was you when they grabbed me, so I probably had a taste of the same treatment, yes," I said. "They beat me up a little and put me on the waterboard. I didn't last all that long."

"Me neither, I don't think anyone does," he said. "I strung them along for quite a while before they started all that, though. Noah was hungry to know about it all, so I took him all around the houses with the supporting theories, we had a good meal and a proper night's sleep. It was all very hospitable for a while. Actually he seemed like a nice guy, and genuinely excited about my work."

"I knew you'd come up with a canny plan. Nicely done," I said.

"Incidentally, about something Noah said. Is it true you don't know what the Fields Medal is?" he asked. There was an annoying hint of superiority about his tone.

"Why not just tell me?" I replied, a little defensively. "Is it such a big thing?"

"I suppose not. It's just interesting. We both thought it was quite funny at the time. Anyway, the humour was short-lived. I ran out of time this morning which is when things became more unfriendly rather quickly. Once they had my passcode out of me, they dumped me back in my room and that's all I knew about it, until you made your miraculous appearance."

"We tracked the boat down the coast," I said. "We didn't realise that we were being tracked ourselves."

"Well it seems to have worked out," he said.

"Did Izzy say?" I asked. "It turns out that Persi works for the US government."

"Ah, I should have known," he said, almost to himself. Then after stopping for a moment to think it through, he looked up again: "I imagine that's something to do with your being able to call down a missile strike on us."

"Don't flatter me. That was only to the extent that she told us to get the hell out of there. They knew half the story, knew about Noah's crew and why you were in the States. After you'd gone missing they worked out we were following the *Diva*. They were desperate to stop Noah passing your stuff on to the rest of his criminal pals. Obvious reasons."

"What if I'd been in the house with him?" he asked.

"I wouldn't like to say, bro. You're too valuable an asset though, aren't you?"

We came out onto a point where a large pod of pelicans had congregated by the bank, and there was a flurry of activity as the surprised birds scrambled towards the middle. We sat and watched them circling for a while, enjoying the peace of the riverside and each other's company, as we had done all our lives. The heat of the day had begun to ease.

"That's the strange thing," Magnus said, breaking the silence after a while. "The universities were pretty interested in my work, more so the second group in California, and they took it seriously, but it didn't seem like enough of a surprise to them."

"You mean, like they'd already seen it? Someone had hacked your stuff already?" I asked.

"No, not like that. More like they wanted to know how much I knew. As if I'd rediscovered something they already knew, or half-knew. I don't think I'm the first." The disappointment was written all over his face, like a child who discovered there was no Santa and that he was the last one to find out.

"Bloody hell, they've kept that quiet," I said.

"They also offered me a research fellowship, by the way," he said. "I expect that way I can find out what they know already, but there'll be conditions attached."

"You'll be sworn to secrecy?" I asked.

He nodded glumly. "If they already know the stuff, it's hardly mine to share anymore, is it?"

"So what you're saying is that they can already hack the Internet," I said, filling in the rest of his story for my own benefit. "There are no so-called safe places, and they don't need backdoors to snoop around. They go through all that political shouting just as a cover?"

"It depends on who you mean by 'they'," he said. "I don't suppose many people can be in on it. It's a very big secret. All that Five Eyes shit, I don't suppose they're sharing a half of it. They'll want to keep onto their lead for as long as possible. You surely wouldn't want any politicians to know about it."

"Not even the President or the National Security wotsits?"

"Especially not any of them," he said. "Think about it for God's sake."

"That was a joke, bro. What are you going to do about it?" I asked. "I mean, you're in a worse dilemma than before, aren't you? Maybe you ought to go back to Basil with it."

"I'm not doing anything, not for now," he said. "I need to

go home and have a bit of time to think. Actually the next thing I'm going to do is ask Izzy to marry me. Do you think she'll agree?"

I gawped at him. In my head was the sound of tyres skidding to a halt on gravel, followed by a thunk like a car door. What should I say to him? What lengthy list would I have to leave out of the best man's speech?

"Are you sure she's the right girl for you?" I asked him.

"It's easy to love her. You can understand why," he said. "She's too gorgeous for words, and sexy and talented." Then, as if the thought just occurred to him: "Although I love her, I don't always like her very much. She still hasn't told me she lost her job – did you know? – and I think she's been unfaithful to me."

"Blimey, bro. You don't mince your words. What're you saying? There are more pros than cons, in your opinion," I said to him, desperately trying to avoid catching his eye.

"That probably applies in both directions," he said. "It seems there's something about me that lights her candle, surprising as it may seem. I suppose we're both a bit nutty, in our different ways."

I should have guessed that this moment might come, but I felt conflicted still, and I wasn't sure if it was because their match seemed to be doomed, or if a part of me still hadn't finished letting go of Izzy, like an ex-smoker who couldn't throw the last packet away with a cigarette still in it.

"Well best of luck to you. I mean it," I said, pushing my reservations to one side. "And you remind me I've got some sorting out to do with Persi, on the personal front," I said.

"Oh right. We thought there was something bubbling under there," Magnus said. "Couldn't understand why nothing came of it. Maybe she was applying the brakes."

"She may have had professional reasons," I said, "but I

suspect she was ready to compromise them. It's more that I kept buggering things up whenever I talked about my personal problems. I shouldn't have indulged myself. Feelings aren't my speciality."

"Nor mine," he said. "But you were always more the love 'em and leave 'em type."

"Maybe this one's a bit different," I said. Neither of us was quite sure how to follow that up, and we fell into silence.

"I think we're keeping our lift waiting, by the way," he said.

I turned around and saw a red Jeep and three rather ordinary-looking vehicles waiting on the bridge, and some guys dressed like civilians. But for their military haircuts, scarcely concealed weapons and a certain swagger one might never suspect they could be a special operations tactical team or private contractors, or both. In the near distance, Izzy and the boat crew were already climbing up the bank towards them. Maybe the sound of cars stopping hadn't been entirely in my head.

My poor brother had really been through the mill. He stumbled as we climbed the bank to the road and he needed a push from behind while another pulled him up from above. Izzy identified him to the officer in charge who steered him towards one of the cars, and Izzy to another. The two ship's crew claimed to be US citizens, even though they didn't have their papers, and were taken on board too. That left only me.

"You're Marc Miller, are you?" asked the officer.

"Yes, where are we going?" I asked.

"We're going to a landing strip less than a mile from here," he told me.

"So we're flying back to the States?"

"I'm sorry, Mister Miller, I've told you everything I can," he said.

♈

The airstrip wasn't much more than a patch of concrete on the mudflat, with a tubby twin-prop plane parked at one end of it, its passenger door open with a ladder hanging out and its engines turning over noisily. It looked like a miniature version of a C-130 Hercules transport.

Our officer headed over to meet a small huddle of people for a brief conference beside the plane, and I recognised Persi among them, looking serious behind her sunglasses. Her hair had blown loose in the plane's backwash, which also fanned the pages on the clipboard which she held.

I could see Magnus was still sitting in his car, but Izzy had got out of hers and was chatting happily with the rest of the tactical team. They were getting on very well, and from her animated figure I could tell she was enjoying herself being the centre of attention. Then she gestured a blow to the neck to one of them and I saw they were swapping stories about their adventures.

Eventually, Persi's group broke up and I saw her walking towards me, nervously trying to straighten her hair with her one free hand. I wasn't sure what kind of greeting was appropriate, but she fixed that by giving me a brief kiss on the lips, before standing back and waiting for my move. I took her hand and she gave it willingly, tugging me down the runway, away from the cars and the plane, where we could have a few moments of privacy and relative peace.

"I didn't realise we'd be seeing each other again so soon," I said.

"Yeah, there's a reason for that," she said. It was much quieter down at this end of the landing strip. She lowered her voice and stood closer to me.

"Thanks for everything, by the way," I said. "I'm sorry for being upset with you, things have been a bit confusing lately." I was talking too much, a sure sign of agitation. Feelings were so much more complicated than sex, and there was something else I needed to say: "When I said we should talk some more, I did mean more than once," I said at last. "Maybe something a bit more regular."

Her smile grew broader. "Happy to give it a go," she replied. "And if we understand each other right then I might consider falling in love with you, after a suitable period of probation."

"Yes, I think that could work two ways," I said, fairly sure that I meant it.

"You could kiss me now, and I won't arrest you," she said. And so I did, and for a moment time stood still while we were lost in our embrace. She tasted as sweet as the scent of her skin. When we broke apart, she smiled and pulled herself up to my chest and laid her head on me that way she did.

"That was the good news part," she said.

"Very good news," I agreed. "Was there some bad news?"

"Yeah, I can't take you back to the States with the others," she said. "Actually, you're prohibited for entering for five years, minimum, just for not turning up at the courthouse today."

"Bloody hell, you're not kidding are you? So what am I supposed to do now?"

"We'll leave you the Jeep, and enough cash for a plane home," she said. "You can go south to the state capital and get your embassy office to sort you out with some ID."

"Actually, I got my passport back. That doesn't help with seeing you, though. When are you back in the UK?"

"I'm not sure," she said. "When I go back to Europe I've got a new posting, based in Malta. Come and see me there and you can stay. And then I'll tell you my real name. You've got my old number. It still works."

"You mean your name isn't Persephone?" I asked, and she laughed at me like that was the funniest joke. I thought it was a shame, though. The name really suited her.

♈

The plane was revving up its rotors and the tactical team officer was waving to us, or rather to Persi, with some urgency. We set off back towards them. Half the group was climbing into the plane and the remainder clustered round the car which Magnus had ridden in.

"The professor's been taken ill," the officer said when we reached him. "We thought he was asleep but we can't rouse him. He needs medical attention right away. The sooner we get airborne the better."

One of the tactical team, acting as a paramedic, was organising the others to lift Magnus over to the plane. I looked on helplessly until I realised Persi was pressing an envelope and a car key into my hand, looking anxious. I could hardly hear her above the plane engines.

"I'll call you with news," she shouted to me, then turned to go on board the aircraft.

"Can you really not sneak me on board?" I called after her, now desperate with worry. Most of the people I cared about were suddenly being torn away from me and I felt very alone at the end of the airstrip.

"Trust me, it's better that you don't try." I read her lips as much as heard her.

I walked away from the plane and saw Izzy running up towards me, seemingly the last person apart from me still on the tarmac, and with a glare that shot daggers.

269

"Keep your fucking hands off that woman," she shouted. "She's a snake in the grass. I'll never speak to you again."

I was knocked off balance for a moment while she fulminated. It came so unexpectedly. But there was no point confronting her, I just tried to ignore it. I suppose relations between the two women had degenerated rather badly, and if this was turning into a shooting war between them, then I was best keeping my head down, even if I was at the centre of the dispute. If there was a higher power looking down, spare me, I prayed.

"She says I can't come with you," I said, changing the subject. "I've been banned from the States."

That surprised her a little, and her mood changed in the same instant. "It figures," she said, after a pause.

"You do know Magnus has been taken ill, don't you?" I asked her.

"Yes, of course," she said. "Don't worry, I'm sure he'll be all right. He's a precious asset, they have to take care of him. And he got the job, we'll be moving to California before you know it. It's a shame they say you can't come to see us, but I'll find a way of sneaking you in." She giggled and gave me a knowing look.

I didn't see how she could seem so certain about Magnus, and found it disconcerting that she took it so lightly. But then reality was subjective to her and she never doubted herself. It was a great strength, as well as a weakness.

"Look after him, will you? And yourself too," I said. "Stay with him and let me know how you both get on. He's got something important to tell you."

"I'm not letting him out of my sight till I've prised those sods away from him. Don't trust them an inch," she said, and then saluted me in a frivolous kind of way and bade me farewell: "Good luck to you, soldier. Be seeing you."

I wish she'd looked more distressed, but I could never tell what she was hiding under the veneer, or even whether there was very much under it at all. People like her have no empathy, Persi had said. But she judged her too harshly, even if a lot of it was true. Izzy was just – what did Magnus call it? – a bit nutty, to make the best use of British understatement.

Izzy ran off and was the last person to board the plane. As she disappeared inside the fuselage, they pulled the ladder up behind her, the plane's engines reached their highest pitch and the ungainly monster lurched off down the concrete, gathering pace rapidly until it left the ground, heading north.

I watched them for a while, until they had almost disappeared into the hazy sky. It was time I turned into an optimist, I thought. I made a wish for a quick recovery for my brother and hoped the law of averages would improve his luck from here on. Why not?

Then I turned back and walked over to the Jeep they'd left behind for me. I looked inside the envelope and reckoned I could afford some new clothes before the journey, wherever I was going next.

She'd said Malta would be her next posting, hadn't she? I'd heard the diving was pretty good there.

Acknowledgements

First and foremost I must thank my wife Liz, for her forbearance while I wrote, dreamt and talked endlessly about this book, and for her contribution as copy-editor. A special thanks too to Sam Watson at Exeter College for her encouragement and support.

To the rest of my family, friends and work colleagues, can I also thank you for your enthusiastic interest in the book, which was really motivating. And to "the class" at Exeter College, thanks for a fun year and for listening to me practise.

Lightning Source UK Ltd.
Milton Keynes UK
UKOW04f0633260917
309887UK00001B/6/P